RUNNER'S HIGH

A PAUL GREY MURDER MYSTERY

CHERYL RITZEL

TOLLING BELL BOOKS
ATLANTA

Printed in the U.S.A.

OTHER BOOKS BY CHERYL RITZEL
BEGINNER'S LUCK

COMING SOON!
TEACHER'S PET
OPEN HOUSE
GOING POSTAL

ISBN 978-0-9740583-6-8

Library of Congress Control Number 2005926913

RED HERRING PRESS
IMPRINT OF TOLLING BELL BOOKS
ATLANTA, GA

For my family, with love.

PROLOGUE

D avy Kimble couldn't understand why some people chose to run the six miles of the Peachtree Road Race as a way of celebrating the fourth of July. Running for fun never made sense to him. He had done too much running in boot camp to want to do it for sport. And running in this heat—it was so damn hot, even for July. Davy shifted, uncomfortable in his uniform as droplets of sweat trickled down his neck. No sprinklers running this year, at least not at his post in front of Colony Square. A little cool mist every now and then would've been nice. He pulled at his collar.

Watching the tens of thousands of runners go by made him feel nauseated—so many, so close together, heads bobbing up and down like waves. Queasy, he had to turn away. Across the road an apartment complex towered. Davy squinted and looked up. Someone above had taken it upon themselves to provide motivational music for the racers. He caught a reflection of a chopper in the green glass of a nearby skyscraper. Over the roar of the crowd, the runners, and the boom box, he could hear the thumping of helicopter blades cutting the air. A police chopper hovered, as if time stood still.

A small boy dressed in red and white patriotic garb tugged gently at Davy's sleeve, wanting a photo. Davy shot him a gruff look that said no.

"Well, you shit," he silently cursed himself. "You don't have to ruin other people's fun."

He softened his look, shrugged at the boy, and then smiled. *At least it's a break.* He took the boy's hand. As he knelt down to be photographed by the boy's mother, he glanced up one more time into some glare off the apartments. The boy waved his tiny flag, the camera whirred, and over the mother's shoulder Davy saw a large object, a person, fall behind the fence and trees of the Magnolia Apartments. *A person?* he thought, shaking his head. It couldn't be. Piercing screams and shrieks rang out, followed by children's cries.

A few people fled the scene, but a growing herd of spectators gathered quickly at the spot, pulling in more and more people from up the street and even some of the runners. At the same time, word of what happened spread out away from the scene like a stone's ripples in a pool of water. A senior police officer on the other side called for Davy to assist him. Davy left his post, leaving the barricades unguarded. Naturally, the audience on his side pushed in, following him. The race was at a stand-still. Davy looked up through the mass of people at the balconies above. Spectators stared down in horror at something he hadn't seen yet, something up ahead. He radioed to the top of the hill to stop the race and barricade the road since hundreds, maybe thousands, still raced forward.

"Police, coming through!" He pushed his way in, pausing to set up barricades with another officer.

Although he knew what it would be, he wasn't prepared for what he saw. A body heaped up on the pavement. The arms and legs twisted and contorted and barely recognizable as such. Silvery pants and white shirt contrasted sharply with the burgundy pool of blood beneath the body. Parts, he didn't know what, had escaped the woman's abdomen. At least he thought it was a woman with bloody, blonde hair.

"She's not alive, is she?" Davy asked, unable to look away, until his stomach swirled and his gag reflex tightened up.

"No," the officer replied. "Now help me keep this crowd back."

With the assistance of a third officer, the three men used the race barricades to block off the scene. An ambulance had been stationed nearby for heat-exhausted runners. The viewers parted to let the ambulance in, flowing back in behind. The EMT's jumped out, but merely shook their heads; nothing could be done.

"We'll have to take the body to the hospital to be pronounced dead," the EMT commented.

"I'll go," Davy volunteered.

"Can't go yet," another officer replied. "We have to wait for the detectives before we move the body."

"Until then, don't let anyone touch anything," the senior officer said. "We need to write down everything we've seen and done. We need to isolate the best witnesses and start getting statements."

Davy turned on his heel and looked around. There were hundreds of people—-all witnesses. "You're kidding, right?" He felt the heat at his neck multiply.

A runner burst through the crowd. His voice trembled. "I heard about the fall. I live in this building. I think from the description I heard in the crowd, I might know her. Let me see; let me see."

Davy allowed him through the first set of barricades.

When the man reached the crime scene barricade, he dropped to his knees and held the bars, looking through them. "Oh, God," he cried.

"Do you know this woman?" Davy approached.

The man nodded. "She's my wife."

CHAPTER 1

Vacationing for the past week hadn't left me looking forward to the pile of catch-up work on my desk when I returned. My two partners would have completed their fair share, but they'd be sure to leave plenty for me. I'm Paul Grey, an insurance investigator, and I was working in the research department of Morehouse Fidelity Insurance in Atlanta, spending my days researching claims for insurance payments. Did the person really die? Did the house burn down on its own or did it get some help?

Shawn and Glenn, my two partners, and I were more like spies than pencil-pushers. We found it rewarding to catch someone committing insurance fraud. While I wanted to do private detective work, the law required me to work for another company for at least two years before striking out on my own, even though I was fully trained and licensed. *Six months to go*, I thought as I picked up my stack of mail and notes from the office message center and headed for my office. Flipping through the stack I rounded the corner and plowed into Virginia Higginbotham from Underwriting.

"Watch it, Mr. Grey," she snapped.

She reminded me of a Doberman pinscher, only not as lean. She had dark, short cropped hair exposing pointy little ears, and her dark eyes seemed to have no pupils. She was about thirty years my senior. People around the office often discussed what motivated her to stay on staff since she really seemed to hate everything and everyone.

"I heard you got the case," she said, flashing her teeth.

"What?"

"The fourth of July jumper," she replied over her shoulder as she strode down the hall.

"Must be some celebrity case," I mumbled as I went on my way.

A celebrity case was any investigation of a claim making the nightly news. I'd been out of town, so I had no idea what the case might be. My wife, Lindsey, and I had gone to visit my cousins in North Carolina in the little town of Oriental along the coastline. It was a vacation with few distractions——no malls, no traffic. Remote and isolated.

I took the elevator to the second floor. The research offices were on the far left side of the building. Glenn had nicknamed our niche the "dungeon" for obvious reasons——the whole left flank of the building had been obscured by a newer, larger building. We had no view, unless a wall constitutes scenery. We had been delegated this section of the building along with any others who didn't rank in importance. The powers that be reasoned the investigators, like me, spend a lot of time out of the office and aren't important enough to need sunlight.

The research offices consisted of three rooms. The first was used by our support staff——a secretary, a receptionist, and a battle-worn copier. The second office stored files, videotapes, photographs, and the all-important coffee maker. The third office, also the largest, was shared by Glenn Green, Shawn Bramblett, and me.

As usual, Glenn had both feet propped up on his desk as I strolled in. He nearly fell over in the chair as he abruptly shifted them off the desk. "Damn, it's only you," he chuckled and ran his hand over his slick, bald head. "I nearly killed myself there."

"I think you screwed up your equilibrium when you shaved your head."

"You like it?" He bent down so I could see the shine.

"It'll take some getting used to. What possessed you to do such a thing?" I threw my mail down in the "In" basket and leaned against the front of the desk.

"I think it makes me look like that famous actor," he smiled. "The ladies like it."

Glenn didn't look a day over twenty-three but was actually in his mid-thirties like me, only much more athletically handsome.

"I think it makes you look like a bowling ball," Shawn challenged. "You need to keep any hair you can at your age."

Glenn rolled his eyes at her, the whites an even sharper contrast than usual with the excess of exposed ebony skin.

"Thirty ain't old and just you wait," he said. "You'll get older, too."

"Glenn, leave her alone; she doesn't have anything to worry about," I said.

Shawn, still in her early twenties, was average height and weight, and attractive. Her smooth, honey-colored skin required no touch up. Her long, luxurious hair shone like a copper penny, twisted into one large knot and held in place with a pencil. The men from upstairs were always asking her for something to write with so they could watch her shake out her soft, shiny hair. Unmarried, she frequently dated guys from the office and then talked about how she shouldn't date guys from the office.

"I'm glad you're back, Paul. I can't handle him sometimes." She glanced over at Glenn, who'd gone back to work, then whispered jokingly, "I'm glad to see you kept your hair while you were away."

"Yeah, but he's getting some whites in amongst those black ones and losing it slowly, a little empty spot near the top." Glenn couldn't let it go. "Age catches all of us one day."

"Glenn, you're the only one tall enough to even notice a thinning spot," she retorted.

"Enough, you two. So what's up?" I sat down at my desk. "I heard I've got a new case."

"Paul, you're such the eager beaver, always straight to work with you. We want to know, how was your vacation?"

"Fine, not much to talk about." I shrugged.

"That's it? Fine?" She folded her arms and tried a different tactic. "You look like you got some sun."

"Yes, I'm not my normal pale self. I did tan. Now, tell me about the new case."

"Ugh, Glenn, you tell him." Shawn turned her back to me.

"Paperwork is there on your desk, big fella." He pointed. "A celebrity case, made the national news. Some woman fell to her death on the fourth of July during the Peachtree Road Race, no less."

"A suicide?" I shuffled through the papers looking for the correct file. "We don't pay for suicides."

"Not so fast. It's not straight up."

"Didn't you see it on the news?" Shawn turned back around to face me.

I shook my head.

Shawn's eyes widened as if she were enlightened. Perhaps the definition of 'not much to talk about' seemed to hit home with her now.

"It may have been an accident," Glenn said.

"So then we pay." I found the folder and crumpled up the sticky note off the front of it.

"But it's also possible the husband killed her for the insurance since he's the beneficiary." Glenn was playing with me.

"So then we don't pay." I flipped the papers one by one.

"The husband hasn't been arrested." Glenn dodged the sticky note ball as I threw it at him.

"I'll read it for myself!"

Information on the case was scarce. The file contained only a few pages——a quick summary of why the case warranted investigation, a summary of key witnesses' statements, a transcribed police interview with the husband. It was up to me to research the case to determine whether Morehouse should pay the claim or not. I was in charge of handling all suspect claims concerning life insurance. Glenn researched claims for auto accidents. Shawn was in charge of fire and disability. Usually we dabbled into each other's cases as need and curiosity inspired us to either ask or offer to help.

According to the case file, Mark Sills was filing a claim for life insurance on his wife, Nikki. Nikki had apparently fallen to her death from their seventeenth-story balcony. I noted the address. I would first visit the apartment complex and with the medical examiner.

"So you saw this one on the news?" I began skimming the other case files to rank them in priority order by cause of death. Accidents or suspicious deaths are researched to try to save the company money. It's all about money.

"Yeah, we saw it. It brought the Peachtree to a stop," Shawn replied.

"Helicopters from all the news stations were already there covering the race. They were flying over the scene before the detectives could even get there," Glenn added.

"It says she fell. She didn't jump." I looked up from my organized stack—no other cases took priority at this point. "There wasn't a note or anything? No suicidal tendencies?"

"Shit, man. It's your case. How am I supposed to know?" Glenn thumped his pen rhythmically on his desk.

"Glenn, you can't fool me," I looked over the file again to be sure I hadn't missed anything. "I know you read over the case. You love this crap."

"It doesn't say, man." He shrugged.

"I guess I'll be adding her doctor and the police to my list of visits." I stood up to go.

"Leaving already?" Shawn asked.

"They certainly don't pay me to stick around here to talk with you two." I gave her a little salute.

"Keep me posted, will ya?" Glenn asked.

"Of course." I nodded. "And if I need any help, I'll know who to ask."

On my way down to the lobby, I stopped off at the first floor——

Records. The lady who ran the department was Myra Selewski, a staunch feminist the bosses judged as a little too off-beat considering she had dyed her hair banana yellow and wore a nose ring. They had her transferred to Records knowing she, like the filing cabinets, wouldn't see the daylight either——no clients would ever see her. She claimed she could sue the company for discrimination and win, but her paycheck was too good.

Myra looked up from her desk as I approached. I wondered how she got her hair to stick out the way it did. It looked like a sea urchin.

"Hey, Myra," I greeted her. "I need to check some records."

"Hey, Paul. Glad to finally see a man down here..." Her icy blue eyes seemed to lose their chill and she added, "...doing some work."

"I thought you hated men," I teased as I logged onto a computer terminal. She seemed to like me for some unknown reason.

"Mostly." She smiled. "What I mean is they haven't yet totally segregated the men from the women up there."

"What do you mean?" I typed in Mark Sills' name, then Nikki Sills'.

"Open your eyes. Look around. You and Glenn are the only guys working menial desk jobs around this place. Most of the men are insurance salesmen with their own offices or boss-men up on the top floor."

"Maybe Glenn and I aren't real men." I instructed the computer to print.

"Whatever. Women do all the gritty work around here like underwriting, records, answering phones. It's all women from the first floor up—"

"Mostly women," I corrected.

"Until you get to the top," she finished her thought.

By now the computer had printed the screen I had looked up. It listed the microfilm locations of all records on Mark and Nikki Sills. I took the printout to Myra.

"I need copies of all these files."

"Help yourself." She waved me access to the storeroom. "Holler if you need any assistance."

I didn't need any help. I was quite handy at the microfilm reader. Within a few minutes I had gathered the reels I needed and loaded the first one on the machine. I was going to be looking for several details.

It wasn't long before Myra was looking over my shoulder. I noticed her reflection in the microfilm reader.

"Shame on you, seeking out the company and attentions of a man,"

I said.

"Hell, I'm bored to death." She pulled up a chair and straddled it. "Whatcha lookin' for?"

"I'm looking for life insurance policies on Mark and Nikki Sills." I scanned the reel.

"Oh, the jumper." She nodded knowingly.

"Everyone knows more about this case than I do." I sighed. "Ah-ha. Looks like Mark and his wife each had $500,000 term life insurance policies."

"Is five hundred grand enough money to kill for?" Myra pondered.

"I'm not sure. People have killed for less. I assumed there would be more."

"Well, keep looking. We're not all computerized yet. There could be other policies taken out later," Myra suggested.

"I found three references on two reels. I need the reel." I indicted the one she was holding.

"One of these days we'll have this all computerized. It's hard to believe we're in the twenty-first century and still relying on this crap."

She tossed the roll into the air, and I caught it up with a snap.

"Yeah. How come it's not already on computer?" I asked. "And how long will it take for these to print?"

"It has to warm up. And the reason we haven't been brought out of the Stone Age is because those boss-men on the top floor spend all the company money on their stylish office furniture and pretty office assistants, that's why." She threw out her arms in exasperation. "And bigger salaries for themselves."

My copies finally printed. I rewound the first reel and put the second reel on. Myra sat in thought for a few moments, perhaps brooding about those at the top of the corporate ladder. I zoomed through the film, stopping only to get a frame number in my search.

"Oh, wow," escaped my lips as I scrolled back and forth a few times.

Myra crowded next to me to get a look.

"More policies. Three of them, all separate policies on Nikki Sills. A half a million each."

Myra whistled in appreciation. "Two mil."

"In all, yes, and all taken out about six months ago." I pointed to the dates on the screen.

"I smell a fish." She snorted as if there were a stench in the room.

I pressed the button for copies.

"Why do you think Mr. Sills had four smaller policies instead of one large one?" she asked.

"Perhaps to avoid medical tests, which I'll look into next. Or so they didn't have to make a financial statement. We check out the finances of anyone wanting a policy over one million. I guess to see if they are over-insuring. Or maybe it saved money on monthly payments for him to do it that way."

"So he didn't want you looking at her finances or medical background?"

"It would appear so. She may have had a disease and a full medical evaluation would have revealed it. Smaller policies only require a mouth swab. The more money we may have to pay out, the more medical tests we want them to pass. If he knew we weren't computerized, he probably figured he could get away with the four smaller policies. They might not ever be discovered. May be why he chose us as his insurer in the first place."

"She must have been rich, like a movie star, to be worth two mil."

"I doubt it. My guess is she wasn't worth anything. Which may explain why Mark Sills used four policies instead of one."

"But it would be discovered at payout time, like now."

"True, but this investigation is only a priority because we don't know cause of death—-suicide, accident, or murder. When I opened the file, I had no idea how much payout we were talking about."

"So if she'd died in a non-suspicious way, there may not have been an investigation."

"Probably not."

"Interesting." Myra mulled over this for a moment.

"I need to write a memo to my boss about this problem. There are probably other policies like these," I said.

"Yeah, maybe you could get a promotion to the top floor."

"I don't want to be on the top floor, but I do think they ought to get all this computerized so they can double check for other policies like this one."

"So you don't think Nikki Sills was worth a lot of money?" Myra returned to the case at hand.

"No."

"She's not worth anything alive, but she's worth a pretty penny dead."

"Exactly and it seems suspicious the way he went about it, and Mark Sills only had a $500,000 term life policy on himself."

"Sounds like he knew he wouldn't be going anywhere, but Nikki would—right over the railing—SPLAT." Myra used her hands to demonstrate.

"Yuck." I laughed at her distastefulness. "He's got an alibi, according to the police."

I took the reel off and threaded yet another.

"Alibi schmalibi." Myra crossed her eyes. "He could have hired someone to do her in."

"You're spending too much time in here. Your imagination is in overdrive," I teased. "No really, that is a good assumption, but it could all be a coincidence."

"Umm, Paul the Purveyor of Truth steps in."

"Paul the what? Never mind." I shook my head in confusion.

"What are we looking at now?" She leaned closer to the screen.

"I'm checking to see if we did medical tests or pulled medical records. At that rate of insurance we should have done both at least on a small scale.

Myra waited patiently as I read the medical records. I printed them also.

"Anything?" she asked.

"Nope. Both the Mr. and Mrs. were perfectly healthy as far as they reported—no diseases, no mental illness. Medical exams and a mouth swab, were done on the first policy for both of them. The additional policies on Nikki were applied for within sixty days so they didn't require a re-evaluation. The agent selling the policies knew what was going on. He didn't order new tests and he knew about the separate polices."

"So someone on the inside helped him?"

"Well, inside, or eager to make some sales. I'll probably still check with the doctor, but I'll need to get an official copy of their signed medical information release forms first."

I gave her the best brown puppy dog eyes I could muster.

"I'll get it for you. It'll be on your desk tomorrow." She smiled.

"Great." I gathered up the reels.

"I got it." She took them from me. "You go on. And thanks for letting me rant earlier. You won't tell anyone, will you?"

She tilted her head and faked a pout.

"Not if you tell me something," I said.

"What?"

"How do you get your hair to stick straight out? I figure it can't be regular hair gel."

"It's hair glue. You should try it sometime."

"No, thanks. I'll stick with hair spray. And my lips are sealed." I pretended to fasten my lips and threw the imaginary key to her.

I took my copies for my file, signed the log sheet on the front desk, and left. I was off to see Betsie Jordan, my contact at the medical examiner's office. She and my wife, Lindsey, were good friends and would have lunch together every other week or so. Lindsey tried to keep me updated on her current look so I wouldn't be shocked each time I saw her. Betsie liked to change her appearance frequently and some of her attempts were outlandishly funny. The last time I'd seen her was a little over two months ago so I was prepared for anything. The only sure way to know I was in the right place was the glow of her peach colored walls and overabundance of plants in her office.

This time her hair was braided in tiny rows. She had startling green contact lens to mask her deep brown eyes. Her skin was the same dark cinnamon color as before.

"Betsie?" I asked with some hesitation.

"Yes?" She looked up to see who the visitor was.

"It's me, Paul Grey." I reached to shake her hand.

"Oh, yes. I knew it was you, or else a dead ringer." She laughed at her own joke.

Medical examiners seem to have their own brand of humor. It comes from spending so much time with dead bodies. On her desk were some particularly gruesome photos of a man split open from neck to hips on the autopsy table.

Seeing the look on my face, she quickly covered them. "Sorry. I see it every day and I'm totally desensitized, well usually anyhow. What brings you here? Another insurance claim?"

"Yes, the woman who fell from her apartment on the fourth of July, Nikki Sills."

"Oh, yeah. Not my case, but let me see if I can find the file." She stepped around her desk to the door. "I'll be back in a sec. Make yourself comfortable."

How comfy can you get in a building full of dead bodies? Sitting alone in her office reminded me of movies like *Night of the Living Dead*. You wouldn't find me around a place like this after dark, even though her office was bright and cheery.

Betsie returned in a few moments with the file.

"Let's see, as with all accidental deaths and suicides, we did a complete medicolegal autopsy." She thumbed through it. "Nothing much to say on this one. Nikki Sills—no alcohol, no illicit drugs, no signs of a struggle."

"They scraped under her nails?" I asked.

"Yes; no tissue from any assailant was found. No unusual bruises or scratches either, from what we could tell."

"What do you mean?"

"You see, the body was in terrible shape. She was almost completely unrecognizable. We identified her from fingerprints and dental records."

"How did the husband know it was her? Didn't he identify her?"

"Yes, by her clothing, but we went a step further."

"What about toxicology?" I asked. "You said there was nothing in her system?"

"A minute amount of Antivert, a prescription drug. Nothing else."

"What is Antivert a prescription for?" I noted down the drug name.

"Various things like nausea, motion sickness, dizziness, vertigo."

A visit to the doctor was definitely in order.

"The official cause of death?" I inquired.

"Broken neck." Betsie pulled out an x-ray and pointed. "See, the fall snapped her neck. She also broke fifteen major bones, too many small ones to count, and ruptured several internal organs."

I wrote down all the information.

"Of course," Betsie added, "she would have died even without the broken neck."

"What was the manner of death? Has it been ruled an accident?" I asked.

Betsie nodded and pursed her lips sourly.

"It couldn't have been a suicide?" I sensed she disagreed with the ruling.

"Not in my estimation." Betsie frowned as she thought. "She didn't land feet first the way most jumpers do. A suicide is usually a controlled fall and can be survived even from heights of 100 feet. She was in an uncontrolled fall, like when you slip."

"She was caught off guard, so she landed awkwardly." I leaned forward.

"Exactly."

I absorbed this information and its ramifications for a moment. "An uncontrolled fall could be the result of either slipping or a push. Which do you think made her fall?"

Betsie shrugged. "It wasn't my exam. The police will be a better source since they had a detective present at autopsy. Evidently the woman was standing on a chair and it shifted out from under her. The examiner lists the manner of death as accidental."

"You don't agree?" I asked.

"It's not my place to disagree with the other medical staff on my team." She avoided an answer. "I wasn't in the autopsy room. I don't know what information the detective had."

"You don't agree." I sat back and folded my arms across my chest. "You think it was a homicide. Tell me why."

Betsie got up, crossed the room, and shut the door to her office. She leaned against the closed door and sighed. I turned in my chair so I could face her.

"I don't think she would have been up on a chair. She suffered from vertigo or dizzy spells, hence the medication in her blood." Betsie paused to let this sink in, then leaned down and whispered close to my ear, "Besides, a pregnant woman is usually more careful than that."

CHAPTER 2

"She was pregnant?" I whispered. "You said there wasn't anything interesting about this case."

"Why is a pregnancy so interesting?" She shrugged and continued in hushed tones. "The husband knew it was his baby."

"You're right; a pregnant woman with a history of dizzy spells or blackouts isn't going to be climbing around on chairs seventeen stories up." I gripped the armrests of the chair, holding back excitement.

"Am I right? I don't know. People do stupid things and get hurt...or killed." Betsie sighed and let her head drop back against the door.

"Your medical examiner didn't think it was strange?" I asked.

"The police detective had other evidence I didn't see." She stared blankly at the ceiling. "It was ruled accidental."

"O.K., maybe she was up on a chair. I've done stuff that could've gotten me killed, but it *is* suspicious."

"Very suspicious."

"Did you do a paternity test or take his word the baby was his?"

Betsie brought her eyes back down to meet mine. "We did a test. It's his."

"How many months along was she?" I was taking notes again.

"A little under five months. She was probably starting to show."

"Anything else I should know?" I prodded.

"No. Just keep the information about the pregnancy to yourself. The husband requested it be kept confidential."

"Why?"

"I don't know." She shook her head.

"Who else knows about it? Family?"

Betsie shrugged, her information tapped out.

"Thanks for your help." I dismissed myself. I figured I could stop by and see my wife, Lindsey, for lunch before going to the police station.

Lindsey had finished serving her first year as a state Senator and was working at Robert Mayson's law offices until the next legislative session began in January. She had won election to the seat almost a year ago. It had been her lifelong goal to serve in politics. Like many legislators, she worked somewhere else April through December because a Senator's pay was not enough to live on.

Robert Mayson's law offices were located on the northern side of the city. Judging by the elegant appearance of his offices, I knew Mayson must charge his clients a sizeable chunk of change for representation. The entrance with twelve-foot ceilings and marble floors gave way to more modest nine-foot ceilings and plush carpets in the waiting area and offices. All the cherry wood furniture, upholstery, and artwork had been picked by an interior decorator. Bright sunlight filtered through the gracious windows in every room.

The firm boasted three senior law partners and five juniors specializing in mostly criminal law, but dabbling every now and then into other areas if the money was right. Lindsey worked as right-hand woman to Mayson. She did preliminary work on all his cases and was present with him in court when defending a client.

Today she was hunched over her desk, a frown on her face. The door to her office was open so I rapped on the frame to get her attention.

She looked up impatiently. "Wha—"

Her frown faded with an emerging smile.

"I came to take you to lunch, to whisk you away." I swooped my arms through the air for effect.

"I'm so glad." She grabbed her purse and tossed her chestnut hair aside before placing the purse strap over her shoulder. "I wasn't going to have lunch since there's so much catching up to do after our vacation. And my stomach is feeling weak. It's a good thing you came along."

"You're too caught up in your work," I chided.

"You should talk. I'll bet you're here because you're in between stops on a case." She threaded her arm through mine and took my hand.

"Actually, I missed you already." I gave her a kiss.

"Yeah, right. Come on. I know the perfect place." She tugged me down the hall.

We went to a small sandwich shop and each got a BLT with pickle spear, cookie, and a drink. BLT's are one of my all-time favorites. I love the way the bread sticks to the roof of my mouth. As I made my way through my sandwich, I told her about my current case.

"I think the police go for the fastest, easiest solution." She shook her pickle spear at me. "Easy isn't always right."

"They know." I snapped my teeth like I was going to take her pickle.

She snatched it back defensively. "I know they know. They have time constraints, money problems. They can't give a case like Nikki Sills the time it may deserve."

"I know someone in government who could work on getting the police department more money so they can spend the time." I winked at her.

"Huh. Don't even try to get me riled up." She smiled. "Your idea would get my vote, but about a million people in this city wouldn't go for it. Besides I don't work on the budget committee."

She finished the pickle and licked her fingers. Her lips puckered with its sourness. To me, those simple actions were pure seduction. She was so beautiful. Her hair was particularly shiny and she smelled good. She innocently wiped her hands and mouth with a napkin and looked up.

"What time will you be home?" I asked with interest.

"After six; why?" Her golden-green eyes sparkled.

Her eyes, normally a darker brown, changed with her mood—one way I could tell if she was receptive or not.

"You look yummy."

"Thanks." She smiled appreciatively. "You, again? After last night?"

"Sure." I smirked. "Last night was great. Different, didn't you think?"

"Different as in better? Or simply good because you were deprived while we were visiting relatives?"

I shrugged. "So is that a yes?"

"We'll see." She took the straw of her drink into her mouth in a manner most sexy.

"Umm."

We finished our meal and then I took her back to her office and gave her a long, lingering kiss to remember me by before I headed over to the police station.

Detective Martin Jeffries was a stout man with fair, freckled skin and dark hair which I believed he dyed because it didn't go with his complexion at all. He was not expecting me, yet he seemed pleasantly surprised to see me approaching. He was on the phone, standing behind his desk, as I arrived. He smiled and signaled for me to wait.

"To what do I owe this unexpected visit?" He replaced the phone. "Coming to invite me out to a ball game or something?"

"I wish, but I'm investigating the death of Nikki Sills for an insurance claim," I replied.

"Exactly what I thought." He shuffled some things around on his desk and then added, "I'm glad."

"Really?" I raised one eyebrow. This had to be a trick or a joke. I awaited a punch line or an onslaught of some kind.

"Yes, really." He nodded. "You know me well enough to know I'm not pulling your chain."

"You want me to snoop around. Why?" I folded my arms across my chest.

"I suppose you'll want to see the crime scene." He picked up his hat and took his keys out of his desk drawer.

"Well...yes," I responded, confused at his cooperation.

Martin Jeffries was a friend, but he was still first and foremost an officer of the law. I learned from my previous investigations the police don't like a private eye sticking his nose into a case. It's nothing personal. They don't like to share information. They'll let you see a crime scene, but only after they're absolutely certain they don't need it anymore. They don't appreciate it when you point out oversights or mistakes. They take criticism about as easily as you'd get them to swallow poison.

"I'll take you." He put on his hat.

"That's really not necessary," I argued. "I know the address—"

"Nonsense. I know better than to send you on your own. Remember the time you were at one of my crime scenes alone and you removed evidence?"

"Yes, I remember, nearly two years ago. Will I ever live that down? We've worked together since then and I've not done anything of the sort. Besides, it was planted evidence; it was false."

"Yes, well, I need to talk to you anyway," he insisted. "Come on."

We decided it would be best to take two vehicles in case Detective Jeffries got called to another crime scene. I followed him to the Magnolia Apartments where Nikki Sills had lived.

The apartment building complex consisted of two grey stone and cement structures about thirty stories tall and a smaller five-story building off to one side. Its design was pleasing and consisted of simple architectural angles and accents. Five balconies stuck out along the front face of the towers, four on the sides. The buildings faced 14th Street, across from the Colony Square Hotel.

The entrance drive was paver stone and took one either around a loop or down below to parking. Detective Jeffries parked in the circular drive, in the fire lane, and I followed suit. On the left side of the circle, two maintenance men were down on the ground scrubbing down the paver stones with sudsy buckets and a hose.

"Are they cleaning what I think?" I asked Detective Jeffries as I gathered my papers, got out, then slammed the car door shut.

He nodded and walked off in the direction of the entrance. I craned my neck to look up the height of the building above the men with the buckets. I counted the floors. *What a fall.* The door buzzed to give us access to the building so I hurried to catch up to Detective Jeffries who held the door open for me. We both signed our names to the visitors' register at the front desk.

"This is the insurance investigator, Paul Grey." He showed his badge to the petite Asian girl at security. "He's with me."

The girl nodded to us. A woman walked by, headed for the elevators.

"Excuse me," she hollered to the woman. "You're not a resident are you?"

"No," the woman replied.

"If you're not a resident, you'll have to sign in, please," she said.

I wondered what the girl would do in a real emergency or if someone refused to sign in. She was thin and tiny framed, not at all commanding. She couldn't hurt a fly.

We passed the woman as we went to the elevators. While we waited on the elevator, I noticed a surveillance camera monitoring the front entrance. Off to the right were the stairs and a side entrance for tenants only as well. The elevator opened and we both silently entered. The building had thirty floors, no thirteenth floor. Detective Jeffries pressed the seventeen.

"So you wanted to talk to me? About what?" I asked around the twelfth floor, figuring I had waited long enough in silence.

"Notice anything about the security around here?" he asked.

"Yes. It's good."

"I thought so, too." He rubbed his chin.

"What is it you wanted to discuss?" I asked again as the elevator stopped and we got out.

"It's this way." He motioned for me to follow. "Why are you on this case?"

"The husband had a hefty insurance policy on the late Mrs. Sills. Her accidental death is a little suspicious."

Detective Jeffries led me through the crime scene tape and unlocked the door. He held the handle, but didn't go in.

"Yes, strange. I thought so, too," he said. "But accidental seems to be the only explanation given the evidence. You'll see."

He swung open the door and motioned for me to enter. Hands behind our backs we began a walk-through of the apartment. The small foyer opened up into a living room and dining area, more gracious than most apartments, and decorated lavishly—leather sofa, marble dining table, valuable antiques.

"How much does a place like this cost?" I crossed the room directly to the living room balcony and peered out. Another balcony was farther to the left over the men who were scrubbing.

"More than you or I could afford, my friend," he replied, following my gaze.

We went quickly through the kitchen which was precisely color coordinated with tile floors and backsplash and granite counters.

The first rooms we came to off the hall were the spare bedroom and bathroom. The spare had been used as an office. The hall bathroom looked like it had never been used, matching towels meticulously folded and dainty carved soaps. The last room in the apartment was the master suite. Numbered tags from the photo and crime scene crew were still in place.

"Everything is exactly the way we found it the morning of her death," Detective Jeffries explained. "The husband's been at a hotel."

I opened the balcony door. Standing in the doorway I observed a chair next to the railing on the right. Also on the right was a decorative terra cotta pot broken in several pieces where it had been dropped. The macrame hanger was still on it. On the left of the balcony hung a matching plant and pot. I stepped gingerly around the fallen plant to look over the edge. *This was it.*

"What do you think?" He stood in the doorway behind me.

"It looks exactly the way it was described to me. She was up on the chair, lost her balance, and fell."

"Mm-hmm," Detective Jeffries agreed.

"You know she took medications for dizziness?" I turned to face him.

"Yes."

"What was she doing with the plants?" I bent over to visually examine the fallen one.

"Don't know. The husband said they'd been hanging here forever. He had no idea why she'd be moving them."

"Was it in the way of her view of the race?" I checked several viewing angles and concluded it was not.

Nothing else was on the balcony.

"Where did the chair come from?" I moved back to the doorway to scan the bedroom.

"The office." Detective Jeffries moved aside to let me in.

I faced the bathroom. The sink and make-up vanity were visible from the balcony. I counted off the paces to the vanity.

"What are you doing?" He raised one eyebrow.

I returned to the balcony and counted off the paces to the office.

"What are you doing?" he demanded to know.

I returned to the bathroom, Detective Jeffries following every step of the way like a lost puppy.

"I was wondering why she would go all the way to the office to get a chair when there was a make-up chair in the bathroom. The office is twice as far—"

"I don't know, but before you go all crazy thinking it was a homicide, let me explain why it wasn't."

I pulled latex gloves onto both hands and returned to the bathroom.

"O.K." I listened as I checked the contents of the cabinet, gingerly turning a medicine bottle to read the prescription, but mostly looking and not touching.

"The front door was double bolted when we arrived. Only Mrs. Sills and her husband had keys so no one could have gotten in here."

"No forced entry?" I looked up from my stooped position.

"No. Besides, we checked all the surveillance tapes and every person on them has been checked out. Same for the sign-in sheet."

"What about the husband? Is he accounted for?" I shut the cabinet and opened the drawers.

"He was running the Peachtree Road Race. No one saw him in or around the building anytime before her death, only after."

"Immediately after, right?" I asked.

I saw his nod in the mirror's reflection.

"His alibi is tight," he added.

"O.K., what about enemies?" I shut the last of the drawers, pulled off the gloves, and headed for the closet.

I noticed a used towel in a pile on the floor. Either she or Mark Sills had showered, probably her.

"She didn't have any friends or enemies. She didn't know anyone well enough to give them a motive. She was aloof, but nice. Not enough personality to motivate murder. Either way, no one could have gotten in past security and without a key."

"You're sure?" I entered the aromatic cedar closet.

"I'm sure."

"What about someone who was already in the building? Perhaps it was someone who lives here."

"Possibly, but like I said she didn't know anyone well enough and their way in was locked."

"Tell me more about her family," I requested.

"We couldn't find any family."

"What about her personal shopper at Saks?" I joked, taking stock of the extravagant clothes and furs.

"Expensive upkeep, huh?" Detective Jeffries asked.

"Yeah, I thought my wife was a clothes horse." I nodded agreement. "Did Nikki Sills have a career? A job?"

"No."

"Would you say she was lonely? Depressed?" I shut the closet and went back to the living room.

Detective Jeffries shrugged. "I didn't see any 'happy' drugs on the report. Her doctor reported good mental health."

"Not recently diagnosed with any incurable problems like cancer?" I hinted. "Or unwanted pregnancy? Nothing?"

Detective Jeffries smirked. "You already know. How do you do that?"

"Lucky, I guess." I shrugged. "I must ask the right questions. Who else knew she was pregnant besides her husband?"

"No one, except her doctor, but he said she was ecstatic about it."

"Why didn't they tell his family?" I looked at the photos on the bookshelf and coffee table.

"I don't know. Don't know if he had any family either."

"Who are these people in the photos?" I picked up a photo of what I thought to be Nikki Sills—pretty smile, blonde hair.

"Don't know."

"Any marital problems? Either Mr. or Mrs. Sills having an affair?" I asked.

"Not that we could uncover. Of course our investigation never really got far. It's been rather cursory since it seems obvious it was an accident. The medical examiner agrees."

"So you think it was an accident? I guess you're right." I shrugged. "There were no warning signs of any trouble?"

"There doesn't seem to have been any problems." He shook his head glumly. "If only all married folks were so lucky. They were a storybook couple."

"Doesn't it seem a little too flawless?" I replaced the photo frame.

"Yes, they were the perfect couple—like Barbie and Ken."

"So the perfect couple is having a baby. They fill out papers for two million in insurance on Mrs. Perfect, who doesn't work and isn't worth anything, and then she ends up dead? No friends or family to tell what she really felt and what she was really like."

"It's strange. And it's what I wanted to talk to you about. I have this gut feeling," he confessed.

"A gut feeling it wasn't an accident?" I asked.

"Yes. Something is wrong, despite the husband's alibi and the incredible security here."

"You think she was murdered?"

"Call me crazy, but yes, I do."

CHAPTER 3

"Why didn't you say so in the first place?" I looked around the living room again.

"I wanted to get your unbiased feelings first. My opinion isn't too popular at the station. It's not cost effective or time efficient." Detective Jeffries shrugged and flopped into the armchair. "I wanted to see if anyone else thought it was weird."

"It's weird." I patted him on the shoulder reassuringly.

"I knew you'd come through for me." He smiled.

"So the circumstances are bugging you?" I motioned for him to follow as I headed back to the bedroom again.

"Yeah, the same details you picked up, although I hadn't noticed the thing with the chair," he confessed as he jumped up.

"All right; let's go over what you think happened." I put my hands on my hips and stood in the middle of the bedroom.

"Someone with a key came in, managed to surprise her, and threw her over the balcony." He walked over and slid open the balcony door.

"Autopsy report suggested there were no signs of a struggle, so it was a surprise attack," I agreed.

"There also weren't any witnesses." Detective Jeffries looked over the railing and down at the men who were scrubbing.

"How do you think the person was able to get hold of Nikki Sills and get her over the rail so quickly?"

"Well..." Detective Jeffries turned to face me and rubbed his chin, thinking. "She might have been sitting, but I assume she was probably standing or leaning into the railing to watch the race."

"Like this?" I stood about a foot from the railing, bent at the waist, and rested my folded arms on the top rail.

"Something like that. Then the person reached down and grabbed her lower legs." Detective Jeffries bent down and grasped my ankles, lifting slightly.

"Whoa, stop." I held tightly to the railing. "Enough of a demo. A swift yank up and forward would have sent her flying over."

"Only one problem." He released me. "The balcony's sliding door had to be open for someone to get behind her unnoticed."

"True." I slid the door to test its noise factor. "Was it open or shut when the investigators arrived?"

"Shut."

"It doesn't really matter," I reassured him. "The person who killed her could have shut it. And you think that person was the husband?"

"I think so, although I'm not exactly sure how he had the time or how he avoided detection."

"Where are the cameras located?"

"There are four cameras: one in each of the two elevators, one in the lobby near the front entrance, and another at the door where you buzz in from the parking deck."

"Are they recorded?" I asked.

"Yes."

"What about cameras on each floor or in the halls?" I bit my cuticles nervously.

Detective Jeffries shook his head. "Negative."

"Are there cameras in the stairwell?"

"No; maybe be the only way Mark Sills could get in without being seen. He didn't show up on the tapes, but he could have come in the side door where there isn't a camera and dashed up the stairs."

"Would security have seen him?"

"If she was looking, I guess."

"What about his alibi. Was he in the race?" I asked.

"A witness saw him at the starting line, before the race. They were in the same color group, but the witness didn't see him when crossing the starting marker at 8:12."

"Would he have had time to run all the way to the apartments, get inside, throw her over, and get back out in time?"

"I have to say I don't know. He claims he runs a nine-minute mile. The apartments are five miles from where he was last seen so he could have arrived there by 9:00, assuming he could even run. The Peachtree race is so crowded. He was seen after she fell at 9:03."

"Maybe five minutes of unaccounted time in there," I figured. "O.K., let's forget all that for now. What about the chair and the plant?" I squatted down to examine the pot again.

"I think they were put in those places immediately after she was thrown over to make it look like an accident."

"Otherwise the pot would have gone over the side with her. And wouldn't the chair have tipped? No one would notice the evidence being, excuse my pun, planted, because all the action was down on the ground," I agreed.

"The only problem with the theory is it seems a little risky to me."

"Who might have been able to see anything?" I looked left and right. Four balconies seemed to have good viewing vantage points.

"No one else was on the balconies this high up," Detective Jeffries replied. "We questioned everyone in the building."

"A reason like someone didn't see it doesn't mean it didn't happen," I said.

"Like the tree falling in the woods, huh?" Detective Jeffries joked. "I haven't exactly been winning any popularity contests at the station with these ideas. No wonder everyone's laughing at me—it sounds crazy."

"Crazy, yes, but I think close to the truth. The chair would have been placed out here after the plant was broken."

I tipped the chair back to look at the bottom of the legs. Tiny grains of the pot fragment were stuck to the rubber feet. I pointed them out to Jeffries. He bent down to take a closer look.

"That doesn't make any sense," he frowned. "The chair had to be in place first. Either Nikki Sills used it or the killer used it in order to get the plant down to break it."

"You're wrong." I crossed the porch to the other plant, still hanging. Without standing on tiptoe or stretching in the least, I reached out and took down the second plant.

"You're tall," Detective Jeffries explained, commenting on my six-foot-three height.

"I think you could comfortably reach." I gauged his height to be almost a foot shorter than mine.

I offered him the plant to try. Not on tiptoe, but with a stretch, he was able to replace it.

"Why would there be a chair out here at all if it's easy to reach?" I asked. "Maybe the plant was broken long before and the chair was brought out for viewing the race. She was pregnant. She'd probably want to sit down some."

"Husband said the plant wasn't broken before he left. It's possible Mrs. Sills didn't want to reach or she didn't think she could, so she got a chair. But it still doesn't explain the slivers."

"Standing on a chair way up here would be scary." I looked over the railing and down. "With her medical disorder I think if she was tall enough she would have done without the chair. Or why move the plant at all?"

"What exactly was wrong with her?" Detective Jeffries pulled out a pack of gum and offered me a stick.

"No, thanks. I don't know what was wrong with her. Something along the line of dizzy spells. I'm seeing her doctor tomorrow," I replied.

"If she was sitting, my theory doesn't work. How could someone toss her over?" He unwrapped his piece and popped it in his mouth.

'Maybe clunk her on the head?"

We scanned for large, heavy objects and saw none.

"Do you know Nikki Sills' height?" I asked.

"She was about my height. I'm five-foot-seven. We can check for sure."

"How tall is Mark Sills?"

"Taller. I don't know exactly, but I can find out for you."

"For me?"

"Mm-hmm." Detective Jeffries looked around for someplace to put the crinkled up wrapper and headed inside. "None of this does me a damn bit of good. My hands are tied. The police have closed the case. At least with you working on the insurance claim you may find enough evidence to keep the bastard from getting the money."

"What are you talking about?" I stepped back into the apartment. The heat on the balcony and Detective Jeffries' announcement had me sweating. "You aren't going to re-open the investigation?"

"No way. Chief Blumberg doesn't want to hear any more on the subject. I've already chewed his ear off about it so much he's ready to bust me down to traffic duty if I don't shut up," Detective Jeffries called out to me as he spoke over the flushing toilet where he had relieved himself and disposed of the paper. Returning to the bedroom, he continued, "I was hoping you might uncover something more solid I could use later to re-open the case."

"Me? No. I can't. If it's declared an accident and you don't re-open the case my employer won't keep me on it. Ninety percent of the time it'd be a waste for the company."

"But you'll try, right? I hate to think someone's going to get away with a crime and the money."

We headed back towards the living room.

"Why don't you spend some of your free time trying to dig up something?" I suggested.

"Chief Blumberg has done everything but order me off the case.

He'd have my ass if I got caught. I had to sneak the apartment key from Detective Silverman's desk."

"So, you're serious about me helping?" I looked him straight in the eyes. Our relationship could be adversarial or cooperative, depending on the day.

"Yes."

"Then I'll tell you what I need you to do..." I picked up the photo frame with the picture of Nikki Sills again.

"What? Anything."

"You need to leave me here alone for an hour. I'll search everything." I unlatched the back of the frame.

"We already did a search," Detective Jeffries insisted.

"Did the police make up a victim profile for Nikki Sills? For example, her activities this past month or her educational background?" I put my hands on my hips and surveyed the area.

"No—"

"O.K. then. I need to do my own search; I want to learn everything I can about her from what brand underwear she wore to the type perfume she preferred."

"Here. Use a pair of gloves if you'll be moving stuff around." He offered me a pair of white cotton gloves, much better than the latex ones I usually used.

"Was there anything removed from the apartment?"

"Yes, some drink glasses for fingerprints. The balcony door handle had no good prints."

"Did they check the railing?"

"Nothing there either."

"Heard anything back about the fingerprints on the glasses?" I worked on the removing the photo from the frame.

"They found some prints that don't belong to Mark or Nikki Sills; no match to anyone yet."

"Where were the glasses?"

"Out here in the livingroom." Jeffries pointed to the coffee table.

"I'll let you know if I take anything." I held up the freed photo. "I'll need this."

"I really can't allow..." he began, but seeing my perturbed expression, he said, "O.K. Take what you need. Be sure to make a list so we can put it back later."

"I'll document everything," I reassured him. "While you're gone, do me a favor. Check with the Department of Motor Vehicles and get copies of driver's licenses for both Mark and Nikki Sills."

I knew I could get heights and weights from the doctor, but driver's licenses might also give me their Social Security numbers and be faster.

"I have to come back to lock up the place when you're done. Beep me when you're finished." He wrote down his number for me. "I'll try to have copies of their licenses by then."

With Detective Jeffries gone, I was free to roam. This activity was probably a complete waste of time as tomorrow morning the insurance company would more than likely close the case and pay the claim. *But, I'm already here. What's it going to hurt to have a little look around?*

What was I looking for? Anything to help me construct a more developed picture of the lives of Mr. and Mrs. Sills. In the past, things proving valuable were photographs, phone bills and messages, address books, calendars, and the like. Even a trash can could hold priceless clues.

I began my search in the kitchen, making records of my every move for Detective Jeffries in my pocket notebook. The kitchen usually holds the least clues and the messiest trash. I took off the cotton gloves, put on the latex ones, and went through the trash first. Remnants of what might have been the last meal Nikki Sills prepared, some junk mail, and paper towels were all I found. I removed the latex gloves. On the fridge was an invitation to a Fourth of July barbeque, which I confiscated because the hosts might be friends or family I could question.

In the living room I jotted down the valid numbers appearing in the memory of their cordless phone with Caller ID. Many were telemarketing calls from out of area and one from a private caller. The few displayed photos and an album provided me with persons whom I would like to interview. Nikki had labeled each page with captions including names of persons and dates. I wrote down their names. None appeared to be family members.

Next I went to the office. I collected two old messages from the tape machine, one from a business colleague and the other from a storage rental facility wanting to know if Mark was going pay his account and empty his unit. His account was overdue and the contents would be auctioned if he didn't contact them soon. The storage phone number matched one of the numbers off the Caller ID. Their desk calendar showed no appointments or activities scheduled for July. I couldn't find the June page which was already torn off, and I searched everywhere for it. Then I found the filing cabinet tucked away in the closet, and I knew

I'd be occupied for a while. Filing cabinets usually hold the most information—that's what they're for.

Most people don't realize the amount of important information they file away about themselves. My private investigator training had taught me, anyone with any time to snoop, like a housekeeper or babysitter, can find out more than anyone would want them to know. With the simple items I found in most filing cabinets I could wreak serious havoc on credit lines, illegally refill and use prescription drugs, and order checks I could use to empty a checking or savings account. Of course, I would never do those things, but the information is there waiting on someone who will.

Mark Sills' current tax return was enlightening. I got his Social Security number and his late wife's. He made a six-figure salary the last year and had a hefty write-off for gambling losses against his earnings. I checked my file. Mark Sills worked as a stock broker at Houghton Lofton.

The spare bath had nothing to offer and I had already searched the master bathroom. I knew from Nikki Sills' clothes closet she appreciated the finer things in life even before I searched the bedroom and found an old birthday card in her jewelry box on the dresser. "Nothing but the best for my darling Nikki," it said. Some expensive piece of jewelry had no doubt accompanied it. There were several pieces in there fitting the bill. I had barely finished searching the bedroom when I heard the front door open. I went to check who was there.

"How's it going?" Detective Jeffries asked as I came around the corner.

"I thought I was to beep you when I was done." I folded my arms.

"Need more time?" He ignored my display of annoyance.

"No." I sighed and looked at my watch. It had been over the one hour I had requested. "I'm about done."

"Find anything?" He looked around the room to be sure everything was still in place.

"Sort of. I have a better idea of their lifestyle now. They didn't have many vices except gambling—no porn, non-smokers, no alcohol, not even any caffeine in this apartment. All of their money was spent on household bills or Nikki's department store dependency. They have exceptional financial records, which is to be expected from a stock broker," I read from my notes. "Oh, and they pay their taxes honestly every year."

"Really?" Detective Jeffries was impressed.

"Yes. They weren't socialites either judging by their address book and Caller ID. They didn't have any plans for the entire month of July, except for a barbeque on the fourth which they never got to attend."

"Are you going to take anything?" he prodded.

"Mostly I copied down anything I thought I'd need. I've got some names and faces from photos, some phone numbers, and such that I'll want to question. I took this invitation, but I've got the name and number so I can leave it." I emptied my pockets.

"So the only thing you'll need to take is the photo of Mrs. Sills?"

"Yep, that'll do it." I snapped my notebook shut. "Did you get the driver's licenses?"

"Oh, yeah. I got those." He handed over the creased papers.

I unfolded them. Mark Sills was on top. His height reported as expected, about five-foot-ten. Nikki Sills was shorter than I thought. She was five-foot-six—probably still tall enough to reach the hanging plants.

"Well, good news," I said. "It would appear the chair was part of a set-up."

Detective Jeffries saw the look of excitement on my face. "But it still allows for other explanations. She might have broken the one taking it down and brought the chair out afterwards to get down the other one."

"But the chair should have been by the other plant on the other side."

"True."

"Could an officer have moved the chair enough to get those fragments under the legs while conducting the investigation? Or might the chair have been tipped over and someone straightened it up?"

"It's possible. I'll go back and check our notes."

I folded the pages in half and put them in my file. I gathered my things and followed him to the door.

"Hey, did you say something about them gambling?" He held the door open and let me pass.

"Yes. They wrote off some gambling losses on their taxes."

"Were Mr. and Mrs. Sills in financial trouble?" He scanned the room one more time before leaving the apartment.

"Based on their records they were in debt, but who isn't these days? With her upkeep they were probably squeaking by on his income, unless they had some underhanded loans or undocumented problems, if you know what I mean."

He nodded and locked the door. "I know what you mean, but I don't have any information."

"You putting the crime tape back up?" I asked as he left for the elevators.

"No. We're done with it." He kept walking. "Want to go get some hot wings and beer?"

"Actually, I'm going to do a little more work here. I'm going to take the stairs down and find out if I can avoid being seen."

Jeffries pushed the 'down' button. "I appreciate what you are doing, Paul."

"I told you I'll do what I can," I reassured him. "I'll take all my information to my boss in the morning and see what he says."

I went around the corner to the stair doorway.

"Hey, Paul?" Jeffries called out from the elevator as it opened.

I stuck my head back around the corner. "Yeah?"

"What kind of underwear?" He teased.

"Victoria's Secret," I replied nonchalantly, then turned on my heel and pushed open the door. I stepped into the stairwell and let it fall shut with a clang. The staircase went up on the right and down on the left. As I descended I came to a landing where the staircase turned 180 degrees and continued down to the floor below. The stairs were cramped and narrow, not well lit. I felt claustrophobic, one of the few times I'd ever felt that way. It didn't hit me until I descended about four or five floors. It was compounded by a phobia of heights, since each step was not a solid piece, rather made up of two metal beams placed side by side, allowing you to see between them to the level below. Beneath each descending staircase ran another and another. I felt like I was trapped in an M.C. Escher drawing. I held the railing tighter and tighter. I wondered what would happen if I fell. I wondered how Nikki Sills felt when she realized she was falling. I slowed my steps.

When I reached the sixth floor my grip on the rail relaxed a little. I knew I was more than halfway down. As I passed each landing, I felt more and more relieved. Finally, I burst out into the brightly lit lobby. An expression of panic briefly crossed the security girl's face as I emerged from the stairwell. It probably wasn't well traveled.

I re-introduced myself as I hung over the side of her desk and watched the TV surveillance of the cameras. "Paul Grey."

"I'm Sue." She smiled, showing very white teeth.

"How many cameras are there?" I asked.

"Four."

I watched the cameras silently and ran some math through my head. If Mark Sills could run a little faster than nine minutes a mile, say eight minutes a mile, then there would be ten minutes unaccounted for. Maybe he didn't run at all. No one actually saw him running. But then there was still the issue of whether or not he would have been seen at the apartments.

"Could a tenant come in the side door and get into the stairs without you seeing him?" I asked.

"On a day like today?" She tilted her head to her shoulder. "I doubt it. It's been so slow, I've seen everything."

"What about on a busy day?" I prodded. "Like the fourth of July. Were you busy then?"

"The fourth?" She nodded. "Oh, yes! People were trying to get in all day to use our restrooms, plus tenants were in and out of the heat to watch the race themselves."

"So, someone could have gotten to and from the stairwell without being seen?"

Sue frowned. She knew she shouldn't admit security had its failings. She carefully framed her answer. "The stairs are enclosed by soundproof walls and doors, so tenants don't hear people clanking up and down the stairwell. I wouldn't be able to hear anyone on the stairs once they are in them. Security is tight here so I doubt anyone could have gotten to them without being seen, but I never say never."

"Has the apartment complex had any problems since you started working here? Are there ever any crimes committed here?"

"No crimes at all, sir."

I didn't believe her. In the effort to sell apartments it would be counter-productive to say anything derogatory about them.

"Detective Jeffries and I feel there has been a crime committed here, possibly a first. I need your help," I encouraged her.

I have a theory anyone who takes a job with security has the private detective itch. These individuals are dying to have a mystery to solve and usually are more than happy, sometimes downright ecstatic, to help me solve mine. I had never been wrong about this theory, and I wasn't wrong with her either.

"How can I help?" She raised one eyebrow.

"I'm going to try to run up to the seventeenth floor in three minutes," I told her. "Time me."

She grinned at the game. "O.K."

She set my stopwatch, said "go", and I ran. The first flight took only seconds at a moderate pace. The second and third flights took about the same, but then the stairs began to take their toll on my timing. Each successive flight took a second longer than the last. Ascending the stairs in this manner all the way to the seventeenth floor would take incredible stamina and athletic prowess.

On my run from the eleventh to the twelfth floor, I was almost breathless, legs like rubber bands. All my efforts were tied into keeping a full-bore run going. Halfway up this flight I tripped over my own feet and was going to stumble into the stairs. I tried to balance and catch myself using my arms and hands and found instead I had over-corrected and was flailing backwards like a windmill. My knee buckled out from under me and I came crashing down, sliding, tumbling down the half-flight of stairs, crashing in a heap at the bottom against the landing wall. My vision narrowed as the dim lights of the stairwell grew even dimmer, then dark.

CHAPTER 4

When I opened my eyes, I had no idea where I was. Above me, fuzzy, distorted views of the stairs became clearer, and I remembered. Lying supine, on my back, up against the wall, I shifted onto my elbows and lifted into a sitting position. My legs felt worthy so I pulled them under me and hauled myself up to a crouching, then standing position using the railing for support. I brushed off my clothes with uncontrolled, shaky hands. Running any farther was out of the question. With effort, holding the rail, I hobbled down stair by stair to the eleventh floor door. Taking the elevator seemed like the best idea at this point. It let me out where the security girl was waiting expectantly.

"You took long enough," she huffed.

"I know; I quit for today," I replied not caring to embarrass myself by explaining. I took my watch from her outstretched hand.

"No pain, no gain." She leaned over the edge of the desk and watched me limp away.

"I made some gains," I replied over my shoulder.

Only an athlete would be able to run seventeen flights of stairs in three minutes. Someone with minimal exercise or training, like myself, would be doomed.

I seemed to have jammed my ankle, so once at home I propped up my legs. I was icing it when Lindsey arrived. A look of disgust crossed swiftly over her face causing her lips to momentarily purse like she was going to blast into me about the importance of job safety. But then her eyes lifted from the ice pack to meet my sheepish grin. She smiled, briefly.

"Klutz." She dropped her things and came to sit down beside me. "What happened?"

"A little twist, that's all," I insisted.

"How?" she demanded.

"Honestly? Well... I was part of a major arrest today, part of a large insurance fraud bust. One of the suspects was escaping so I tackled him before he got away, and in the process I twisted my leg."

She raised one eyebrow suspiciously and lifted the ice bag to inspect the bruising. "Really?"

"No, I'm just kidding, Lin." I laughed. "Actually, I fell down a flight of stairs while doing a little research on a case."

"Detective work is all one big joke to you, isn't it?" She got up from the sofa and crossed the room. "It's all a joke until someone gets hurt."

"I *am* hurt, and I'm still laughing. Don't be so serious; it's kinda funny the way it happened."

She folded her arms, her brows knitted up tightly. "Paul, I am serious. I don't want you doing investigative work where you get hurt, you know that, so don't play around with me."

"This could have happened anywhere."

"No, it happened because you were experimenting somehow."

"Lindsey, you're right. You should be angry."

"What? Are you trying to use reverse psychology on me?"

"No. You're right, I was working on a case. I should be more careful. My investigations may seem tame and harmless, but when the insurance claims are in the millions of dollars range I am definitely at risk. These perpetrators will kill their own family members for money; they certainly would have no qualms about killing a complete stranger like me."

"I know, like the one before you who had to quit after being beaten so badly by a baseball bat he was in the hospital for two weeks."

"But the fact of the matter is nothing happened today. I twisted my ankle on a set of stairs. I could have been anywhere."

"But you were on the job."

"Lin, I know you don't like it, but this is what I want to do. It makes me happy." I moved towards her and took up her hand in mine.

"What you want?" She squirmed away. "How about me? You used to say all you needed was me and nothing else mattered."

"Well..." I began but I didn't have an answer. I could feel the color rushing to my face, flustered.

"Your job is important enough you don't care about the consequences." Her voice grew higher in pitch. "You don't care if it upsets me. You don't care it something happens to you."

"Don't be ridiculous! Of course I care about those things. And you *are* the most important thing to me."

"Really? You don't act like it sometimes." She wiped her eyes, hating for me or anyone to know she was crying.

"I just took you on a vacation. What do you want from me? Do you want me to quit my job? What is it you want?"

She didn't look up at me, and she didn't reply

"What's wrong with you? Are you hormonal today?"

"Ugh. Don't even go there, no."

"You want me to go back to a job like I had a DataCOM and be depressed? Do you want me to quit my job?" I continued.

"I would quit my job if you asked me to," she answered softly.

"Oh, Lin, you're not being fair." I shook my head and walked away.

"Where are you going?" she asked as I picked up the car keys.

"Out. I don't want to have this argument anymore."

"It's too late. We've already started; don't go away angry."

"I don't think we can settle this one." I shrugged.

"We have to try," she insisted, turning a brief second to wipe her eyes once again.

We stood in the living room in stony silence for a while. I was waiting for her to speak while she was waiting on the same from me.

"You would really give up your work in the Senate if I asked you to?" I questioned.

"Yes," she replied.

"No, you wouldn't. That's stupid. I mean, why? Why would you give up a job you love?"

"Because you're more important to me than a job, and I feel the marriage has to come before the individual."

"The type of job I have has nothing to do with how healthy our marriage is," I insisted.

"It can play a part." She shrugged.

"I disagree. If I asked you to give up your job, I would hope you *wouldn't* do it. If you did, it would only mean you don't value yourself or your happiness."

"Not true. It means making you happy makes me happy."

"There are better ways of making each other happy," I insisted.

"Like what?" she demanded.

"Sex?" I laughed.

"Be serious, Paul. Every time you make someone else happy you have sacrificed something."

"Not true."

"Give me an example of when that's not true."

I couldn't think of anything on the spot. "Well, the point is..."

She tapped her foot expectantly.

"The point is," I continued, "I don't think the marriage should come first."

"You don't put our marriage first, over your work?" Lindsey's face flushed red.

"No, what I mean is I don't want the marriage to take over to the point the individual loses all sense of self. You and me, I want us to be happy. Neither one of us is superior to the other. The individual and the marriage are equal, one is not superior to the other. A marriage can't be happy if the individuals in it aren't happy with themselves first."

"So you are saying if you don't have a job you like, you won't be happy and then the marriage will suffer? You would take it out on me?" Lindsey's voice escalated louder.

"No, let's don't shout. Remember, I have never taken things out on you. Even at DataCOM, I never did. But what I'm doing right now, this case, it isn't dangerous. We shouldn't even be arguing."

"Your work is dangerous."

"So you want me to quit?"

"Yes," Lindsey said, then backed off. "Well, no. I just don't like it."

"And you may never like it, but I do."

"So I should sacrifice to make you happy." Lindsey flopped into a chair.

"That's your theory, but there won't need to be sacrifices. What do you feel you have to sacrifice?"

"I don't know, my sense of security?" She shrugged.

"Feel secure knowing I love you and I am careful." I knelt down beside her and took her hand.

"I love you, that's why I worry." She let her head fall against my shoulder. "I guess I'm just in a bad mood, I'm sorry."

"Look, I fell in love with you, an *individual*." I lifted her head by the chin and looked into her eyes. "I would never ask you to do something to change the person inside, the person I love. And the person I fell in love with would never ask that of me. Am I making any sense here?"

Lindsey's eyes lowered, because she understood. I took her in my arms. Her kisses begged forgiveness, soft and warm and tender. She smelled so good as she pressed her form against me, nuzzling my ear, my neck. The setting sun had left the room in dusky darkness, and I lost myself in her.

Make-up sex, the kind you have after an argument, is undeniably, invariably the best. I don't know why, but it is.

*   *   *   *   *

Early the next morning, I awoke, got ready for work, and by 8:30 A.M. waited outside the plush top-level office of my boss, Logan Moore, for an audience with him. Mr. Moore was not easy to get to know or talk to. He was often short on words, finishing your sentences impatiently, and appeared too busy to care about anything much except getting away from you. However, I confidently believed in reality he wasn't as pressured as he appeared. In fact as I sat and waited on him, I was certain he kept me there in limbo, intentionally perpetuating the myth he scarcely had time to breathe. In these days of cutbacks, it probably wasn't a bad idea to put on a front for the benefit of those more elevated in the hierarchy. *Surely if Mr. Moore is so busy we can't fire him or cut his position*, I could hear the bosses say. *Besides he does so much, we'd be lost without him. We don't even know what all he does. Perhaps we ought to get him an assistant or offer him a raise*, the scenario would go.

When Mr. Moore appeared anxiously in the doorway I took my time moving into the office, still babying my twisted ankle. Papers were everywhere, the way one might rearrange the food on one's plate to make it appear as if something has actually been eaten. The papers made it look like he was neck deep in a project of some kind.

"Did we have a meeting? Was I expecting you? What is this about?" came tumbling out of his mouth.

"I'm here about a life insurance claim investigation," I explained.

He motioned for me to take a seat across from him as he glanced at his watch. "Go ahead, go on."

"I'm working the claim for the death of Nikki Sills—"

"She jumped during the race, yes, yes," he rushed.

"At first look it might appear to have been an accident. And I'm fairly sure it wasn't a suicide. I feel it might have been a murder..."

Mr. Moore drummed his fingers impatiently, rapping them in an even clicking manner in reverse from the pinky finger in— an annoying and distracting habit.

"So why are you here?"

Regaining my train of thought, I continued, "Official police reports indicate an accident; however, I'd like to get permission to continue investigating—"

"Permission denied." He rose. "Is that all?"

"Yes, but did you hear what I said? It might have been a murder—"

"Yes, I heard you. Permission denied." He motioned for me to leave.

"At least may I interview the husband first?" I stood up and was shooed toward the door.

"No, go on to the next case." He ushered me out.

"But, why not?"

Mr. Moore was probably not accustomed to being challenged. His abrupt manner usually put people off, and they were easily scared of him. Reports of him flying off the handle during periods of high stress had circulated the office.

"Why?" he repeated my question, and, like a parent reprimanding an inquisitive child, he added, "Because I said so. Because further investigation would be a waste of time, like my having to explain myself to you is an even bigger waste of time."

Scolded enough, I gave up and retreated to my dungeon with Glenn and Shawn.

"Myra dropped off a medical information release form for you" Shawn indicated the ever growing pile of papers on my desk.

"Too bad I won't be needing it." I picked it up off the top of the stack and dropped it into the trash can.

"What's wrong cowboy?" She pouted her lips and then grinned. "Bad news?"

"Why are you smiling?" I went to work organizing my desk. "You revel in other people's pain."

"No, I don't!" Her brown eyes sparkled as if relishing the moment even though she shook her head in adamant denial.

"Then why do you like to hear about it so much?" Glenn added.

"Taking his side, huh?" She smiled. "I see how it is, guys against the girl."

"The company closed the Fourth of July jumper case." I flopped into my chair. "They're going to pay the claim."

"Oh." Shawn's grin dropped.

"You look more disappointed than I am."

"I am disappointed. I like it when a case has some twists and mystery, you know?" she said.

"Yeah, I know. Believe me, it has some mystery, but Mr. Moore said to go on to the next case anyway."

"He's a bean counter, whad'ya expect?" Glenn said. "You should have kept investigating and never said anything to him about it."

"It doesn't matter anyway. Even if I could pursue the case further, Mark Sills has an excellent alibi," I said.

"How?" Glenn asked.

"He was in the road race. The timing seems too close for him to have been able to run those five miles, leave the race, run up to the seventeenth floor, kill his wife, plant evidence, then get back downstairs, all without being seen."

"Have you ever run the Peachtree?" Glenn asked.

"No; have you?"

"Yes, and let me give you a little insight into the ordeal, O.K.?"

"O.K., enlighten me."

"People sometimes purchase their race number and never intend to run the entire six miles. Somewhere along the last two miles, when they see people with their color tags running by, they'll go through the barricade and into the race. Then they run through the sprinklers to make themselves look like they are all hot and sweaty and have been running the whole time."

"So they hang out at the end, and no one sees them do this?"

"Of course they're seen. But they make-up lame excuses like they had to use the bathroom or something. In the spirit of the day, no one really bothers with them."

"Not bother? They're cheating, and why do it if they know they cheated?"

"No one ever turns them in. At the end of their two-mile sprint, they get a free T-shirt like the rest of the pack, so why not? It's one-third the effort for the same prize and prestige."

"So what you're saying is Mark Sills might not have run the five miles; he could have been hanging around the apartments. When the timing was right he pushed her over, then joined the race up by a set of sprinklers and pretended to have been running the whole time."

"Exactly." Glenn leaned back in his chair and laced his hands behind his head.

"No, that still doesn't work. He was seen at the start of the race."

"Maybe it wasn't him. You must see twenty to thirty thousand different faces in one day. Over fifty-five thousand people run, and even more are there to watch."

"Well, it's a good idea, Glenn. It could explain why security at the apartments never saw Mark Sills come in. He could have been in the building the whole time. I'm sure security doesn't pay as much attention to people leaving as they do those entering. Mark could have slipped right out. Plus all the chaos outside would have already begun."

"Makes sense."

"But he was on the scene so quickly also. He couldn't have had time to go up hill and wet down and then return to the scene. I wonder where the sprinklers are along the route—how far from the apartments, I mean."

"I think they were no more than a block up the hill the last time I ran the Peachtree, years ago. You'd better contact someone from the race, like the organizing committee." Glenn propped his feet up on the desk.

I nodded then shook my head. "What am I saying? This doesn't help. The case is closed anyway."

Glenn shrugged. "Can't help you there."

"To investigate more, I'd be going against company policy—"

"Thbbbht," Shawn raspberried. "It's always better to do it and beg forgiveness than to ask and not receive!"

"O.K., Confucius." I shook my head and laughed. "I'll consider it."

"Well, Confucius has to go out to an arson sight. I'll catch ya'll later." Shawn swung her purse and a camera over her shoulder and picked up the camcorder bag.

I set to work sorting my papers and cases. Maybe she was right. Maybe I should continue to work the Sills case, and if I got caught I could simply ask forgiveness. As long as I kept my other cases up to date Mr. Moore might not ever know. I fished around in the trash can for the discarded medical information release form.

"What are you looking for?" Glenn asked with curiosity.

"Med release form," I replied.

"I see." He smiled knowingly. "You don't have to worry about me."

"I know." I folded the retrieved document and put it in my pocket. "I'm going now."

"And I don't know where." He winked.

I really wanted to rush right over to Mark Sills' office and ask him a barrage of questions, but I knew seeing the doctor and some friends first was the right thing to do. Those people would enlighten me concerning Mr. Sills' character, hobbies, and lifestyle, which I could never discover on my own. Armed with information I could frame better questions or perhaps not even have to see Mr. Sills at all.

Therefore, my first order of business would be to see the doctor—Dr. Claborn Lazar, OB-GYN, to be exact. His waiting room area was beginning to thin out as the lunch hour approached.

"I'd like to speak to Dr. Lazar for a few minutes if at all possible," I explained through the sliding glass window in the reception area.

The girl looked at me dubiously, glancing down at my hands and even farther down at my feet, noticing I had no briefcase or sales bags.

"You're not with a pharmaceutical company?" She frowned.

The office probably didn't receive many male visitors unless they were drug reps.

"No, I'm with Morehouse Insurance," I replied, pulling out my wallet for a business card and handing it over to her.

"Insurance? What kind of insurance? Are you selling?" She guarded the doctor like a bulldog.

I shook my head. "No, no. I'm here to speak to Dr. Lazar about an ex-patient of his."

She examined the card like she was checking for a fake ID on a teen at a nightclub. "Sit over there." She motioned and disappeared behind the frosted glass panes.

I seated myself in the corner far away from the female patients, next to a side table filled with parenting magazines. Oddly uncomfortable in this room and not wanting to make eye-contact with any of the ladies, I flipped through an issue of *American Baby* to pass the time. Waiting rooms are the earthly equivalent of the Catholic Purgatory—a place of indefinite limbo between heaven and earth, between the doctor and the outside world.

A young lady who looked like she was carrying a basketball under her dress was called to the back by an assistant. As the nurse held the door open for the woman, the booming voice of the doctor rang out clearly. The door closed behind them, and his words became muffled. The higher pitched voice of the receptionist joined in. They jabbered a while before a nurse came to the door to escort me to Dr. Lazar's consultation office.

I glanced at my watch as I sank into the plush sofa chair, hoping the doctor would have some information I could use. There's nothing worse than waiting around for disappointment. After laying out the medical release form for the doctor to see, I picked anxiously at my cuticles waiting for him to appear.

At last, a Hispanic man of medium build and dark eyes rounded the corner, his white lab jacket flapping open, his stethoscope around his neck. Portions of his thick, wavy, dark hair fell forward barely above his eyes so he ran his fingers through it to pull it back. Only about thirty years old, I guessed, and handsome in his face. His physique was massive, in a muscular way, with dark, smooth skin. I was sure most of his patients didn't miss their appointments. Single, too. I noted no ring on his left hand as he extended his right to shake mine heartily, although these days a bare finger was not always a reliable marker of one's eligibility. I made a mental note to find out if Lindsey used his practice.

"Good morning. What can I do for you, Mr. Grey?" he asked, deeply rolling the *R* 's, which I'm sure was added delight for his clientele. I indicated the form on his desk, and he nodded.

"Ahhh, yes. Mrs. Sills, poor senorita. A sad story." He shook his head. The tone of his voice showed much despair and sympathy.

"Perhaps you could share the story with me," I suggested. "I was hoping you could tell me about Mrs. Sills' medical history. Her records indicated she used you as her primary physician."

"Yes, yes." He nodded. "I was her doctor—"

He paused, and I wondered if he might add 'and her lover' to the end of his statement, but he only sighed. I could see where the attractive Mrs. Sills and the young, suave doctor might have matched up.

"I'd like to know about any problems she had, physical or mental, any medications, and particularly I'd like information about her pregnancy," I insisted.

"You know about her pregnancy?" Dr. Lazar seemed to pull himself out of his melancholy state.

"Yes. It was recorded on the autopsy report when they examined her body. The husband said they had been keeping it a secret. Do you know why?"

"That's not possible." The doctor shook his head.

"What's not possible?" I asked, baffled.

The doctor knitted his brows. "About her husband. She hadn't even told *him* about the baby..."

CHAPTER 5

'Why wouldn't she have told her husband?' was the obvious question running through my brain, but I took a slightly different tact, guessing the answer to that question and skipping on to the next inquiry.

"She didn't tell him because they were having marital problems, and she wasn't sure she was going to keep the baby. What were the causes of their marriage problems, do you know?" I asked.

Dr. Lazar hesitated, his black coal eyes squinted, staring deep into my mind trying to read it. Did I really know this or had I been fumbling blindly and made a lucky strike?

"Yes," he began slowly. "There was a possibility of a break up, but I don't think abortion or adoption were ever considered by Nikki. She was a moral, level-headed woman—"

Did I see tears in his eyes? I couldn't help but notice he had slipped and called her by her first name.

"She was having an affair, and the baby wasn't her husband's," I declared, although I was certain this wasn't the case. I wanted to see his reaction anyway. Was there more between them than a doctor-and-patient relationship? I wasn't sure.

"It was nothing like an affair, at least not on her end," he assured me. "I think she refrained from telling him because she didn't want him to feel obligated to stay with her. However, the point is mute, because you said the husband knew about it, so she must have decided to tell him. I was a little surprised, that's all."

"Maybe she didn't tell him. He might have figured it out on his own or possibly he only knew when the autopsy was complete and pretended to know."

Dr. Lazar made no further comment; he seemed to have slipped back into his depression.

"Perhaps they reconciled," I suggested, again to see his reaction. There was none. "Do you do paternity testing here?"

"Only if it is requested."

"Was there a paternity done for Mrs. Sills?"

"No." Dr. Lazar fidgeted with a paper clip.

"O.K.," I confessed. "I know it was Mark Sills' baby anyway. The medical examiner tested."

The doctor stopped playing with the silver clip and gave me a harsh glare. "So you are then wasting my valuable time? Playing games?"

"No, no. I want to see if you can corroborate facts. I want to know what you know, and frankly, you aren't telling me much."

"She didn't want to tell him because she didn't want him to stay with her for the child's sake. She didn't want a loveless marriage. But she never told me what the problem was between them. I'm her doctor, not her therapist."

"Was she distraught or depressed about the possibility of divorce?"

"I'm sure she wasn't happy about it; people seldom are when it comes to these things. It was added stress for her, but she was not clinically depressed or anything even remotely close."

"But you said you were not her therapist, so how do you know?"

"I know. Doctors know these things." He flung his arms up, and I knew I had to back off or the interview would be over.

"There are two theories about what happened to Mrs. Sills. Either she jumped or as the police have concluded, she fell accidentally while standing on a chair. Do you believe either of these?"

"What about murder? Has no one thought of murder?" The doctor seemed agitated, perhaps from my presence, perhaps because of what he felt to be police incompetence.

"The Antivert drug in her system led the police to think she got dizzy and fell," I said. "Why was she given a prescription? And when pregnant?"

"I prescribed it for her, an extraordinarily low dose because of the fetus and possible side affects, but still enough to keep her from falling off a balcony, by God."

"Why did she take Antivert?"

"She experienced inner ear problems which caused her to get dizzy and, on rare occasions, black-out. She should only have been taking the medicine if she'd had a spell, not every day."

"So if she was dizzy that day, she might have fallen?" I asked.

"Anything is possible, but she was very cautious. Obviously you've never had a vertigo spell," he said.

I shook my head in the negative.

"Well," he continued, "the room will start to spin, slowly, then gaining speed. Everything begins to close in on you, and the room gets dark. Your ears ring, a very high pitch, so much you can hardly hear anything else, even people right next to you. Then you find it is nearly impossible to stand so you must lie down or crawl to somewhere where you can lie down, until the spell passes. Eventually, the ringing will subside and the spinning will stop and the room open up and lighten. The key is, it is gradual. A vertigo spell comes on over a short time, but long enough for people who have experienced it before to get somewhere safe, like a bed. If Mrs. Sills was feeling bad enough to take her medication, she wouldn't have been outside on her balcony standing on a chair."

"So in your opinion what happened to her?"

"I think the husband or someone might have pushed her, but I don't know. Not my field of expertise. I leave those decisions up to the police." He shrugged. "Now, if you'll excuse me, I have patients waiting."

"Of course." I shook his hand as he departed.

I headed over to a local deli for a sandwich and to make some notes. With Nikki's photo propped up between the salt and pepper shakers I stared into her sea blue eyes hoping somehow they could tell me what happened to her. Although flat and two-dimensional, her eyes were haunted in the photograph. She didn't appear to be looking at the photographer but rather staring over and past him like a third person was looking on. It gave the photo an eerie feel; her eyes followed you. Her smile was enigmatic, reminiscent of the Mona Lisa—happy, yet sad. What did I really know about her? She had no friends, no family, no job according to Detective Jeffries. But since when did I listen to him?

I pulled out the phone numbers from her Caller ID and the number for the couple who had sent the invitation to a Fourth of July barbeque—Ramona and Chad Nash. Calling from my cell phone, I determined the other names and numbers were nothing, but the Nashes were friends and a different story. When Ramona Nash answered, I introduced myself with an alias and a false cover story I worked for the press—risky business, impersonating a reporter. Press reporters are so pushy sometimes people feel like they are required to talk with them, and those who don't feel obligated to speak sometimes react violently. Both types of people dislike the press with equal hatred—a hatred usually reserved for spiders and snakes.

Mrs. Nash did not hang up, did not seem anxious to talk to me judging from the edgy abruptness in her voice, but she was cooperative.

"I thought this would be old news by now," she said.

"Well, it's not front page anymore," I confessed, "but may I ask you a few questions anyway?"

"Will my name be in the paper?" she asked.

"Do you want it to be?"

"I suppose, but I can't take long. I have to pick up my son from preschool."

"O.K., I'll be quick. A couple of background questions first. Were you and your husband friends of Mr. and Mrs. Sills?"

"Yes."

"How did you first meet Mr. and Mrs. Sills?" I took a tiny bite off my sandwich and twisted the receiver away while I quickly chewed and swallowed.

"My husband works with Mark—Mr. Sills. We met out one night for dinner and became friends."

"How long have you known them?"

"Since before our son Caldwell was born, so about six years."

"Did you ever speak privately with Mrs. Sills about her marriage or other things in her life?"

"On occasion."

"Did she ever mention any marital problems to you?"

"Not recently. They went through a time, right after Thanksgiving, when things weren't real great, but she was never one to talk about it much. Most of what I know came from my husband and his conversations with Mark."

"So what was the source of their problems?"

"I think Mark was having an affair, but neither one of them ever said. You're not going to quote me, are you?"

"Not if you don't want me to. Could their problems have been financial?"

"I don't know. Mark was a gambler; of course a lot of the rich are highrollers. And she was a spender—not a good combination. But Mark seemed to make enough to support both. They lived quite extravagantly. She was never left wanting for the finer things in life."

"How well do you think you knew them?"

"Very well."

"For instance, did you exchange Christmas or birthday gifts?"

"Not always, but sometimes."

"Do you know what kind of perfume Nikki Sills might wear?"

"What? Perfume?"

"I figured if you knew Nikki very well, you would probably know what kind of perfume she liked. Don't women usually know those kinds of things?"

"She didn't wear any," Mrs. Nash defended. "I believe she was allergic to most of them."

Despite Detective Jeffries' claim Nikki had no friends, Mrs. Nash was close enough. She knew what I had discovered in my search of the apartment—Nikki Sills had no perfumes.

"What kinds of activities did Mrs. Sills like?" I asked.

"Are you kidding?" Mrs. Nash laughed. "Shopping."

"Was she a member of any groups or clubs? Like fitness clubs? Or a church?"

"No, she was a loner, of sorts."

"Any hobbies?" I asked.

"Shopping" was the witty reply.

"What do you think of the rumor Nikki Sills was killed by her husband, Mark?"

"I think it's trash. Mark would never do such a thing. Besides if there was any substance to the rumor, he'd already be arrested and charged."

"There's quite a bit of evidence collected that points towards him."

"Well, you'd need some heavy-duty conclusive proof to convince me he had anything to do with it because the last time I saw him with her it was like two teenagers in love. I've never seen him happier."

"An act?" I suggested.

"I've got to go now," she insisted, put off by my last comment.

"Please, Mrs. Nash, do you think he could have been putting on an act? Perhaps he was planning to kill her and he needed to make himself look good?"

"I don't think so."

"Did you know he stands to inherit $2 million in life insurance from her death?"

There was a pause, then a shocked, "No."

"What do you think about that?"

Another silence was followed by, "Well, it's always the ones you don't suspect, isn't it, Mr.—I'm sorry, I didn't catch your name."

"Greg Kramer, thanks for your time."

My decision now was to set up surveillance on Mark Sills. Mrs. Nash had not painted Mark in the best of light—a philanderer and a gambler, ready to inherit. And where there are money and love triangles there's bound to be murder.

CHAPTER 6

Before I could begin surveillance I needed to pick up some equipment, try to convince some poor sucker to join me (surveillance is always more fun with company), and see Lindsey. All the legal spy equipment I could ever possibly want to use was readily available at Morehouse, and I was sure I'd find my sucker there, too. It wasn't hard to convince Glenn into keeping me company. He was single, adventurous, and had already expressed an interest in this case. We arranged to meet at Mark Sills' office at quarter 'til five. Not sure of what equipment I would need, I probably took more than was necessary. I took video and SLR cameras with film, a handheld tape recorder, walkie-talkies, and a pair of binoculars. Feeling very James-Bondish I packed the car. If my boss noticed the check-out sheet, there'd be hell to pay. Speaking of hell to pay, convincing Lindsey of the necessity and importance of a twenty-four-hour surveillance would be a challenge. So for the second time in a week I stopped by her office, only this time she didn't greet me with a smile.

"Let's see, it's too late for lunch and too early for dinner." She glanced at the clock on her desk. "So you're here for some other reason."

"Gee, try to contain yourself, Lin. Don't look so happy to see me."

"Wait, don't tell me. I can guess," she continued in her smart-aleck way. "Some kind of investigation case takes priority over coming home tonight."

"How'd you know?" Sometimes I'd swear she could read my mind.

"First of all, your timing is a good indication. Second, I can see it in your eyes, an apologetic, puppy-dog look you get when you have done or are about to do something wrong. Third, you've got a stupid camera dangling around your neck."

"You make a decent detective yourself, Lin. Want to join me? You and I, alone in the dark—"

"Eavesdropping on other people's conversations, following culprits through shady parts of town, no thanks, and I wish you wouldn't either."

"We'd make a great team, I think." I ignored her jab. "I could tell Glenn to take a hike."

"Glenn, huh? It's a good thing I'm not the jealous type or I might think you're having an affair or something."

"With Glenn?"

"No! Not with him, with another woman!" She laughed.

"Another woman? Where? You mean other women would actually have something to do with me?"

"I doubt it." She rolled her eyes. "So give me the bad news and spare me the sugar coating."

"Glenn and I are tailing Mark Sills for twenty-four hours. Hopefully this will be more effective than trying to ask him a bunch of questions."

"Twenty-four hours, huh?"

"Yes."

She nodded reluctantly. "I guess I'll be ordering dinner in for myself tonight. I mean how can I resist those pleading brown eyes of yours?"

Glad to have her approval without a confrontation, I kissed her lightly on the cheek and lips.

"I'll have my cell phone if you need me," I said.

From her office I dropped by the grocery store for some supplies. An overnight tail would require some munchies. Once I had the snacks compiled, I stashed them in the backseat and arrived at Mark Sills' office and waited patiently for Glenn. Unaware of his stealthy approach from the rear, I nearly flew through the roof when he pounded his fists rump-pa-tah-tah on the trunk of my car before sliding into the passenger seat with every tooth in his head shining forth. Heart thumping, I searched for something to say, but all I could do was shake my head.

"Silent and deadly, like a panther." He smiled more, if possible. "Some detective you are."

"Yeah, well thanks for demonstrating. If I was on the lookout for such an attack I wouldn't have been caught unaware. Unfortunately your skill at causing cardiac arrest is not needed tonight."

"Excuses. What are we going to do? Follow him around or what?" Glenn asked. His smile dropped and his expression became serious.

"I'd like to get a bug in his office. Let's go in and scope out the place and see if we can come up with a plan."

"What? What are you saying? You know that's illegal."

"How else can I get any information about him?"

"Well, we can think of something else besides a bug. You know you're talking about a felony? You took your private investigation training and they told you this, right?"

"Relax, I don't have a bugging device. I know I can't really tap his phones or his office, but let's go in and look around. Maybe we can come up with a better plan," I suggested.

We both entered the Waterford Building and traveled to the second floor where Houghton Lofton was located.

Scanning the maze of cubicles hustling and bustling with activity—phones ringing, people pacing up and down the aisles, papers shuffling—I concluded it would be easy to search Mark's area without being noticed if we could get him out of his cubby for about five minutes.

All the stockbrokers wore the same droopy expression, like they were suffering through these last few minutes of the trading day. I could sense the stress level was peaked off the meter. Occasionally someone would pop up out of one of the cubicles like a gopher and say something to someone, then disappear down below again. I located a woman close by who looked like she might be willing to point out Mr. Sills and leaned over her cubicle wall.

"Can I help you?" she asked.

"Which of these people is Mark Sills?" I asked.

She stood up and pointed. "Fellow in the corner, see him?"

I followed her finger to the corner of the large room—about six rows over and three rows down in the cubicle city. Mark Sills was a disheveled-looking man with slightly stringy, almond hair, untucked shirt tails, and loosened tie. I backed up to conference with Glenn.

"What do you think? Snoop his cubicle?"

"I don't know. I still don't like it. If we get caught, we're both out of jobs and not just at Morehouse. We'll lose our licensing; we won't work investigation again anywhere."

"But what's the point of having this job if we don't get the bad guys at least some of the time?" I insisted. "We can bend the rules a little. Just a little snooping."

Glenn was silent.

"I'll take that as silent agreement. If I get caught you can deny knowing anything. We need to get Mark out of here," I whispered.

"Could you get Mr. Sills to come over here and speak with me for a minute?" Glenn asked the woman.

She had sat back down, but, with a look that said "I'm not a secretary" and a huff of disgust, she got up and went over to him.

Mark Sills stood hastily, tucked his shirt, brushed the front of his suit, adjusted his tie, and glanced with anxiety to see who had beckoned him. He smiled uncomfortably as Glenn, a big, formidable man, approached. I had separated myself from Glenn and as Mark Sills came from one side of the cubicles, I wound my way around the other side to his cubby. Glenn would detain Mark while I had a look around.

The cubicle contained a computer, a rather complicated looking phone, books, files, and other papers. Assorted notes and papers, including photos of Nikki, were adhered to the cubicle wall with stick pins. Staying low, I took a quick glance around. I flipped through a stack of papers and scanned his loose files. I saw nothing of interest to my case.

As I passed behind Mark Sills on the way out of the office, I gave Glenn the thumbs up and headed for the elevators. I waited for him there.

"What did you talk to Mark about?" I asked.

"Oh, I made up some questions about investing, said I got his name from a friend. He seemed relieved that's all I wanted."

When we got back to the car, I summed up what I found. "Nothing."

"So what's the plan?" Glenn opened his car door and climbed in.

"I really wish I could bug his office." I got in and pulled my door shut. "But I can't."

"How about something simpler?"

"You mean like a tape recorder?" I turned on the car power to put down the windows.

"No, even less technological. Tape recorder, whatever, it's still illegal. I think we should go no-tech and follow him around."

"What can we learn by following him?" I asked.

"I don't know, but we're about to find out." Glenn pointed.

Mark had emerged from the building, crossed the parking lot, and climbed into a black SUV.

"Are you going to follow him?" Glenn asked.

"Yep. You lie down in the seat," I commanded as I started the car and pulled out behind him. "I don't want him to recognize you and realize we're behind him."

"Do you know where he's going?" Glenn whispered.

"Why are you whispering? He can't hear you," I chided. "I think he's headed home so I'm going to follow him from the front."

"Do wha'?"

"I'm actually going to get in front of him since I know the way to his apartment. He'll be following me, but I'll still be watching him in my rearview mirror." I passed him on the right and pulled in front. "Most people never suspect or worry about the car in front of them. They worry cars behind them are following them."

"What if he's going somewhere else?"

"Well, then I'll probably lose him. No one ever said tailing was easy."

Glenn indicated he'd like to sit up. "Can I?"

I was two cars ahead of Mark Sills now and traveling in the same lane. "Sure."

On this occasion, one of very few times, the tailing was without incident. We arrived at the Magnolia Apartments and parked across the street in a small maintenance lot by the Colony Square Hotel. Mark Sills came up right behind us and turned into the Magnolia parking deck.

"We're not going to be allowed to stay parked here," Glenn commented. "What about getting a room?"

"It would take too long to get down and back to the car to follow him."

"Yeah, you're right. What do you suggest then?"

"I think we could park over at the apartments across the street. There are a few spaces down there; maybe we could even get a space inside." I got out of the car and walked down the way to take a look.

Glenn followed, hands shoved deep into his pockets. "Looks promising."

"Of course, we could park at the Magnolia." I looked back across the street to the cobblestone circular drive.

"Whatever you think, man. I'm just along for the ride. Personally, I prefer somewhere air-conditioned."

"No, this won't work." I indicated the small apartments we had walked down to. "Even if we could get a space facing the street, we couldn't get out to the car in time."

"So we need to sit in the drive of the Magnolia or the lot of the hotel where we're already parked?"

"Seems so. I'll call Jeffries and see if he can work some of his police magic and get us permission to sit in one of those places."

I was calling on my cell as we returned to the car. Already someone was standing by our car, a cabbie.

"Yous cannot park here." He waved his arm at the car.

"Why not?"

"These is for cabs, like me," he explained.

"We'll see," I said as I got Jeffries on the phone.

Jeffries agreed to "secure" a place for us at the hotel maintenance drive. "If anyone questions your presence or asks you to leave, give me a call," he said.

I told the cabbie he was out of luck, and he wasn't too happy about it. In fact he might have cursed us in Turkish, or maybe Arabic, upon his departure. Glenn and I climbed back into the car to settle in for the duration.

"How are we going to surveillance that anyway?" Glenn looked up the skyrise. "There's no way to see inside."

"I don't need to see him, as long as I know where he is. I'd love to be able to hear him though," I said wistfully.

"Again, illegal," Glenn said.

"I know, I know."

Thus it was an uneventful evening, which we filled with idle conversation as we filled our bellies with Fritos, crackers, and chips.

On two occasions we were asked to move along by city police and once by a hotel employee. Each time a quick call to Jeffries fixed the situation. Then word must have spread we were legit, and no one bothered us after about 3 A.M.

We took turns monitoring while the other slept. While it was my turn to keep watch, I went through my compiled file on Mark Sills. I needed to call the race organizer, the police officers who were on duty, and the runner who had spotted Mark at the race start. I plotted my plans of approach for all these and carried on dialogues in my head, rehearsing how the interviews would go.

At 5:45 A.M. Mark Sills appeared in jogging clothes and headed for Piedmont Park.

"Should we follow him?" Glenn asked as I nudged him awake.

"No, not in the car. When he gets through the park gates I'll follow him on foot and watch him from a safe distance." I took the binoculars. "When I see he's on the way back I'll get back to the car."

I hovered near the park entrance. Some low-hanging trees and shrubbery provided good cover while Mark Sills ran through the park. I needed a plan to get close to Mark without him knowing who I was, but I hadn't an inkling how to do it yet.

After about forty-five minutes Mark returned to the apartments, and I was back in the car. Glenn and I then followed him to work. We sat around waiting all morning and got nothing. While Mark ate lunch, I put in a call to the Peachtree Road Race organizers after getting the right names and numbers from information. Glenn knew the Atlanta Track Club organized the race, saving me from having to call the City of Atlanta where no doubt I would have received a typical governmental run-around where I was transferred from one worker to the next. I was able to get Hannah Baxter with the Atlanta Track Club, who was eager to give me information about how the race was set up and help solve the murder.

"Every year we set up the race in about the same way. I mean, if it's not broken don't fix it, I say. Once we find something works, we stick to it. Runners without official race times are randomly put into one of eight groups based on the unofficial times reported to us. The group is given a set of numbers and a race tag color, but those change from year to year. The particular runner you're looking for, what was the number or color?"

"31178, red with black numbers," I recited from my file.

"Let's see, that would be time group eight, and yes, they were red this year."

"Can you explain how you know that and how the groups work?"

"There are ten total groups to run. The first group begins at 7:30 and is made up of runners who have official race times. Then we have groups one through nine. Group one is also runners with official times. Each group starts successively, so start times are staggered. We can't have fifty thousand people all start with the gun; someone would get trampled. So they let one group go and the next moves up and so on. Group eight would have been the ninth group to start at approximately 8:10 A.M., and most should have completed the race by 9:30 A.M."

"Except for the delay because of the police and the crime scene."

"Right, except for the delay."

"How do you assign a color? Do the runner's know in advance when they will be starting?"

"Colors are assigned differently each year, but the runners within a color group are random, like I said. They get their color and number in advance, so they know the lineup and approximate start times before they get down to the race in the morning."

"Is there any way to get a runner's reported time, even unofficial?"

"You mean from their application or from the actual race?"

"From their application. You said they would give unofficial times."

"Well, yes, we could probably find one, but I can tell you the runners must finish the race in about an hour after crossing the start in order to earn their race T-shirt. It's a 5K race, which is 6.2 miles."

I did some quick math. "So about nine or ten minutes a mile."

"Sounds right to me."

"Are any steps taken to prevent people from cheating in the race?"

"Cheating? You mean starting early, before your color group?"

"No, I mean only running the last mile or not at all and trying to claim a T-shirt."

"We try to discourage those behaviors. The race path is mostly barricaded to prevent car traffic or pedestrians from crossing over the race course. The police patrol all along the path, but runners sometimes leave the race along breaks or by the portable restrooms, and we don't question those going back into the race."

"So it is possible for someone to run only a mile or two and still get a shirt?"

"Yes. We keep our eyes on the race numbers and times when they come to collect, but we rarely confront anyone. It goes against the spirit of the day. We do, however, mark their number so they can't come back and get another shirt."

"Do you have sprinklers set up along the route anywhere in front of the Colony Square Hotel?"

I heard papers shuffling in the background. "Umm, I believe there should have been sprinklers about five hundred feet above Colony Square Hotel. You might want to ask someone on your list of witnesses to be sure. We used to have the cameras there, but now they are at the start of the race."

"Cameras? For what?"

"A company takes photos of all the runners near the start line."

"May I have their phone number?"

"Certainly." She rattled it off, and I jotted it down.

"Do other places along the race course have cameras?" I asked.

"Well, at the start of the race we have an overheard crane where the news teams can set up to take film or still shots."

"Do they film all the runners or only the beginning ones?"

"I don't know; you'd have to call the stations individually and ask. But the photography company does take everyone's still picture. What does this stuff have to do with the murder?"

"Nothing directly, but don't worry. You've been extremely helpful. May I call if I need more information?"

"Of course," she replied.

Then I called the race witness who reportedly saw Mark Sills at the starting point. After the many days which had passed, his story had changed somewhat, memory fading. He couldn't accurately describe Mark Sills or what he'd been wearing. So his testimony, now wavering, became weak at best, which was actually good for me. It meant I could support my theory Mark Sills hadn't run at all, that he wasn't at the start line.

I called a few television stations to see if they had any film footage I could review. They claimed they didn't keep old footage and had turned in what the police had requested. Then I called the photo company about the runners' pictures taken at the start line, and I gave them Mark Sills' running number. The company representative said it would be a few days before they could get a copy, assuming he'd actually been in the race.

The day was long with no activity on Mark's end. Thank goodness Glenn and I both had things we could talk about. By the end of the day I was ready to bug his office.

"He seems clean," I said, discouraged. "No contacts with anyone important much less anyone shady or underhanded, at least from what we can tell out here in the car. Let's call him and rattle his cage."

Glenn shrugged. "How? Have you any clue as to what to say?"

"He had gambling issues. I'll call and ask him where my money is. If he comes across innocent, I'll pretend it's a wrong number."

"Okay."

Glenn sat in silence as I made the call and was connected to his extension.

"Mark Sills," he answered.

"Where's my money?" I demanded.

"What? Who is this?" he asked.

My ploy didn't seem to be working, I didn't respond as I raced to think of what to say. Who says those who hesitate are lost? In the moment of silence, Mark added snappily, "Why are you calling me at work?"

"Where is my money?"

"I'll get you the money. I'll have it soon," he hissed.

Glenn having heard the comment, made a 'cha-ching' gesture.

"Soon isn't good enough," I said gruffly.

"I know, O.K. I'll get it." He slammed down the phone.

"Jackpot!" I said to Glenn. "He sounded really angry."

"Dude, the man's wife died and someone's harassing him about money, wouldn't you be pissed, too?"

"You sound like my wife—a logical explanation for everything."

"Except for why she married you."

"Ow, I'm hurt. Now, come on, I saw your eyes light up, too. Admit it."

"Yeah, it sounded pretty bad, I'll give you that. So what are you going to do about it?"

"I don't know," I replied, and it was the God's honest truth.

Before I could put any more thought to the matter, Mark appeared in the parking lot and hastily got in his car.

"I suppose we're following him?" Glenn asked, the gold flecks in his brown eyes sparkling.

"Are you kidding? Of course we are!"

I put the car in gear and cautiously pulled out of the parking spot. Looking both ways I followed him as he took a left out of the lot. Several blocks later he took a left, appearing to head towards his home. My cell phone rang, nearly startling me out of my car lane.

"Relax, man." Glenn handed me the phone after I fumbled around aimlessly reaching for it for several rings.

"Keep your eyes out for me," I said to Glenn as I answered the phone. "Hello?"

"Hey, it's me," Lindsey said, full of spirit.

"Hey," I replied, not taking my eyes off the road and my prey.

"Whatcha' doing?" she asked.

"Oh, nothing much." I pulled into the left lane behind Mark Sills. Glenn rolled his eyes. "Tell her you'll call her back later."

I gave him the "hush" signal.

"Are you going to be home for dinner?" she pried. "I've got some good news."

"Good news? I don't know."

"What do you mean, you don't know?"

"It depends," I said. "Can I...uh...can I call you back?"

Mark Sills had taken a left, and I was close behind, too close. Tailing is an art. Too far away, lose your quarry. Too close, be detected. Tailing requires totally dedicating my attention, and I wasn't able to do so while talking on the phone at the same time.

There was a huff and a silence, then she replied, "Call me at work."

Mark Sills arrived at his destination—a fast food parking lot. He parked by the dumpster area which was surround by fencing and a huge hedge of Leland cypress trees. He got out of his car and sat on his trunk and waited.

"He's waiting to meet someone and we're not going to be able to hear anything from here on our own," I said.

"Eavesdropping is illegal," Glenn reminded.

"Oh, Glenn, shove the legal stuff, will you? This is a public place, we're okay."

I moved the car to an area in the parking lot next door, on the opposite side of the cypress hedge. Mark Sills was blocked from view when I re-parked. Glenn and I quickly sprang from the car and ran along the hedge to the backside of the dumpster area where we would remain out of Mark's line of sight. Using a small compact mirror, I propped it open and set it inconspicuously around the corner. Mark Sills still sat on his trunk, his back to us.

A few minutes later a dark blue Caddy pulled up next to Mark. Mark dismounted and leaned in through the blue car's window as the tinted glass electronically lowered.

"Eddie, you in there?" Mark shielded his eyes to look into the car's depths.

"Yeah."

"Eddie, man, how you doing?"

"I'm good," said the deep, mellow, faceless voice.

"That's good, real good. Hey, I'm going to need another loan." Mark nervously kicked at some pebbles.

"Another loan? How much?"

"A hundred and sixty thousand."

"What are you doing? You just paid me back," the voice chided.

"Yeah, I know."

"You need more and more each time. You're not stuck, are you?"

"Stuck? What do you mean?" Mark balked.

"You're going between two lenders, don't bother to deny it," the voice spoke condescendingly, like a parent being lied to, as Mark shook his head. "I know your whole financial situation has been turned upside down; you were caught in the act, and I'm real sorry about your wife. I don't care about any of that bullshit as long as you're good for the money. You are good for it, aren't you?"

"Yeah, I'm good. It's only until my insurance money comes in."

"How long?"

"It shouldn't be too much longer, two weeks maybe." Mark shrugged.

"Ten percent," the voice stated.

"Ten percent fee, Eddie? A little higher than usual, isn't it?"

"I'm not your friend, Mark. You took forever to pay me last time. I thought I was going to have to collect in other ways."

"I know I took a long time to pay last time," Mark whined, "but ten percent for two weeks? Come on."

"No, you come on. That's the cost. Do you want the loan or not?"

"Yes...I want the loan."

Mark shook the extended black-skinned, dark-haired arm and sealed the deal.

"The usual account?"

Mark nodded. The agreement was made, and the Caddy left. When Mark left, Glenn and I didn't bother to follow. I had other plans.

"It seems Mark is having to borrow from one loan shark to pay off another," I mused. "I wonder how he got started?"

"I don't have a clue, but I know you'll find out," Glenn said.

"If he was so far into financial trouble it was quite lucky his wife died leaving him a bundle, but I hardly believe it was luck."

"What do you suppose the guy, Eddie, meant about being caught in the act?" asked Glenn, as I drove him back to his car where we had left it the day before.

"Don't know; could be a couple things." I shrugged. "Maybe a woman, maybe embezzlement?"

Glenn nodded in agreement to my suggestions. "And what about the comment about other ways of collecting?"

"I suppose it means leg and arm breaking or something similar." I pretended to shiver. "Yeah, scary stuff."

Glenn laughed. "Nothing we haven't seen before, like poor Wendell who had the job before you and the baseball bat."

On that thought we both set to silent imaging, minds wandering over the various ways one could collect payment without money. Then my mind drifted to formulating a plan to get close to Mark Sills, right under his nose, to infiltrate his personal life without him knowing who I was.

I dropped Glenn off and called Lindsey back on my drive home. Lindsey had prepared a thirty-minute lasagne and garlic bread, probably to make me feel even more guilty for leaving her alone the night before.

"There are stars in your crown in heaven for putting up with me," I said.

She laughed and dished out plates. "I know. Is this a big case you're on now?"

"Well, it's going to take some time, like last night. I desert you and you feed me an elaborate supper, what's the lesson here? I should leave you more often?"

"No." She lightly smacked my butt as I sat down at the table. "I had lots of time on my hands last night so I made this. All I had to do tonight was warm it up."

I dug in ravenously. Twenty-four hours of Fritos and donuts had left me craving something good to eat.

Lindsey watched me eat for a while, then asked, "Will this case be dangerous? I mean they always could be, but do you see this one as being dangerous?"

"I'm not sure. Maybe. It has all the elements: a murder, money, a loan shark. This lasagne is delicious." I switched topics. And it was delicious.

"I made it with turkey meat and fat-free artificial cheese."

"Now, why did you have to tell me? You know telling me normally ruins everything."

"Normally? You're still eating," she said.

"Well, it's either truly good or else I'm just hungry enough to eat it."

"It must be truly good." She smirked.

"You're not eating much," I commented after a few minutes.

"I'm not so hungry. It is good though."

"Speaking of good, what was the good news you mentioned?" I asked as I finished up.

"What?"

"Earlier you said you had good news."

"Oh, it's about work, nothing really. What's your plan for tomorrow?"

"Why are you so interested in this case?" I asked.

She shrugged and hopped up, heading for the kitchen with her plate.

"I'll be getting up early tomorrow," I explained as I cleared my dinner plate. "I'm going running."

"Really?" Lindsey's hand and sponge stopped mid-circle on the dish. "Your twisted ankle up for running?"

"Yes." I nodded.

"What about your psyche?"

I hadn't run at all since I was injured in the accident—a car explosion on my way to the park. The running and the explosion had nothing to do with each other, but it was a little association game my mind liked to play. Every time I thought of going to run, I'd get sick to my stomach and sharp pains would pierce the backs of my legs where I'd received stitches. Lindsey was probably sure I'd never run again—I psychologically couldn't. The thought of running made me queasy, but it wasn't only the exercise I was after. I had something else in mind.

I was up like an early bird after his worm, but at 5:00 A.M. even the worms aren't out. The neighborhood, eerily quiet, appeared deserted, like some great catastrophe had taken all the human lives and left only empty streets and dark houses. Dressed in my running clothes, I drove to Piedmont Park by 5:30 A.M. A short distance from inside the park entrance I jogged in place to warm up while waiting for Mark Sills to make an appearance.

When I saw his figure coming down the dimly lit street to the park, I began stretches. I was a short sprint down the path from him. He turned and headed towards me. He nodded acknowledgment of my presence as he approached. I stood up and signaled like I wanted to speak to him. He slowed his step, but didn't completely stop, probably wary of a stranger in the park. This area of town is not known for being particularly safe in the dark.

"How far is it if I run all the way around the park?" I asked.

"I guess about two miles, depending on which paths you take," he replied, picking up his pace.

He ran at a moderate speed. I followed behind him at a distance which I considered close enough to be uncomfortable, but not threatening to him. He kept looking over his shoulder to check my location. When he slowed, I slowed. I would have preferred he ask me to run with him at the start, rather than play games. Since he didn't know me and couldn't see me I knew my actions were risky. I had no way of knowing what he was going to do. He could have stopped and pretended to tie his shoe or turned and ran in the other direction. I would have been forced to run on past or do whatever it was I was going to do to him if I had evil intentions.

But instead he turned around and jogged backwards a few steps, his jungle-green eyes, a little wild-looking, assessed me from top to bottom in an effort to figure me out. Finally, he stopped and put his hands on his hips and, panting ever so slightly, he said, "What do you want?"

I stopped. I hadn't thought through a confrontation. What did I want? I wanted to go back in time and have him offer to show me the trek or to run beside me instead of letting me tail him. I didn't know what to say, so shrugging I gave him a look which could be read many ways—embarrassment, ignorance, sheepishness—all in one.

He repeated his inquisition more firmly.

"I don't want anything," I claimed.

"Why are you following me?" He stepped from one foot to the other in an irritated manner.

"I'm sorry." I waved both hands, palms out, apologetically. "I wasn't trying to follow you. I'm new to the area and don't know the park. You seem to know it, and I was trying to pace myself to you. You seem to know where you are going. I had hoped you'd offer to show me."

"Uh-huh." His disbelief was evident, hands still on hips. "Where did you move from?"

"Mississippi," I replied quickly. "I'm renting a place off North Druid Hills."

"Why did you move?" he asked.

"I got a divorce and wanted to get away, far away."

Mark's stiffened posture relaxed as he let his arms fall to his sides. I took a step forward to introduce myself.

"Stop," he commanded.

I stopped.

"You're not trying to pick me up are you?"

"No," I said defensively.

"There's not anything wrong with...to each his own, but this park was known for...and I'm not..." He paused. "Oh, never mind. Mark Sills." He reached out a hand.

"Greg Kramer." I used my alias on the chance he'd seen or heard my name in relation to his life insurance claim.

"So Greg, how long have you been running?"

"I haven't for the last year. I really thought I'd try to get back into it, you know—release some demons, a new town, a new start."

"I could use one of those myself," he muttered.

"Should we run?" I indicated the path before us.

Our steps took us from light to shadow and back again as the sun slowly lightened the park. Pinkish and amber hues painted an aura and made me remember how much I loved to run through sunrise. The conversation between Mark and I became strained from there on since both of us were exerting ourselves. We focused on the short and trivial, like jobs, weather, sports teams. Nothing too deep or too personal. I had to falsify details of my life to keep my cover, hoping all along I'd be able to remember what I'd told him if it became necessary to put on the facade for any length of time. At the end of our run, we made plans to meet the next morning, assuming my aching, screaming muscles would allow me to live until then.

CHAPTER 7

Before my next running appointment I wanted to talk to the police officer who had directly witnessed Nikki Sills' fall. I called the station to see if he was in and arranged to meet him after a short stop at my house for a shower.

The station was bustling with activity, people moving around and talking and phones ringing. I was able to bypass the front desk and take a seat in the conference room, a large room empty except for a few old wooden chairs that looked as if they would break if too much weight were put on them and a huge beat-up wood table. Davy Kimble was prompt, appearing only moments later.

"Let's discuss your report," I said after introductions. "You were at your post as part of crowd control when you posed for a photo with a five- to six-year-old boy. Right after you saw the blur of the last of the lady's fall and heard people screaming. Were the screams first or did you see her first?"

"I saw her falling first."

"You don't say much else about what happened before the crime."

"True. I didn't notice much beforehand. I'm a self-centered guy, a little selfish. I was more concerned about how hot and uncomfortable I was than observing people or doing my duties. The heat was un-frickin' believable."

"That's not in your report," I jested.

Davy smiled, seemingly more at ease with some humor.

I continued. "Is there anything you've remembered? Or anything not in your report?"

"No. Believe me, I've been over it all myself again and again."

"Could we discuss the events of the day without the report?"

Davy shrugged, a reluctant agreement.

"The last thing I want to do is waste time for us both, but I think something may turn up," I explained.

As I questioned Davy about his actions, he retold his entire morning step by step from helping put up barricades to the moments of

Nikki Sills' death.

"So you did look up at the apartments across the street?"

"Yes. There was a chopper at one point, and someone turned on some really loud music for the runners. I looked to see where it was coming from."

"What about close to the time of death?"

"The self-made DJ had just changed the music. He—I think it was a he—he was up pretty far so I couldn't really tell. Anyhow, he put on Neil Diamond's "America", and I looked up then and noticed the helicopter."

"If you had to guess, which floor was this guy on?"

"I don't know." Davy shrugged. "About ten floors maybe. His statement is probably in the police files, along with about a hundred others. In most of the statements people didn't see anything until she'd already fallen. No clues really."

"Have you read them?"

"Me? No, but I've been told."

"So how long after you looked up until Nikki Sills fell?"

"Less than two minutes. I posed for the picture, and that's when it happened," he explained.

"Any chance the photo background would hold a clue?"

"We requested people turn in their film and videos. Copies are also in the police files, but again as far as I know they were dead ends."

"Any reason to believe you might have noticed anything way up on the seventeenth floor?"

"I don't think so."

"What about the runners and the actual race? Do you remember any details?"

"All those bobbling heads were making me queasy on top of the heat. I remember a few of the more outlandish or unusual-looking runners, but that's about it."

I thought for a minute. "O.K., this is going to sound bizarre, but have you thought about trying hypnosis?"

"What? I don't get it."

"Police have used hypnosis to help solve cases before by using it on witnesses. Why not on yourself? If you were looking up, you saw something. You don't remember it, but under hypnosis you might remember the details, perhaps someone you saw."

"I guess it's possible." Davy slouched back in his chair.

"Does the department have someone they use for this?"

"I'm not aware of one, but we can find out." Davy stood up and stuck his head out into the hallway and called, "Hey, Aaron. You ever heard of the force using hypnotism to solve a case?"

"Not here. I've heard of it being used though," Aaron replied.

"So, if we wanted to we could use one?"

"Check with the Chief." He shrugged.

As luck would have it Chief Blumberg was present and available. A large man with a stern look in his eyes and stiff jaw, Chief Blumberg was formidable to approach. His facial expression appeared to be saying "no, are you crazy?" As we made our proposal his face changed almost imperceptibly and to our surprise he approved the request.

"You have to find someone who's trained and authorized to conduct forensic hypnosis. And get Jeffries in on this along with any of the others who were working on the case."

"If we find new evidence, will you re-open the case?" I asked.

"Depends." Chief Blumberg shrugged as he gave his non-committal answer.

"Thank you, sir." I nodded.

"Oh, and let me know if it works. I've always wondered if I should try it to help me lose weight."

"Yes, sir," Davy said, as we stood to take our leave.

"And one more thing; no playing around with post-hypnotic suggestions. Kimble, I don't want you running around here like a chicken or anything." His deep chuckle resonated in his chest, then made him start to cough.

Davy and I both laughed at the Chief's rare humor as well. With his permission we did some consulting and found a forensic hypnotist in the Atlanta area and set up an appointment for the next Tuesday. With five days of waiting time, I would continue to investigate in other ways in the meantime.

I then spent many tedious hours looking through statements of witnesses, videos, and photos. As Davy Kimble had heard correctly, they were all worthless.

No one pointed their cameras up. None of them had caught Mark Sills on his approach or doing anything suspicious. Even the news footage was no good, so many people I couldn't even tell who was who. That didn't mean Mark wasn't still my suspect; it simply meant no one had caught him in the act. Several witnesses mentioned the man with the music, who was on the twelfth floor, but nothing about Nikki Sills or the seventeenth floor. And who could blame them? The focus of the day was the runners on the street. All the excitement was at street level, even up to and including Nikki Sills' death. A few people reported glancing up to see where Nikki had fallen from, but saw nothing except anxious tenants from above looking down.

When I left the station it was well past sundown. Thursday was my weekly karate lesson. As I worked through my Private Investigator training I thought learning how to defend myself was a good idea. I'd taken the classes for over a year and had some good moves, swings, and kicks. I hoped I'd never have a chance to need to use them. The night's lesson was in Ashi Harai, the object of which is to sweep the legs out from under my opponent. My partner for this exercise was an over-zealous forty-something female named Megan whose growling and lip-licking were intimidating enough to make me want to run. Never mind that week after week she managed to kick my butt even though she looked as though she would snap like a twig. Occasionally I would hold the upper hand, but typically she was better. Her movements, water-like and fluid caught me unaware. I couldn't anticipate them. I asked her to take it easy on my sore ankle, and she obliged. On my turn my movements were more jerky and gave my intentions away. She swore up and down it was her ten years of ballet training giving her the advantage.

She always managed to land softer, too. On the other hand, I came crashing down like a cow being tipped, appendages flailing. Again she said all those years of male dancers dropping her during practice taught her how to fall properly.

Part of our karate training had been learning how to fall without injury, and although I rarely got hurt, I still felt awkward. Megan wasn't pretty, but she had grace. She was a flamingo, an unattractive bird, yet with poise and balance. I was a hippo.

After receiving my weekly dose of ass-whooping, I headed home. Lindsey hadn't waited around for me. She knew it was the night of my lesson and had gone out for dinner and shopping with her girlfriends. I had a terrible headache from scanning all those papers earlier in the day, so I prepared an ice pack for my head and a heat pack for my ankle. And finally drifted off to sleep under the influence of some leftover prescription pain pills.

*   *   *   *   *

Groggily, I pulled myself from the bed at the alarm and drove to the park. I knew I'd regret a second run more than I already regretted the first. I'd carefully wrapped my injured ankle and was doing my stretches when Mark showed up.

We ran again like the day before. My muscles, although helped by the pain medication, still begged for mercy. I winced slightly with each step.

"Did you hurt yourself yesterday?" Mark asked about a quarter of the way around.

"Yeah, I did." I panted.

"Want to quit for today and get some chow?"

"Sounds good," I accepted eagerly, not only for my body, but also because this was exactly the opportunity I needed. An opportunity to talk to Mark on a closer level. We took separate cars and arranged to meet at Waffle House.

Waffle House was packed with construction workers and contractors all getting their fill of eggs, greasy bacon, and black coffee. Mark headed for a booth in the back.

"Oooh," I uttered involuntarily as I stooped to fit into the booth.

"Sore? Things must have been pretty bad for you to want to run like you did. You're punishing yourself."

"Nah." I denied it.

"Yeah." He nodded and smiled. "You are. Something determined drives you. Like you said, getting out some demons?"

I shrugged and the waitress approached. We ordered, and I took the opportunity to change the topic to him. "What about you? What drives you?"

His eyes turned downcast and his smile faded. "I don't like to talk about it."

"I'm sorry," I said, knowing full well what I was doing.

"Oh, no, don't be. It's O.K. I might as well tell you, my wife died recently."

"I'm sorry. How recent?"

"She died six days ago. I still can't believe it. Only now is the idea beginning to sink in, I think." He shrugged.

"It was unexpected?" I probed.

"Yes," he replied.

In the ensuing awkward pause, I waited for elaboration, but there was none. Our drinks arrived, and we each had a sip. I plotted my next prong of attack. If my mother could have heard me she would have killed me for my lack of etiquette. She had taught me much better manners, but in detective work manners are optional.

"How did she die?" I asked bluntly.

"I'm not sure I'm really ready to talk about it. I feel so guilty about her death. See, she fell from the balcony of our apartment. And I wasn't home."

"How horrible. She fell?" I took another drink to hide my smile because I knew he was going to come through for me.

"A long way," was the sullen and distant reply.

"Do you think if you'd been home you could have prevented it?"

"I don't know." He hung his head shamefully. "I think so, but I don't like feeling it was preventable. It makes it harder to take. I'd rather like to think it was fate."

"I understand. Were you at work?"

"No, it happened on the fourth of July. I was running the Peachtree Road Race. I'm surprised you didn't hear about it." Mark played with his straw but hadn't taken a drink.

"Well—" I paused to think a split second. "I was busy moving and all. I hadn't gotten my cable hooked-up."

"She was watching the race when she fell. The Peachtree is this massive race every year with fifty thousand runners. In some places you can hardly call it a race because it's elbow to elbow."

"So she fell while maybe looking for you? How?"

"Yes, she was on a chair—or so the police say. I'm still angry with them because they thought I pushed her over, and I don't think they did as much investigating as they should have."

"They thought you killed your wife?" My eyebrows flew up in mock surprise.

"Yes. I couldn't believe they suspected me, but they did. They've concluded it was an accident now, but I'm not convinced."

This was the first thing Mark had said that came as a surprise.

"What do you mean?" I asked.

"I mean someone might have pushed her. Not me, but someone."

CHAPTER 8

"Someone? You think someone pushed her?" Did Mark have a suspect in mind?

"Yeah, someone." He shrugged.

"What makes you think she was killed?" I asked as I used syrup to drench the stack of pancakes placed in front of me.

"She was afraid of heights so I don't think she'd have gotten on a chair on the balcony. I think the chair was set up afterwards."

"Have you told the police? Have the police checked on this?"

"Yes and no. They say security is so tight at my condo building no one could have done it, including me. So they didn't investigate further."

"Yet you still think it was a murder?" I asked then stuffed a huge bite of the fluffy pancakes into my mouth.

"I think some people have ways of getting things done when it might seem impossible. They can get things done and do it without drawing suspicion," Mark said. He still hadn't touched his food.

"What kind of people are we talking about? Not you?"

"No, not me. Oh, I don't know. I'm talking nonsense." Mark finally took a long drink of his juice. "So, why did you get divorced?"

I wasn't prepared for the swift change of topic. I finally thought I was getting somewhere and the trail ended.

"She was a big spender." I made up something to bring us back to Nikki Sills. "I got tired of arguing over money and bounced checks."

"My wife was a money spender, too, but I actually miss the nights when I would come home, and she'd have something new she'd bought to show me."

"You miss the arguments about money?" In the back of my mind I thought about how much Lindsey and Nikki seemed to be alike, just on different scales. Both attractive, both loved to shop.

"Well, we never argued about the money." Mark shrugged. "I let her spend what she wanted."

"You must have more money than me." I laughed. "I couldn't let my wife, er, ex-wife, do that."

"Oh, we had our fair share of money problems; still do. I'm angry though. Angry with God and the whole world when all I can really do is blame myself. If only I'd been there..."

"Why don't you eat something?" I suggested.

"I can't. I think I'm going to be sick."

His face turned green, like a honeydew melon. Mark's eyes glistened with tears. He tried to blink them away and one ran.

"Excuse me." He gagged as he spoke, jumping up and heading for the restroom door which was right behind our table.

I heard him vomiting—gut wrenching. My stomach turned, too. Had his friends been right? He certainly carried around a burden of grief. He was convincing if it was all an act. He returned a few minutes later.

"Sorry," he said.

"No problem," I replied. "The last thing I wanted to do was make you sick. You should eat. You still don't look good."

"I'm not good. How could I be? Someone killed her and I feel guilty for it."

"But who would have wanted to kill her?"

A stranger, a woman walked up to the table.

"Hello, Mark," she said. "You okay?"

"Hello, Ramona," Mark replied. "I'm fine, thanks."

The name had barely enough time to sink in before it was too late and we were introduced.

"Greg, this is Ramona Nash. Ramona, this is Greg Kramer," Mark said.

"Greg Kramer." She shook my hand. "Do I know you?"

"No."

"How do I know that name? Oh, yes, the reporter!"

The hand was laid out like five card stud, only I couldn't bluff my way out of this.

"Reporter?" Mark hopped up from the table and launched into a finger wagging tirade. "And you were asking all those questions as if you cared. Is that why you supposedly 'met' me at the park? This is wrong...very unethical of you to try to become my friend to lure me in. You *don't* have my permission to use anything discussed here, and I'll sue you if I have to."

"But," "I can explain," and "that won't be necessary" were some of the assurances I tried to give, but Mark continued.

"Who are you working for? Which news? Who is your boss?" he demanded.

"Please, lower your voice," I suggested, as his friend made a quick disappearance.

"I will not! What paper do you work for? Do you have to be licensed to be a reporter? I'll get you fired. I'll get your license revoked."

"I'm not a reporter," I confessed hoping to end the one-sided shouting match.

"What?" Mark stopped, but still hovered dominantly above me.

"People are staring, why don't you sit back down?" I suggested. Eyes around the room were on us, leaving me to wonder why I always had to be involved when someone created a scene at a breakfast place. "I'm not a reporter," I reassured him.

Mark gave up his threatening stance and reclaimed his seat at the table. People slowly, one at a time, went back to their business.

"So if you aren't a reporter, what are you? Who are you? What are you doing contacting my friends and following me around parks?"

"I work for Morehouse Insurance. I'm an investigator for your life insurance claim." I winced feeling certain the yelling would begin again, but it didn't.

"You're an investigator? Like a private eye?" Mark leaned forward.

"Yes."

"That's great!" He clapped his hands eagerly. "Then you can find out who killed Nikki. You can find out for me."

"Find out for you?" I replied, shocked at his suggestion.

"Yes. I mean I could pay you and everything."

"I'm not a private investigator. I don't have a license to work for private individuals. I work for the insurance company. And besides I'm actually supposed to be investigating you."

"Which doesn't come as a surprise." He folded his arms over his chest and leaned back into the vinyl seat. "The police have checked me out and found me clear. Shouldn't that be proof enough for you, too?"

"Yes, I suppose so." I shrugged.

"Whether I get the insurance money pay-out or not, I still want to know who killed Nikki. Can't you help me?"

"Why don't you tell me what you know or think you know and then let me decide?"

Mark hesitated.

"Well?" I prodded. "The only way I'll help you is on my terms. You're going to have to take a chance and trust me."

Mark began slowly, most likely thinking about what to reveal first or at all. "Well...I've been in some financial trouble, with some people who can be unscrupulous at times."

"Be specific. You can't beat around the bush if you want my help."

"My wife, Nikki, was a big spender. She spent more than I had sometimes. Not that I blame her for all our problems; mostly I never told her. And I have my own vice—gambling."

"So I've heard. How did you afford it all?"

"We were a bad combo when it came to holding onto money. I'd always been able to get money with my betting when we needed it. I'm good at it, better than most."

"Risky, don't you think?"

"No. I've always been a winner. But we did finally run out of money, so I began to look for other ways to support our habits. I took out some loans."

"What kind of loans?" I asked.

"From a loan broker, or a loan shark. No one else would give me credit if they knew what I needed the money for."

"Why not lie to the bank?"

"Well, it's a little more complicated. When I couldn't make the payment, I'd borrow from another, different loan shark to cover it. I soon figured out I couldn't continue for long. I was digging a deeper and deeper grave."

"Borrowing from Peter to pay Paul is not a fun game." I sympathized.

"Anyhow, I eventually fell behind and couldn't get any more money. When I didn't make my payment on time, the loan shark began to threaten me and my wife."

Something about what he was telling me didn't sit right. I studied his face as he explained, and I knew he was lying, but why? And about what specifically?

"The same evidence which exonerates you makes it impossible for a loan shark or one of their henchmen to have killed her," I said.

"What do you mean?"

"Things like the building's tight security, the locked apartment door, and no sign of forced entry make murder impossible."

"No, not impossible, merely more difficult or risky. I believe people like I've been dealing with could find ways around all those obstacles."

"You mean, pay off someone at the apartments to let them in, make a key to the apartment, and then turn the other way when a woman falls to her death?"

"Or something like that."

"Too risky. The accomplice might decide to turn over on them. Besides, would the loan shark even bother? The payoff to an accomplice would have to be a fairly handsome sum—maybe higher than what you owed. The whole operation would be an economic loss."

"I don't think it would matter. People like loan sharks will take a loss to prove a point. For the principle of the issue. It keeps other deadbeats in line and makes them pay up because word gets around and they think something might happen to them."

"Did you think something might happen to you or Nikki?"

No, not really. I had a plan; I thought had us covered."

"What about an accomplice? Who would it be?"

"An employee of the apartments or a real estate agent. He or she may have been forced to do it and scared out of his or her mind, fearing the police and the loan shark and his life all at the same time."

"You sure seem to know a lot about these types of operations. You have it all thought out or else you have experience in these matters."

"I do, but that's not the issue," was the cryptic response. "The point is a murder is not impossible, however unlikely."

"So what do you want me to do?"

"I'm not sure, really. I thought as an investigator you might be able to find out if my theory is correct or not."

"I can't investigate without names. I need names," I prodded.

"Eddie, Shiny, Desiree, and some of their sidekicks. I know only first names or street names."

I wrote down all the names he gave me, not knowing how much good a list of nicknames was going to do.

"So you are going to help me?" he asked eagerly.

"If I was a private investigator, I could. The most I can do is give a call to a police detective I know in homicide. He'll look into it."

"No, no police. If the police get involved, I could get killed!"

"Why a PI? How come I could investigate?"

"As a PI, you're a little more discreet, you know?"

"No."

"So you can't help?"

"I'm sorry," I said.

"So that's it? You're blowing this off, just like that?" he asked.

I shrugged and stood to take my leave. I threw some cash down on the table to pay my bill.

"You don't care?" He continued in aggravated, hissing tones. "You don't even care my wife was murdered, thrown off a balcony, and someone is getting away with it?"

I shrugged again and added, "The only thing I'm concerned about is my life insurance investigation. Probably a small consolation for you, but at least you can rest knowing I'm going to O.K. your claim."

"Money is supposed to mean something to me? What kind of person are you?" Mark stood facing me; he was much too close and poised to strike.

"I can't—"

Mark didn't let me finish. He shouted a name which suggested an anatomical part and doing something to myself with it, and shoved me. When I didn't respond, he stormed away.

I hadn't had time to ask about his marital troubles. Although I was sure I knew what they were, I was still perturbed my cover was blown so early into my game. I seemed to suffer from a bad case of poor timing.

I knew Mark Sills had been lying at some points in our conversation. I had watched his eyes. His eyes didn't meet mine; they kept going up and to the side as if he were trying to come up with a suitable response, as if creating something fictional—lies. Lying or not, I was running out of options. I didn't want to pursue the loan sharks because even though Mark seemed mixed up with them, I didn't find his explanation convincing as a motive for murder.

I felt defeated. Perhaps better to give up than to waste any more time. One more avenue to look down—a credit report. If I could scare up a credit report I'd be able to determine Mark's true financial standing. Would loan sharking even have been a consideration for him?

I called up Morehouse Insurance which had an account with AccuCheck, a credit reporting service for employers and lenders. My request for Mark Sills' report would be ready and waiting in about thirty minutes. By the time I got to the office, it was waiting in Glenn's hands.

"You've been busy. Are you keeping this quiet and to yourself?" Glenn waved the report around.

"I'll get all my work done." I defended myself and snatched the paper from his long fingertips.

"Yeah, yeah, all your work plus a little extra, I see." He smiled.

"You're the one who talked me into this," I muttered as I read down the file.

"Me?" He feigned amazement and surprise.

"Yeah." I continued reading.

Glenn couldn't stand not knowing, being ignored. He came and stood over my shoulder.

"What are you looking for?" he asked.

"This doesn't make any sense," I complained.

"What? Don't you know how to read a credit report?" He smirked to think he might have a talent I lacked.

"No, I know how to read it. I talked to Mark Sills today, and what he told me doesn't make sense."

"You met with your suspect? You talked? What did he say?"

Choosing only the last question to answer, I replied, "He admitted being in debt to loan sharks because he needed the money, but on paper it doesn't look like he'd need it. Not from someone crooked at least."

I pointed out the figures to Glenn on the credit report and continued, "He owed lots of money, but he still had available credit on several major credit cards. He had home equity. None of the lenders issuing credit reported him as delinquent or a slow payer. So why would he deal with loan sharks?"

I slapped the paper down on the desk and sighed in aggravation.

Glenn shrugged. "Maybe he knew he couldn't repay the credit cards? Or maybe we're talking more money than you think. Maybe the hundred and sixty grand is just part of the problem. But even so, it would be better to lose a credit rating or even a house, than life or limb to a loan shark."

"He had to be lying." I shook my head, bewildered. "Why would anyone in their right mind borrow money at ten percent for a two-week loan when they can get it safely from a bank at twelve percent for a year? Then again, why would he tell me? It makes him look bad."

"Yet, we know he's not lying because we saw and heard him make a loan," Glenn added. "It does appear he's not too smart, stupid actually. Or maybe he wants you to think he's really dumb—too dumb to plan a murder."

"He would have had to set up the whole thing, a complex coverup if you ask me. He's involved with loan sharks all right, but not for obvious reasons. There's something else—why he needs to obtain money covertly."

"Yeah, but what? Blackmail? Extortion?"

"I don't know. My cover's blown, so I think I'll have to ask Mark Sills for an answer."

I caught up on some work, including some sorting and filing. Every time I left the office for any length of time I returned to a pile of papers. I'm a clean desk fanatic, a cleared-off desk enthusiast. When my desk is truly organized to my standard, there is nothing on it but an empty mail basket and a simple desk calendar. All papers, even those requiring action, are put into files and kept neatly inside the drawers. Glenn insists my filing system is why I end up with more work; the bosses see my vacant desk and think I'm not busy enough. Glenn on the other hand keeps his papers strewn everywhere. Job security is what he calls it. He feels the bosses will see his desk and think he does so much, he's not expendable. He and our boss, Logan Moore, had this in common, and that was about the only thing.

Once the paperwork and some brief research on a few other files were out of the way I was ready to go head-to-head with Mark Sills. I drove over to his office. I sat in the parking lot and waited. When the day was getting late and I was bored with getting nothing, I went in.

I can't say Mark was happy to see me. The opposite actually. His expression fell into one of those "oh-no" faces. He hadn't been smiling, but his eyes took on a more serious look, suspicious or anxious maybe.

He met me halfway across the room. Glancing over his shoulder he said, "We can't talk here. It's bugged, the whole office. They're listening in."

CHAPTER 9

Mark Sills ushered me out of his office. I knew better than to question him right then, so I let him lead from behind as he escorted me out to the open parking lot. "Your office is bugged?" I asked when he seemed to relax. "Who's listening in, your boss?" He didn't respond. We walked towards the road and took a left down the block. I followed him along the narrow sidewalk. "What do you want? Why are you showing up at my office?" he asked. "I've already told you everything." "Not everything." I shook my head. I didn't clarify or explain. We continued walking. I wanted him to do the talking. We passed a homeless drunkard lying in a huddle in a doorway. A woman on the opposite corner called out for spare change. The streets were otherwise empty except for us and a few parked cars. I didn't like it. "Stop right there," I demanded. "I'm not walking any farther with you—not so you can lure me down some deserted street and clunk me over the head." "What are you talking about? What do you think of me? You think I'm going to try to kill you to get rid of you?" I shrugged. "It doesn't really matter what I think of you or your intentions. What does matter is you haven't told me everything." "You're right. And if you want me to tell you everything you'll have to trust me. We're going someplace private to talk." "This isn't private enough? Two street people and us?" "No, it's not." He walked off. When I didn't follow he stopped, turned on his heel, folded his arms across his chest, and cocked his head. "Are you coming or not?" I weighed the risk. I knew he could be a murderer, or not. As long as I stayed aware. "I'm coming," I replied. We rounded the next corner and approached a demolition site. What had been a small building lay in piles of rubble and behind it an area had been cleared and new construction had begun. Steel beams and concrete rose from the destruction like a Phoenix from the fire. But the site was dormant. The heavy equipment and cement mixer were silent. No workers in bright yellow hard hats milling about. Other old boarded-up buildings surrounded the rubble, giving the area the eerie feel of a desolate war zone and we were the lone survivors.

"So this is your private spot?" I asked, as we picked our way over rough piles of concrete.

"Yes. They ran out of funding for this project, and it's been sitting like this for about six months. All the other buildings are empty."

He worked his way to the center of the new concrete slab and sat down on a rusty stack of re-bar. I sat also but a few feet away, and I waited.

"I suppose you want to know why I was dealing with loan sharks when I had good credit?"

"Yes." I was surprised he would know exactly what I wanted. "I checked your credit."

"I know you did. I can access my credit file at work and saw a check on it today. I put two and two together, but I guess you can't. I thought you'd be smart enough to figure it out."

"I saw you had plenty of credit; you could have borrowed from the bank."

"I know, looks can be deceiving. I couldn't borrow the money from the credit cards or the bank. And I know if I want your help I'll have to tell you everything. It's a long story, but here it is." He clasped and unclasped his hands nervously.

"I've always been a gambler, a risk-taker. I gambled big because I wanted to be able to afford a high-class condo and car and a showcase wife."

"You've told me all this before; tell me something new," I demanded.

"Well, the mob found me. They learned about my gambling and saw an opportunity. They could pay me to do some work for them and in turn I would be able to support my lifestyle, including my bad habits."

"You work for the mob?"

"Not directly. I'm not a career criminal like some of them. I got into the game late, but I've done well."

He continued, "The company I work for is a front for a money-laundering operation for the mob. Illegal dollars come in from various operations like drug dealing or loan sharking, and we clean them by buying and selling a series of legitimate investments in stocks or bonds."

"You're kidding? The whole office? All those people work for the mob?"

"No, no, it's not everyone. The office is mostly a legitimate business like any other, and we do work for ordinary people like yourself, but the top players in the firm and a few like myself take care of the illegal part."

"So the mob recruited you to come work there and launder money?"

"No. I was already working there, but they saw I was the type they needed. Rising through the ranks of corporate America isn't very different from the mob. You have to be in the right place at the right time and be the right fit, but you also have to know how to follow orders. You have to be the type willing to break the law."

"And what about getting caught? Didn't you worry?"

"Not really. I know my way around stocks and could launder the money so it could barely be traced."

"But it could be traced?"

"Yeah, but I never had anyone from the law figure me out," he said snidely. "There was an investigation a few years back, but nothing came of it. I figured if they didn't catch me then, they never would. I've gotten better at what I do since then."

"Gambling and your work, they are both risky. You like risk."

"I saw no risk." Mark shrugged.

"Don't you feel guilty working for people of such low standards and morals? You took drug money. Kids buy drugs. Don't you feel guilty?" I tossed some loose gravel pebbles one by one into a pile of broken up concrete.

"No; that's their problem or their parents."

"What about when cheating on your wife? Did you feel guilt or risk then?"

"First of all, you've gone off on a tangent from your original line of questioning. Second, I never said anything about having an affair, so I can only assume you've picked this information from the brain of someone you consider to be a reliable source."

"You are right on both counts."

"Well, I did cheat on Nikki, but it was over. Feeling guilty would indicate I felt what I did was wrong and it wasn't. I didn't worry about being caught because I'd had affairs before. Nikki didn't care to doubt me as long as she could do her shopping."

I contemplated his low moral standards and his ego, his air of superiority. He was the type to plan what he believed to be a perfect murder so he could kill someone he felt deserved it and feel he could get away with it.

"Still, none of this explains why you needed loan shark money."

"Like I said, I was getting there when you went off on this moral tangent." He huffed. "Thousands of dollars a week flow through Houghton Lofton for the mob, and we take a percent. I did a lot of number crunching and realized the big shots didn't really know the numbers. So I tried helping myself to some of their money. I took a little percent for myself, filtering it through separate accounts and doctoring their numbers so they'd never know."

"Big mistake?"

"Yes, colossal mistake. I don't know how, but they knew. They found out."

"And they were actually the ones threatening to kill you and your wife, not the loan shark?" I guessed.

"Unless I put all the money back in ten days, they said they'd kill her and they'd hurt me so badly I'd wish I was dead."

"Why did they let you keep your job?"

"I still work at the firm but not with their accounts. I guess they wanted to keep tabs on me. Also the one reason why I didn't really believe their threats; they didn't fire me."

"But you fear them now? Is that why we are here?'

"Yes."

"So did you put the money back or not?"

"I tried; I really did. I did pay it back, but not within the ten days. By then it was too late." Mark tugged at his hair, pulling it all out of place. "I mean, I, or we, had spent all the money before I was caught, so I didn't have it to return."

"So have you paid it back now?"

"Yeah, but I'm still not out of trouble. I had to borrow from a loan shark mainly because I couldn't draw attention to myself or the mob without risking reprisals; its not good for business. I needed a lot of money fast, so I couldn't just borrow it all on my credit cards or ask for it at the bank. But then I had a hard time even getting the money with a loan shark because most of them work for the same mobsters as I did. Borrowing from one of them wouldn't be like paying the debt at all."

"How long were you filtering money? And how much are we talking about here?"

"It was about a year, a hundred and twenty five grand."

"And it all got spent on gambling and shopping?"

"Yes, mostly gambling."

"So you found a loan shark. Why was it beyond the ten days?"

"When I finally found someone unconnected I was already after the ten day limit. And, unfortunately, I still need the original loan amount plus about fifty thousand in interest to pay the loan shark. I'm borrowing from one loan shark to pay off another, back and forth. I'll have to keep doing the swap until the life insurance money comes in. This is why I need your help. If you don't help me, I may end up dead."

"If you were beyond the ten-day limit, why did you pay? Wasn't your wife already dead?"

"No, she was fine. She was killed after I repaid the money."

"And yet, you think they killed her?"

He nodded.

"How long after you paid was she killed?"

"My deadline with the mob was in mid-May, so it was about a month and a half later."

"Why now? Why would they wait and then kill her? They had their money."

"To prove a point. To show me who's boss. They know I'm the type who feels a little above the law. To humble me? How should I know?" he hissed.

"A long time gone by to make a point. And you have no proof, nothing to go on, but your instinct?" I prodded.

"And some pretty real threats," he said sadly. "Which I never believed until six days ago."

"You're going to have to give me some new names. Who were the people you were dealing with?"

"I can't give you any names." Mark took a small rusty piece of rebar and traced two names in the concrete dust. Then he quickly scrubbed them.

"Well if you can't give me any names, then I can't help you."

Mark continued to doodle and draw in the dust and never looked up as I stood up and walked away, picking my way slowly through the rubble to the street. Mark had passed a burden on to me. I knew some names he obviously felt I shouldn't know and whom he had recently learned to fear. Unless it was all a put-on. Still I had to wonder, did simply knowing the names put me or Lindsey in danger?

CHAPTER 10

A certain element of danger attracts me to detective work. I am drawn to it, almost without concern, like a storm chaser to a tornado. I have an unshakeable faith I can outsmart any criminal one way or another. Along the way, danger may drift close to myself, my job, or even Lindsey, but there was that unshakeable faith in my skills. The thrill of the hunt, and when the tables are turned, the threat of being hunted—and surviving—captivates me. However, in this particular case I felt little threat of being hunted. I still wasn't convinced Mark Sills was telling me the truth. And so, in my narrow-minded thinking, I neglected what Mark perceived as dangerous and decided to pursue the case. Foolhardy I was to continue working on a case that wasn't even mine, I could have been risking my life, or Lindsey's, or at the very least it could have cost me my job.

I went to the library to see if I could find any newspaper articles with the names of the two men Mark had given me—Vincent Artello and Saul Dedmon. If they were leaders of organized crime, they were probably skilled at keeping their noses clean, but their names were still bound to show up out of suspicion.

I went back a few months to January and began my search forward, hoping to turn up something recent. If that failed, I'd work my way backwards until I either discovered something or got discouraged. I glanced at my watch—5:30 P.M. I had to be home tonight to see Lindsey.

Skimming quickly, I was rewarded on my first search with a May article in the food section of the Sunday paper touting the opening of a new multi-million dollar concept restaurant owned by Vincent Artello. I read on: casual dress, no reservations required. I jotted down the address and the driving directions, then I quickly called Lindsey on the phone. I could kill two birds with one stone as they say.

"Lin, how about going out to dinner tonight?" I suggested.

"Sure, where?" she eagerly agreed.

"A new place, a surprise. I'll see you at the house a little after six."

A nice dinner to patch things up with Lindsey and some detective work at the same time—I had to give myself a pat on the back for this one. I drove home and changed into some fresh khakis and a dark green polo shirt. Lindsey arrived already suitably dressed in dark grey slacks and a crisp white blouse, but she wanted to re-apply her make-up. I didn't think she needed it. Her deep green-brown eyes were captivating, even without eyeshadow or mascara. Still, we were out the door by six-thirty, hoping to beat the dinner-time crowds. Lindsey was navigator and I drove.

"We should be close," Lindsey said, comparing the street number on the paper I gave her to the store we had just passed. "It should be somewhere on this block."

Atlanta city streets can be quite narrow and parking can be scarce. All my attention was focused on the road, depending on her to spot the place.

"Oh, dear. Oh, no," she said suddenly.

"What? What's wrong?" I looked at where she was staring.

"Looks like they had a big fire," she replied.

The roof of the restaurant was completely burned out on the left and charred and collapsing on the right. Windows had either blown out or been broken out to combat the blaze. No smoke or smoldering, no fire trucks or hoses sloshing water. The fire had occurred hours or perhaps even days earlier, and there wasn't anything much left inside except ruin. I pulled into the parking lot.

"Hey, look! A news crew." Lindsey pointed to a van at the edge of the lot.

We stopped the car and got out. I wanted to know more because this place was connected to my case. Lindsey wanted to know more, well, because she was downright curious.

A few people were standing outside the restaurant's remains. The news crew maintained their distance. I approached a woman who looked like she belonged there, like she might know what was going on. She was tall, large-boned, and had thick long, blonde hair, not a natural blonde, dark roots gave her away.

"Hello," I said, approaching. "Is Vincent Artello or Saul Dedmon here?"

Her one eyebrow flew up. "Who wants to know? A reporter?"

"No, not a reporter." I extended a hand. "Paul Grey, insurance investigator."

She didn't take the hand I offered; instead, she kept her arms tightly folded across her chest.

"You're not working on our insurance claim."

"No, no, I'm not. I'm actually working on a case totally unrelated to your fire, but I need to speak to either Vincent or Saul."

"Unbelievable!" I heard Lindsey say. I turned to see she also stood, arms folded, face flushed bright pink, foot irritably tapping the pavement.

"I can explain—" I began. Famous last words.

"Don't bother. I can't believe this, you stinking lying rat—no, rat's too good for what you are! You bring me here on the romantic premise of wooing me, of making things up to me, and it turns out you really wanted to come here to work on a case. If you want to work nights on your cases, leave me out, O-U-T, out of it." She began to stomp off, but then about-faced and came at me again. "In fact, the way you're headed you'll have every night free because I won't be around anymore. I'm not going to put up with this crap anymore. If you want my help or my company, ask for it, but don't lie about your purposes and play with my heart. Give me the car keys," she demanded.

"Lindsey, wait, let's talk about this later."

"There's nothing to talk about. Give me the keys."

I handed them over, and she stormed away. I turned to see the lady behind me grinning, amused.

"Aren't you going after her?" she asked.

"She's not really leaving me here," I looked over my shoulder.

"Are you sure?" the woman watched as Lindsey turned to look back at me, huffed, threw herself into the car, and started it.

"Well, no." I took steps toward the car, but by then Lindsey had squealed out, leaving me behind.

"You should have chased her across the parking lot. You have a lot to learn about women." She patted me flirtatiously on the arm.

"I can't believe she left," I said, bewildered, unable to remember even why I was there. What had been so important?

"So honey-bun," the woman cooed. "What was it you wanted with Vincent Artello? Something about insurance?"

"Oh, uh, yes."

"Well, he's right over there." She pointed to a slender, well-dressed man. "But he's a little cranky today, probably won't want to talk to you."

"And why is that? Because of the fire?"

"Heavens, no. The fire was days ago. He got out of the slammer today, and the press won't leave him alone."

"What? He was in prison?"

"My stars, I thought everybody knew. He was arrested for arson. They think he torched his own place, and it didn't help they later found a body in the ashes."

"A body? Who was it?"

"Don't know yet for sure. Not even sure how the person died, but they think it was Saul Dedmon, the other guy you asked about. Vincent and Saul were rivals, you know, not friends."

"No, no, I didn't know."

"I can see you're overwhelmed, shocked? How come you don't already know about this? It was on the news when it happened." She rubbed her hand down my arm, a cross between sympathetic and seductive.

"When was he arrested? When was the fire?" I pulled my arm away.

"The fire was July first, and they locked up Vincent the next day."

I nodded, understanding. "I was out of town through July fourth. So he got out of jail today?"

"Yes; they dropped the charges. Not enough evidence or some such thing. So what did you want with Vincent anyhow?"

"I have a man who insists his wife was killed by Vincent or Saul, and I wanted to ask them about it."

"You're mighty bold, aren't you?" She winked. "As much as I hate to say it, I doubt Vincent has been involved in any of criminal activity recently since he's been held up for murder anyway. It'd be too risky."

"Recently? Too risky? Why do you hate to say it?" More questions than I wanted spilled out at once.

"I wish I could help you out." She stepped uncomfortably close and whispered, "Here's what I know. Vincent runs some illegal business. Sometimes people die, but the police can't ever seem to catch him. He keeps his fingers clean. However, he hasn't been involved in anything recently because of the risk—he's being watched."

"What about Saul?"

"Poor Saul is dead." She pouted her lips in a cross between sexual and saddened, and my stomach churned with the thought.

"You said the police weren't sure about the identity of the body yet."

"I did. The police aren't sure, but trust me. Saul is dead. Vincent made sure they'd never get an ID on him. He can say some poor slum fellow must have broken in and died in the fire."

"What are you saying?"

"I'm saying Vincent and Saul had nothing to do with your case and you best scram before you get in over your head asking questions like you're asking to the wrong people."

"How do you know all this? How do you know Vincent?"

"I'm his wife." She smiled coyly.

"Then why did you tell me this? You clear your husband of one wrong doing, but you implicate him in others."

"I hate Vincent, but we have an arrangement. It works for me." She touched my arm again and smiled, an invitation to go another route with the conversation, but I didn't respond. "See, I told you, you have a lot to learn about women."

Her eyes told me to leave and not say another word, so I headed to the street to hail a taxi.

"Who was that?" I heard Vincent ask of his wife only a few paces after I walked off.

"Another senseless reporter, honey bun," she replied.

The taxi took me home to an empty house. I was worried, but found a note on the fridge. "Gone to Margie's." Margie was her adoptive mother since her parents died when she was a teenager. And I knew this wasn't good on one hand because she may not come home at all; staying the night at Margie's would be a bad step. On the other hand, if anyone could talk Lindsey through her anger, it would be Margie, who would send her home when she was rational again. I called Margie's and got the machine. I didn't leave a message, although looking back I should have. Outside it began storming; torrents of rain pelted the roof and windows. I worried about Lindsey and hoped she wasn't driving in it.

Other than pace the floor and worry, I had nothing to do, and I certainly couldn't sleep. So I pulled out my growing file on Mark Sills. The probability of Saul Dedmon having killed or arranged to kill Nikki Sills had dropped to very improbable. I wasn't sure about Vincent Artello. It seemed unlikely, which left me back at Mark and his excuses left and right and the glaring two-million-dollar check headed his way. He had everything to gain and nothing to lose from his wife's death, and he certainly had me following a wild goose chase. If he kept me distracted long enough his money would arrive, and he'd be home free.

I pulled all the papers out of Mark's file and laid them out side-by-side on the kitchen table. There had to be something. I rubbed my brow, pulled my hair, paced the floor. None of these "thinking" techniques helped, though, until I looked at the four insurance policies again and then again more closely. I realized something crucial. The four signatures of Nikki Sills didn't match. They were very close, but definitely, on inspection, not the same, meaning only one thing, in my opinion. Nikki wasn't aware she was insured for two million because she only signed the joint policy insuring both her and Mark. She had no knowledge of the other three policies for one and a half million dollars. Mark had forged her signature. He probably had an agent who was a friend who allowed him to take the paperwork home for Nikki to "sign," and then Mark either mailed them in or dropped them off. Agents weren't supposed to allow papers to be signed unseen for exactly that reason, but it happened.

I immediately called Detective Jeffries.

"You're sure they're forged?" he asked. "Maybe she signed three and not the last one instead of the other way around."

Lindsey arrived via the front door, soaking wet, dripping puddles in the foyer and hall as she approached me in the kitchen.

"If she's insured for one and a half million, why hide the other half million? It makes more sense she knew she was insured for the smaller amount. Wouldn't you worry if your spouse wanted to take out a large insurance policy on you all of a sudden?"

"Maybe that's what I should do," Lindsey muttered as she poured herself a glass of juice and continued to drip.

I gave her a look, and she returned it.

"I've gotta go, Martin. Are you going to do anything?" I asked.

"Yeah, I guess so," Detective Jeffries replied.

"Either way, it's fraud," I explained. "Arrest him for fraud now, and we'll get the evidence we need for murder charges later. The circumstantial evidence is almost enough to convict him now."

"All right. We'll get a judge on it, and we'll put out an APB. Any ideas where he might be?" Detective Jeffries asked.

"His apartment or work is all I know. Oh, and he runs in Piedmont Park every morning."

"We'll call you when we get him."

I hung up. Lindsey stood, leaning, with her back against the kitchen counter. Her hair, all wet, stuck to her neck and cheeks. Her drenched clothes clung to her slender form. She looked unbelievably sexy, and she knew it.

"Here, umm, let me get you a towel." I fished one out of the laundry room and went to dry her.

She grabbed it from me before I could touch her. I wanted to touch her. It would have been reassuring—a comfort, somehow everything would be all right.

"So they're making an arrest on your case?" She rubbed her hair roughly.

"Yeah." I nodded.

"I guess good things come out of your work." She shrugged, tossing the towel onto the floor.

"Sometimes. This one is good. The guy killed his wife, and we're going to get him for it."

"Is this the woman on the balcony? This is the case?" She picked up the photo of Nikki Sills.

I nodded.

"She was pushed?"

"Yes, but I have to confess," I said. "I have to come clean and tell you all. Hiding things from you is wrong. You're the one person I should be able to tell everything to, and I don't. I don't know why."

"What are you babbling about?" She put her hands on her hips and surveyed me.

"I'm not supposed to be on this case anymore. The company decided because of lack of evidence to pay the claim, so I've been racing against them to gather evidence to prevent him from collecting. Which is why I've spent the nights working. She was killed—no doubt about it. If I let him get the money, that would be so wrong."

"Why does this dead woman mean so much to you? You would risk your job? Risk losing me? It's only money—company money."

"It's not only money. It's the principle, the moral, oh, I don't know what. She was young, vibrant, and beautiful, like you, Lindsey. She loved clothes and fine things—"

"Like me?" She walked over to the laundry area and picked out some dry clothes.

"Yes, only she was a bit more extreme." I followed her.

"So you saw a little bit of me in her?" Lindsey began undoing her shirt seductively.

"Yes, and every other woman who's married to a terrible man." I moved to help her with her shirt.

She shooed me away. "You're not terrible."

"Yes, I am. I treat you like you're second-hand through this whole case, and I don't even tell you the reason I feel so motivated to solve it."

"And the reason is?"

"I'm trying to do the right thing. The bad guys can't get away with this. I realized what it would be like to lose you and I wouldn't survive it."

"You'd survive. That's the type of person you are. And you are not out of trouble with me yet. You're on probation." She tossed her blouse and bra into the dirty basket and stood facing me half-naked.

"I understand." I smiled.

"You still haven't apologized for the dinner thing," she reminded me. "And you owe me some promises, too."

She bent over to pull off her slacks. Distracted as I was, I knew I better not mess this up.

"I'm sorry for misleading you about dinner. I'm sorry for not telling you about this case. I know if I asked you to be my partner in crime, you would, as long as you know all the facts up front. I promise I won't keep any secrets from you ever again, and I promise I won't drag you along without telling you the purpose, and I promise next time you go to the car angry, I'll follow you."

"If you keep half of those promises, I'll be happy. I guess that'll do." She shrugged.

I approached her for a kiss. She gave me a quick peck, pulled on a T-shirt, and disappeared upstairs. I followed, but the light was already out and Lindsey lay on her side, preparing for sleep. I climbed in and tucked my feet in next to hers. They were warm and comforting, and she didn't pull away. A good sign. I was lulled to sleep by her touch and soft breathing, and the drip dripping of water as the rain slackened off.

In the middle of the night the phone rang. Startled awake, heart pounding, I clambered for the portable phone in the dark.

"Hello?" I asked groggily.

"We found your guy, Paul," said Detective Jeffries.

"Jesus, Martin. You could've called me in the morning." I rolled over to look at the clock—6:30 A.M., technically morning already.

"I don't think so," Detective Jeffries said. "Who'd you say this guy was involved with?"

"I didn't. Why?"

"He's been stabbed about twenty-six times. We found him face down in the bushes at Piedmont Park."

"I'll be right there."

CHAPTER 11

As I pulled up to the Piedmont Park gates, I peered through the newly developed, driving rain and the frantic windshield wipers to see I was about the umpteen-millionth person to arrive. Police cars were parked everywhere, helter-skelter in the grass. Lights and rain made it difficult to determine how many. The rain showed no sign of letting up so I climbed out, no raincoat, no umbrella, and began asking questions.

I wasn't allowed anywhere near the body. Two homicide cops were working the scene and Jeffries operated as the cruise director, telling each officer what to do and when. They worked quickly so as to gather as much evidence as possible before the rainstorm washed it all away. I knew in thirty to forty minutes Jeffries could spare a moment to talk to me. In the meantime I took my own mental notes regarding the scene, location of the body, and what I could see of the wounds as occasionally one of the homicide detectives would pull back the body's cover like a magician revealing his trick rabbit. Mostly they kept him covered to protect his body from the rain.

Mark Sills had been out running as I could tell from his bloodied but unmistakable running clothes—royal blue shorts and a sleeveless USA flag T-shirt which he had worn the first morning I ran with him. From what I remembered as his route, he had barely begun his run when this tragedy had befallen him. He had entered an area of low-lying brush and trees and in the early morning hours would have been obscured from witnesses from most angles as he met his demise. No good vantage points, and I doubted many people were in the park at dawn anyway, especially with the threat of rain. I circled the scene, trying to figure out where the attacker had approached from—front, rear, side—and decided it was inconclusive from the fleeting glimpses I received of the body. I couldn't tell if he had been stabbed front or back or both.

By now I was wet to the bones and it didn't matter anymore. Tiny rivulets of water rushed over my forehead and off my eyebrows like miniature waterfalls. I set to searching the area outside the official crime scene for clues. The murder took place in an isolated spot, but the murderer had to get there and leave and certainly didn't do so through the air, unless Mark was killed by aliens. A flash of lightning, followed quickly by deafening thunder, warned me of the dangers of working so closely under the trees. I glanced at my watch—nearly 8:00 A.M.—and the sky showed no indication of brightening or clearing, although I was sure the sun was up somewhere. I was able to see through the driving rain with the assistance of a multitude of artificial lights—police car headlights, strategically pointing at the crime scene, portable work lights brought in for the investigation, and the park's own lights, which seemed dim by comparison. Outside the police's defined area, my search was aided by a single flashlight which I aimed this way and that along the paths, under bushes, anywhere I thought I might find something. The raindrops reflected the light back like falling, sparkling diamonds. The torrents of rain had probably washed the scene clean. The murderer would have been drenched in blood and would have tracked it everywhere, except for the lucky circumstance it was raining so hard—nature's washing machine.

The ground in many places was soggy from standing water. Water culverts and drains were filled and flooded. I sloshed about scanning the area in ever-widening circles, moving farther and farther from the crime scene. Bursts of excitement and a scurry of renewed activity came from within the police lines. I moved closer to see what had happened, sidling up to Detective Jeffries from across the yellow tape.

"Get that area dry!" he commanded his men loudly.

Two officers erected small artificial dams to divert the flow of water. Two more held umbrellas over the location, while a fifth worked at evacuating standing water.

"This guy must have been a few bulbs short of a candelabra to be out running knowing this rainy mess was coming." Jeffries stood under the cover of a large umbrella. "And what's your excuse?"

"Ha, funny. I don't have an umbrella. Mark was probably trying to beat the rain. Was it raining when the body was spotted?"

"Not yet, damn stuff started right as we got here." Jeffries signaled to another officer with an umbrella.

"What have you found?" I asked as the officer approached us.

"A few hairs which were probably pulled out of the attacker's head. But hair is only good if you have a suspect to pair it with. Any ideas?" he prodded. Jeffries took the umbrella from the young man without saying a word and handed it to me. "Here."

"I have no leads for you. Did you find anything else? Know

anything else?"

"There was quite a struggle on Mark Sills' part judging by how disturbed the earth and grass are in the area around the body. And we found a footprint under one of the bushes." He indicated the group of men trying to save the print from the downpour.

"Will the print be any good in all this rain?"

"We'll see."

"So much for procedures—aren't only two men at a time supposed to be allowed on a scene?" I commented.

"Yeah, well, I gotta do what I can. This damn rain—"

"At least it's slacking off. Tell me about the body. You said he was stabbed. Are you fairly certain Mark Sills was killed here and not dumped here?" I asked.

Detective Jeffries nodded, "Yeah. Like I said, he put up a fight. He was stabbed what looks like about twenty times, but the autopsy will be more accurate. From what we can tell he was hit several times in non-fatal areas like legs and arms. His hands were all cut up from trying to stop the blade in self-defense. The attacker finally got him in the chest a few times, and did him in. But the murderer didn't stop there. It seems he, or she, stabbed Mark a few more times for good measure even after he was down on the ground."

"How do you know?" I asked.

"The knife was long and sharp. In some of the soft tissue areas it pierced all the way through to his back and into the dirt below. To get such an amount of force over and over, the killer must have been straddled over the top of his body. When the knife hit bone, it got stuck, and the killer used a foot on Mark's chest to pry it back out."

"The person must have really wanted to make sure Mark was dead."

"Yeah, extremely vicious killing. One of the worst I've seen. I've called in a police psychologist to make up a profile of the killer, see if it matches any other murders anywhere."

"You think this was a random killing, a stranger like a psycho or a serial killer?" I asked as lightning struck nearby and we both jumped.

"Not really. Most people are murdered by someone they know, so we'll check friends, family, and co-workers first," Jeffries said. "Any suggestions?"

"One," I responded this time. "Vincent Artello, a mob-type Mark owed a bundle of money to. He got out of prison yesterday."

"Yesterday?"

"Yeah; he was going to be tried for murder, but now I think about it, going after Mark within twenty-four hours of his release from prison doesn't seem too intelligent. Besides, it was so messy. I always thought mobsters went for quiet, discreet disappearances and accidents when it came time to do someone in." I shrugged.

"Ever heard of the St. Valentine's Day Massacre?"

I shook my head.

"Never mind; let's ask the expert," Jeffries suggested. "Scott! Scott, come 'ere."

He waved over a tall, older man with a grey goatee and mustache.

"Paul Grey, this is Dr. Scott Helms," he said. "Scott, this is Paul." We shook hands.

"Well, Doc, what do you think?" Detective Jeffries asked.

"May I speak freely?" Dr. Helms indicated my presence.

"Yes, whatever you'd tell me, you can tell him."

"I see a lot of anger. The murderer was angry with the victim about something; I can't say what."

"Money?" I suggested.

"Perhaps, but I'm more inclined to say love."

"Love?" Jeffries and I cried in unison.

"Well, yes. You'd usually only see this severity of violence in two general types of cases, although there are exceptions to any rule. The first type of case would be what you would call a homicidal maniac—someone who is most likely a serial killer with some psychological motivation to mutilate. This type of person could be a Satanist or someone like Jack the Ripper. These types usually have a pattern or a signature or some might say a "calling card" making their murders unique. I don't see that here."

"So you think it's the second type of case?"

"Yes, the second type of case is where the murderer actually loves the victim, but the love is either unrequited or unrecognized, or the murderer for psychological reasons can't sense their love being returned. The victim does something to anger their "lover," something which in the killer's mind is the last straw. The "last straw" can be as complicated as an affair or as simple as an argument over money, but in any case the end result is the same. The "lover" snaps and in a rage commits a heinous crime of such brutality—"

"O.K., O.K. We get the idea, as wacky as it is." Jeffries rolled his eyes. "Go back to work."

"A lover's rage," I said to Jeffries. "That may not be as crazy as it sounds."

"I thought Mark and Nikki Sills were nearly a perfect couple."

"Mark did have an affair about a year ago."

"With whom?" he asked.

"I don't know." I shrugged.

"Well, you don't need to worry about it. Your interest in this case died with Mark Sills." Jeffries turned to look at my grin. "Didn't it?"

"To the contrary. I have even more interest now than ever before."

"And why?"

"Because now Mark Sills' two million will be going to his secondary beneficiary."

"Who?"

"I don't know, but I'm going to find out."

"Whoever it is, they won't be getting the two million. Didn't you say the policies were forged?"

"Yes, but I'll bet his beneficiary didn't know. Maybe this whole thing was a plan or a set-up from the start."

"What do you mean?"

"I mean, what if Mark Sills' other beneficiary, the one after his wife, killed Nikki to make Mark rich, then killed Mark to make himself rich."

"You're as crazy as some of the wackos I put away. You've always got some conspiracy theory going on in your head."

"Putting personal feelings aside, you've got three potential suspects—Vincent Artello, Mark's ex-lover, and his secondary beneficiary."

"You haven't explained this Artello and his connection."

"Mark stole money from him and owed it back and evidently was having trouble getting it."

"Stolen, how?"

"Money laundering, he was skimming. You should check out Houghton Lofton."

Jeffries wrote down the tip. "So, Artello might have had Nikki or Mark or both killed."

"Actually, now I think about this, something doesn't make sense. Mark gave me two mob names, but they were rivals. Why would he do that? If they were rivals they couldn't both be responsible for Nikki's death as he claimed in his version of the story."

"I don't know the whole story, why don't you fill me in?"

"Well, either Vincent's wife was throwing out bogus information to cover the fact he and Saul were in fact part of the same mob, not rivals, or Mark has had me on a wild goose chase."

"Mark's dead."

"Yeah, a complication. "

"With the forgery I might tend to think the stiff here had you on a chase."

I nodded. "Vincent allegedly killed Saul which is a good indicator they were rivals. Mark probably was biding time until his insurance check came in. And then this happened. I'll bet I can figure out which one of the three suspects is responsible for killing Mark."

"Taking my job from me? Why not join the force?" He smirked. "It's tempting to let you do all the groundwork, and then I can steal all the glory. But let me warn you, as I have before, investigating can be dangerous work. You of all people should know this."

I nodded, appreciating his concern. At this point, thoughts about the seriousness of this case had crept even into my closed mind.

"I've got to run home first, but then I'd like to get another look inside Mark Sill's apartment," I said to Jeffries. "Do you think you could arrange it?"

"Why don't you meet me there at noon? I should be wrapped up here by then."

"O.K." I handed the umbrella back to Jeffries. "Thanks."

We shook hands at parting. Leaving the park, I headed home with one task in mind—getting my gun.

I showered, shaved, and dressed in clean, dry clothes, then I retrieved my .357 and holster from the top shelf of the bedroom closet and the bullet clip from the dresser drawer. I never kept the gun loaded out of the fear someone might shoot it off accidentally if startled. When adrenaline is rushing through the veins, one can't think clearly and triggers suddenly become easy to pull. My heart somersaulted in my chest as I pulled the gun out of the case and ran my fingers over its sleek, shiny form, a solid, perfect fit in my palm. Clip in one hand, gun in the other, I began to load the weapon then changed my mind and holstered it empty. Even wearing the gun was an admission I was in over my head, an admission to the possibility I might have to use it. Would I be able to use it? Would I *have* to use it? Fear washed over me like cold river waters rushing heedlessly over rocks, careening toward a waterfall. I had no control, no knowledge of where this was going or how it would end.

The weapon was not concealed, although I had a license to do so. Instead I wore it over my T-shirt and tucked the clip into my back jeans pocket. If I had my gun, I wanted others to know I had it, too. Except Lindsey. I didn't want Lindsey to know. Fortunately, she was already at the law offices working, so she couldn't notice the addition to my attire, but I would still have to fill her in on the early morning wake-up call which had caused me to jump up and leave the house immediately.

"Mark Sills was murdered early this morning," I explained the wake up call to her on the phone.

I paused while trying to pick my words carefully so as not to panic Lindsey, but my pause was long enough that Lindsey exploded into it.

"He's dead, too? This is too much Paul. You need to stay home for a couple of days. Drop this case, let it all blow over, and then go back to work on something a little less dangerous."

"But, Lin—" was all I could get out before a second wave of admonishments.

"No! No, buts, Paul. I have a three-dead-body rule. Three dead people in this case and you're out, no ifs, ands, or buts about it."

"Since when is three bodies a rule? Three dead bodies? Sounds like baseball. How do you come up with three dead bodies?"

"The dead guy in the fire, Nikki, and now Mark Sills."

"How did you find out about the dead guy in the fire? You left."

"You're not the only detective around here. It was front page news today. Vincent Artello arrested for murder, but released, again."

"Oh. But that dead body doesn't count. It's not even related."

"It's related somehow, you were there to investigate. Don't try to pull one over on me. You're into some dangerous shit."

"Pull one over on you? Don't be ridiculous. I will be extremely cautious," I promised.

"No, Paul. You don't know what cautious is. You throw caution out the window. I'm glad you told me, but I have to put my foot down."

"Put your foot down? Lindsey, you're not my mother. We are partners; we are both adults. You can't tell me not to do my job."

"This isn't your job!"

"Yes, it is. Mark Sills had a policy with our company. Now he's dead, too, they will want explanations, and that is my job."

"Paul, I swear."

"Don't do this, Lindsey." I shook my head. "I've told you how important this is to me."

"Well, it had better be damn important, more important than me, because I swear if you keep on the path you're on, you'll be sleeping in either an empty house or a graveyard. And I'm sorry I'd rather be a divorcée than a widow."

"Now, Lindsey. It doesn't have to be either one of those. Those aren't the only possibilities. I'll be at the office, and then I'll be under the watch of Detective Jeffries at Mark Sills' apartment and no where else without checking in with you first."

"Fine," she answered abruptly.

"I'll check in every two hours. Don't panic if I don't call on the dot. And I'll be home by five, no later. Heck, we can even look into getting some kind of Lo-Jack for husbands so you can always know where I am."

"I said 'fine,'" she said angrily. "I'm not saying anything else. You're not getting my blessing on this one."

"Fine," I snapped, equally perturbed.

I was anxious enough without her creating feelings of guilt to add to the mix. Why did she have to be like that? What was wrong with her? Couldn't she just let me do my job? Why did everything have to be an argument with her? I would be careful and everything would turn out fine.

My copies of Mark's life insurance policy didn't list a secondary beneficiary, and I wanted to check our records to be sure. Fortunately, Morehouse Insurance had limited Saturday hours where agents could come in and do some work, and it was still early enough. The clouds were finally starting to clear, and the day was heating up. Steam rose from the city pavement as I drove to my office. Leaving my gun in my glove compartment, I went inside to consult Myra for help with this. I crossed my fingers she'd be there working.

"Oh, great, you're here," I said, rounding the corner.

" 'Great' sarcastic because you didn't want me here, or 'great' you are really glad to see me because you need my help."

"Great, you're here, I need your help."

"Good. I would have kicked you out otherwise." She smirked. "I get time and a half to work Saturday morning. It's worth it. Usually I read." She held up a romance novel with a bare chested man leaning into a reluctant woman. "Still working on the Sills case?"

"Yes. Looking at Mark Sills' policy it appears he doesn't have a secondary beneficiary."

She took the papers and confirmed what I already knew. "But we can see if it's always been this way or if it's been changed."

"Great. How?"

"You say, 'Myra you're a goddess, and I'm forever in your debt,' and I do it for you."

I repeated her words in a sassy tone.

"Why, thank you." She batted her blue-lined eyes.

"When policies are changed, the letter in the policy is changed to represent what version it is. If it ends in an 'A', then it is the only version."

I looked at the policy number—1969F576-11A.

"So this is an 11A, a first version; no previous policy exists?"

"Correct."

"That was so easy. I owe a debt of gratitude for that?"

She shrugged. "I make the rules in here."

"Well, it still can't be," I puzzled. "I was certain—"

"This is the husband, Mark Sills, right? The guy did his wife in."

"Yes, but I'm not sure he killed her. He's dead now, too. Murdered."

"Ahh, how?"

"Stabbed in the park this morning."

"It's connected to the wife. It's a conspiracy."

"I don't know. You're sure no one else gets his money since his wife is already deceased?"

"I didn't say no one gets the money. Someone is going to get two point five million. Their two deaths were far enough apart the first claims for two million for Nikki will go to Mark's estate, and then his policy for half a million will go unpaid or since it would have been paid to Nikki and she's already deceased, the money might go to his estate as well."

"You're right—his estate. His estate would go to the beneficiary of his will. Someone will no doubt benefit from his will. Thank you."

I placed my palms on Myra's cheeks, turned her head downward, pecked a quick kiss onto her forehead, and then, releasing her and smiling, I said, "Myra, you are a goddess, and I'm forever in your debt."

She blushed, which seemed out of character. Maybe she liked me enough she wouldn't press harassment charges for the stunt I had pulled. I checked my desk and mailbox at work to make sure I wasn't missing anything new or pertinent to my case.

At 11:45, I arrived at the Magnolia Apartments. I parked in the parking deck across the street and left my files and gun in the car, but I took my notepad and pen. I waited for Detective Jeffries outside the Magnolia, which gave me time to think. I'd never been convinced either way Mark had or had not killed his wife, Nikki. With his death I might never know. My new theory a third party had killed Nikki and Mark put me back to square one—trying to figure out how he or she got into the building to do the deed.

I watched as tenants came and went and realized if I hovered near them and pretended to be with them for the benefit of the cameras I could probably have gotten inside especially on a busy day like the fourth of July. There would have been lots of guests in town. To the tenant I could pretend to have a key but accept their holding the door open for me. That way I wouldn't have to be buzzed in and wouldn't draw attention to myself.

Once in through the side door, it would only take two paces to be at the stairwell and safely out of sight. I was about to make an attempt when Detective Jeffries sidled up and got us buzzed in by waving his badge.

"I wish I had one of those magic passes," I said.

"No you don't." He held the door for me.

"It'd make life so much easier." I sighed.

Detective Jeffries approached the new security girl with our plans. She nodded, her red-headed curls bobbled, and she motioned to the elevators. Once again we rode to the seventeenth floor together.

"What are you looking for?" I asked him after a few moments of silence.

"What are *you* looking for?" He turned the question on me.

"I asked you first," I replied.

He smiled smugly.

"Oh, I see how it's going to be." I laughed. "A battle of detective wit."

Detective Jeffries merely shrugged. The apartment looked about the same as it did during the last visit I'd made, with the addition of more trash in the kitchen garbage can, dirty dishes in the sink, and general clutter here and there which indicated Mark had been living there since Nikki's death.

"I guess Mrs. Sills was the housekeeper," Jeffries commented.

I began the search process all over again like before, only this time Jeffries was standing over my shoulder the whole time.

"Aren't you going to conduct your own search?" I asked, hands on hips.

He shook his head. "No need to. You're doing a fine job. I'll simply watch."

And that's about all he did—follow me around looking at everything I looked at. Some things he paid more attention to and others less. He made his own notes, as I didn't intend on sharing mine.

In my tour of the office, the blinking light on the answering machine drew me over. The call was a hang-up, an unknown caller on the ID, but I was reminded of the phone message from the machine the previous time—something about a storage rental space. A storage space required keys.

"Did Mark Sills have anything on him when he died?" I asked.

"Unless the killer took something, all we found on him was his apartment key."

I pawed through the filing cabinet again. Detective Jeffries wasn't too interested in this as he shifted his weight restlessly from foot to foot.

"What are you looking for?" he asked.

"Clues," I replied, trying to be a smart-ass

"I'm going to make some calls at the desk, O.K.?" he asked.

I nodded as he moved to the phone. I welcomed the chance to snoop unscrutinized. I found a statement for wills from Jackson, Bowden, and Morris attorneys of family law for $350.00, but no wills. Maybe it was kept in a safe deposit box. If there was a will, this lawyer would probably know about it. I jotted down the name and address. Detective Jeffries motioned for me to pass the papers over.

No files or paperwork on a storage place, and I hadn't seen any keys. If I were a key, where would I be? I might be found in the bedroom on the dresser since there hadn't been any on the kitchen counter or on any hooks. I always left mine on the dresser. I shut the cabinet. Jeffries was involved in a conversation, so I motioned to the bedroom, and he nodded approval.

Out from under his watchful eye, I spotted Mark Sills' key ring, which lay with some spare change as I had suspected—on the dresser. Keys jangling as I examined them, I debated about taking the unusual-looking ones off the ring—there were two—or taking the whole set. When I heard Jeffries wrapping up his phone call, I decided against taking them and ended up my search with a cursory glance in the drawers and the bathroom. Jeffries had appeared over my shoulder again. I informed him I was through.

"Find anything?" he asked.

"Not really," I twisted my lip, undecided about asking for the keys. Better to beg forgiveness than to ask and not receive had been my previous motto; however, I'd be risking my license as a P.I. if I took evidence. Anything I found might not be admitted into court. Besides, Jeffries was my friend.

"Too bad."

"What about those keys?" I indicated the dresser. "Maybe we should find out what they all are? Where they go?"

"Good idea." Jeffries took the key ring and pocketed them. "Any suggestions?"

He had a way of knowing when I knew more than I let on.

"I think he had a storage rental place at a U-Store-It."

"We can check it out." Jeffries pre-empted my next question by adding, "And you can come along."

"Thanks. When?"

"Maybe later this evening. Let me check into it, and I'll call you."

Jeffries escorted me out of the building, and we parted ways. He went to the underground deck whereas I hastily jogged across the street while it was clear and entered the parking garage. My thoughts on the storage unit and what we might discover, I found myself wandering, somewhat lost in the garage, not remembering the exact location of my car. When at last I located it, I took a glance at my watch and discovered nearly an hour had passed. I fumbled around on my belt clip for the cell phone so I could report in to Lindsey. To my surprise, the phone began ringing as I was about to dial.

"Hello," I said into static on the phone. "Hello?"

No answer. The events afterward happened so fast, sequencing them is difficult. I hung up to dial Lindsey, all the while walking towards my car. When a red Honda sports car screeched alongside, fear I would be run down or hit caused me to step closer to the parked cars, only to find myself standing by the double back doors of a blue Dodge work van. Still watching the first car, I caught only a brief glimpse of two figures in masks who had swung open the van doors, and in an instant one swooped my feet right out from under me while the second bagged my head, pulled the drawstring tight, and grabbed my torso. Working together, they toppled me sideways and threw me like a roll of carpet into the van. My yells for help were never heard. They worked with precision and speed; they were experts. A third person whom I never saw closed the van doors. The engine immediately came to life, and we moved off.

CHAPTER 12

I continued to scream, muffled by the thick fabric bag. I was not going to go down without a fight. I was not going to let them kill me. I was not pinned, but I could not see. I twisted and rolled like an alligator. I kicked and thrashed about, throwing punches. Despite my shin kicking and elbow-to-groin maneuvers, I was outnumbered. I'd like to think it took six men to subdue me since I couldn't see my surroundings and couldn't count my assailants. But I only remember feeling three distinct sets of hands tying me up with plastic cable ties. My circulation cut, my vision blocked, face down on the van floor, I flopped like a fish. A clunk on the head hit me square behind the right ear sending me senseless, but not unconscious. I knew I must lay still or the man would strike again. Resistance was futile. I could feel nothing but fright and warm blood and sweat running down my ear and neck. Fear of impending death sent adrenaline through my veins, blocking all the pain as a knot grew behind my ear, pulling my skin tight. The suffocating heat and lack of oxygen made breathing labored. In my suffering silence, I concentrated on the road and where they were taking me. Silence was difficult since my every instinct told me to scream, to scream loud, for anyone, someone to help me, but I feared the repercussions. As I lay there I could feel the stopping and starting of the van as we passed through traffic lights and made turns. My teeth chattered, my whole body shook beyond control, and the loud pulsing sounds of blood in my own ears became a timer counting out the seconds passed in my head. Three minutes. The drumbeat was enough to drown out the sounds from outside the van if I let it overtake me. I felt nauseated and dizzy. I felt on the verge of blackout, yet I knew I must stay conscious and keep track of where I was going.

It took about ten minutes to reach the unknown destination. I didn't know what they were going to do with me when we arrived. There was a parking deck; I could tell by the unique echoing sounds of those massive concrete structures as the van halted and doors opened and shut. One man struggled to lift my six-foot-three body over his shoulder like a sack. Profuse sweating had made me slippery, and I slid to the ground. I yelled out for help; a gun stuck to my side immediately.

"No more of that, buddy," he spoke, two sets of hands lifting me the second time.

An elevator took us up. Carpeted floors absorbed the sound of the men's shoes as the two carried me inside what smelled, even through my head covering, like a new or newly painted office building. A closed, claustrophobic feeling wasn't entirely caused by the bag over my face and indicated we were in a hallway. The men tucked in and walked closer to my sides as if there were less room. We proceeded through several sets of slow-closing doors, the clunk heard long after we had passed. I was tipped upright and slung down into a cozy leather armchair, not what I expected. The two escorts stood behind, each with a hand on one of my shoulders, gripping tightly, the gun at the back of my head.

Uncontrollable shaking legs caused the chair to jiggle. I felt certain my heart would give out on me as my pulse pounded like a stampede of horses. My mouth was parched, dry from thirst and fear. They would want me to talk. A distorted voice of an artificial larynx spoke to me, like a demon.

"Now is the time to tell me the truth. Do not try to cover up or lie. If I even think you are lying or holding back information, I will have you shot and disposed of."

I squirmed in the padded seat until the hands on my shoulders gripped me tighter.

"What do you know about Mark Sills?" the voice asked.

"I know he's dead. He owed some people a lot of money." The words gushed out in fear.

"What people?"

"I don't know exactly." I wished I did know more so I could give better answers. I didn't want these people, whoever they were, thinking I was playing games.

"Then tell me what you do know, all of it." The gun brushed so close I could feel it graze my neck through the covering. I was certain I felt the coolness of the metal, and its touch sent chills to my toes.

"Mark Sills was taking money out of mob accounts, and he was found out. The money was being laundered at his office. He claimed the mob had threatened him, and now he and his wife are dead."

"So you assume the mob did it?" The voice crackled from the electronic distortion. The hand on my left shoulder dug sharply, talons into my collar bone.

"I don't know who did it." I winced under the pressure of the hand. "Mark didn't want to talk about the money; he didn't want to give me names, but he did. He told me the names Vincent Artello and Saul Dedmon."

"Vincent Artello and Saul Dedmon."

"Yes," I blurted.

"What about them?"

"Mark didn't say; he wrote the names down for me as a lead. I was investigating his wife's death."

"A lead for what?"

"To find out who killed her. He thought the mob had her killed as a warning, and he wanted me to check it out. He was being investigated for killing her himself. He wanted to clear—"

"Do you think one of those men killed her?" The voice cut off my details.

"I don't know."

A sharp smack of half closed fist crossed my face, catching the bridge of my nose. My eyes teared immediately; my nose ran. I could not move to wipe either.

"That's a yes-or-no question. You either do or you don't. Do you think one of those men killed her?"

"No," I replied, even though my real answer was still one of uncertainty.

"What do you know about those men?"

"I know Saul is dead and Vincent Artello was arrested for arson but released from prison."

"How much does the cop know?"

"Nothing." I paused. "Really."

"You haven't told the cop any of this?"

"No—well—yes, I gave him Vincent Artello's name. And Houghton Lofton."

"Why?"

"Mark Sills was killed, and he obviously feared Vincent Artello. There was a motive. I gave the police the name as a possible suspect for Mark's murder. But that's all I told him was the name and suggested he check into it himself."

"And Houghton Lofton? What did you say?"

"I told him to check it out, that's all."

"The cop is your friend? Yet you don't tell him everything?"

I felt the gun butt up against my head again.

"Yes, but we don't want to bias each other with our own investigations. If we come to the same conclusion, it is more certainly correct. Besides, we like to compete, a little friendly rivalry. I try not to tell him anything."

"What have you told your wife?"

"Nothing. I've told her nothing." I knew the answer would be trouble, but I wasn't bringing her into this. Not in this lifetime.

The man behind me hit me on the top of the head with the butt of the gun. I would have doubled over and grabbed the top of my head with my hands, but I was firmly restrained from any reaction other than a reflex-like jump. Warm blood trickled down the front of my face, across my nose and lips, down my chin, and into my shirt.

"We don't believe you; in fact, we know it's not true. What have you told your wife?" the demonic voice repeated.

"I've told you everything. Leave her out of this." I struggled against the hands holding me.

I was wrested from the chair and found myself face down on the floor with a foot in my back in short order.

"You're not in a position to demand anything, Mr. Grey."

"I know," I replied into the Berber carpeting. I could feel the bumps, and it smelled new and soapy, like it had been freshly steam-cleaned. "I'm sorry, but I've told you everything."

"Not everything, not yet. Do you know how the money-laundering is accomplished?"

"Not really. Vaguely."

"Do you know which other people at the company are involved and which are not?"

"No."

There must have been some silent signaling and discussion; it felt as if the man standing on me wavered like he was signaling with his hands.

I was scooped up, once again a human roll of carpet and carried down the hallways back to the parking deck and then the van. The van revved and then ventured out on what seemed a meandering route, a long drive with lots of turns. After about twenty minutes we left the busy sounds of traffic and highways. My pulse began to rapid fire again. Were they taking me to some remote spot to kill me and dump my body? I listened as we crunched over the tops of poorly paved roads and finally stopped and idled.

"If you tell anyone anything about what has happened, if you try to investigate and find out who we are or where we took you, if you tell the cop or your wife anything, we assure you, you won't be able to tell anyone anything else ever again. You got it?" a man said.

I nodded underneath my covers and spoke. "Yes."

"If you turn around before the count of thirty, we'll shoot your head off, got it?"

"Yes," I replied as I was shoved out the back, still bound and tied.

The van doors slammed, and they pulled away leaving me shocked, amazed, and angry all at once. I counted past thirty as instructed before I even attempted to remove the straps on my arms and feet or the head covering. I found I was stuck, unable to remove any of it. Not knowing where I was and not knowing who might come to help me, I called out for help anyway. A few moments later I felt hands on me; a knife sawed at the cord on my wrists. As the person undid my feet, I pulled the fabric bag off my head; clots of blood stuck to it, reopening one of my wounds. The scab over my ear throbbed painfully as I opened my eyes to see where I was.

I had no idea where I was. They didn't courteously drop me back off at my car where they had grabbed me in the first place. I saw my rescuer, a small black boy, about eight years old, who shut his army knife and pocketed it without a word. I thanked him, and he nodded a single time before turning on his heel and retreating into a nearby house.

"Did you see what happened?" I called after him.

He paused at his doorway. "I'm not supposta talk to strangers."

"I understand." I smiled. "Are your parents home?"

"They're busy right now. I'm not supposta answer the door either."

"All right," I reassured him. "If you can, tell me whether you saw anything or not, and then I'll be on my way."

He shrugged. "I didn't see nuthin'. I was playin' my video game, and I heard you yellin', and I came to see what's up."

"So you didn't see anyone else?"

"Nope."

"Thanks for helping me," I said and I waved. The boy disappeared into the dark depths of his house, screen door slamming.

My pulse had slowly been returning to normal as I conversed with the boy. I checked my watch—1:35. I searched the poor, run-down neighborhood for a pay phone so I could call Lindsey. Small houses, all similar in size and age, lined the streets in even blocks. Many were boarded up, front porches falling off, chain-link fences around, and

"Beware of Dog" signs posted. People stared from their doorways as I passed. It was a place where you might expect to find a dead body around any corner. I didn't fear mugging; a mugging would be like lighting striking in the same place twice. Archer Street, the first street sign read. No phones in sight. I didn't dare knock on a door and ask to use a phone, so I continued walking until I finally found a phone at a corner gas market. Thankfully I had a change and I dialed. Ring, ring, ring again. The recorder picked up.

Panic filled my system, adrenaline gushed, pulse skyrocketed once again. My hands shook as I replaced the receiver. What if they had gotten to Lindsey, too? I had to call the police. I had to get a taxi and get home.

With not enough change to make another call, I dialed the operator to place a collect call to the police station where Detective Jeffries worked. The charges were accepted, and I was put through.

"Paul, where are you? Are you all right?" Jeffries asked.

"Yes, I'm fine. Have you heard from Lindsey?"

"Yes, she's here with me at the station. She's getting some coffee. She was scared for your safety when you didn't check in. A patrol car checked the garage and your car is still there. Where are you and what are you doing? You sound strange."

"Strange isn't even the beginning, but never mind about me. She's O.K., right?"

"She's fine other than the heart wrenching you put her through. If you say you're going to check in every two hours and you don't, you better have a good reason—"

"I do, but I can't tell you."

"You can't tell? You're asking about Lindsey, and it's not because you didn't call. Do we need to be worried about Lindsey's safety? What do I need to tell her?"

"Tell her to go to a hotel or to Margie's and tell her not to go anywhere by herself, not anywhere. She's to stay there until I call her."

"I'll get a car to take her and then stay in the area. I know I'll be wasting my breath, but you know telling the police is probably the best way to help yourself right now."

"Oh, I don't think so, Jeffries. Sorry. Try to tell her all of this without frightening her too much. If they'd wanted her they'd already have her," I said without adding *I think* on the end even thought it was an aspect I wasn't totally confident about.

"They? They who?"

"I can't tell you. Some things need to get taken care of before I'll feel Lindsey and I are safe again. Trust me, your involvement would be more harm than good."

"Well, how can I help?"

"Take care of Lindsey, and get me into the storage place."

"It was a U-Store-It over on Peachtree Circle. You can go, and I'll meet you there in an hour. I'll call ahead so they know we're coming. If you get there before I do, you can open it up, but be good."

"Yeah, I'll be good."

"Anything else?" Jeffries asked as I was checking my wallet for cash and pockets for my car keys.

"No."

"You're sure?"

"Yeah, thanks," I said and then added, "and Jeffries—"

"What?"

"Watch your back."

"Always."

The corner market restroom gave me a place to clean up a little bit. Looking in the mirror, I hoped not too much bruising would occur. As I washed the blood off my face, swirls of red ran circular patterns down the drain. The bleeding had stopped; stitches wouldn't be needed. I parted my hair around the injuries to examine their ferociousness. I wondered if this tiny, run-down market sold Bactine. My dark, salt-and-pepper hair would hide the scabs and a ball cap would cover the rest. I rinsed my hair, neck, and face a final time and then dried off with toilet paper for lack of anything else.

In the convenience store I purchased a cap, a clean T-shirt, a drink, a snack, and some Motrin to help the headache, pain, and swelling. I grabbed a handful of ice from the drink cooler and packed it into a torn scrap from my old shirt.

"Can you call me a cab?" I asked the wide-eyed clerk who'd seen me come in all grimy, bloody, and generally looking like hell.

"Sure."

"Where am I?" I asked.

"Porterdale. You aw'right?"

I nodded, paid for my things, and went to wait outside. The cabbie arrived shortly and returned me to my car in about forty minutes. The abductors had jumped me so quickly, I'd dropped my cell phone. I picked it up; it was undamaged. I ducked into the car and retrieved my gun. Caressing the sleek metal form, I decided to keep it on my person from now on and wished myself back to the time of the abduction so I could have used it. No doubt I wouldn't have had the opportunity, and they would have confiscated the gun—or worse, used it against me. I also decided the best protection was to become more aware of potentially dangerous situations and stay away from vans.

I checked the incoming call log on my cell phone for the number that had called me before I was snagged, however it was an unknown number and wouldn't show on Caller ID. The call had come in at 12:45. I quickly jotted down what I could remember about the van ride, my assailants, the building, the times, and the locations. I would be looking into those things later, despite the warning not to.

On my way out I stopped, not only to pay my parking fee, but I got out and approached the man in the tiny booth.

"Sir? Can I help you?" he asked.

"Yes, you can. Three or four men in a blue van. Can you describe any of them?"

"Sorry mon? Blue van, what'd you mean?" The man backed up further into his small cubbie.

"You know exactly what I mean. There were several men in a blue van here in the garage a little over an hour ago."

"No, mon. I'm sorry, but I don't know—" The man was visibly shaking.

"Don't bullshit me," I warned. "Tell me what they looked like. Are there cameras? Can I get a license plate number?"

"Uh," he stammered.

I hovered over him with my height as he sat on his stool. I didn't want to physically accost him, but I leaned into him a bit, and put light pressure with my arm against his upper torso. He was pinned.

"You will tell me what you know. Now," I said.

"I don't know nuttin' about them men. Just they pay me good money to not say nuttin' about them."

"What did they look like?"

"I only see one, mon. Man who paid me, he scare me, too. He pay me and tell me not to be sayin' nuttin' or he kill me and me little girl. She only five year old." He indicated a picture of sweet-looking, young girl in the corner of his booth.

I let him up. "I understand. Did you see a license tag? Are there cameras?"

"No, mon. I not be lookin' at them when they go and there are no cameras." The poor man's teeth chattered as he spoke, a sign he was terrified.

"It's okay. I won't harm you. I'm a detective. Tell me about the one man you did see, what did he look like?"

"A big, white guy, like you. Only he younger and darker hair and eyes. He have a tattoo on his arm, a band went all da' way around." He indicated his biceps. "He scared me, somethin' in his eyes, mon."

"It's okay. Don't worry about him. They won't know you talked to me."

He nodded and wiped at his brow.

"You've been helpful. Thank you."

He nodded again and he took my parking fee. Then I headed over to the U-Store-It. Thankfully, I'd written down information about the phone call from the storage company in my notes. Now I had to hope Mark Sills hadn't already closed it up. The storage units were open 24 hours. The key I'd seen had 121 written on it with a permanent marker, so I pulled through the storage entrance and looked for some guidance. Small signs on the sides of the buildings listed the space numbers—1 to 60 on the first, 61 to 100 on the second, and 101 to 140 on the third. The second and third buildings had larger units than the first. I drove to space 121. I shut the car off, got out, and walked around the corner to the rental office.

"Can I help you?" The gentleman in the front office was chewing either gum or tobacco. He mumbled the words, head bent over some paperwork. He didn't look up.

"Yes, I hope so. I'm meeting police detective Martin Jeffries here. We want to get into unit 121."

"Let me see here." He sloshed his mouthful to the side pocket of his cheek.

He typed a few strokes on his computer keyboard, then looked up.

"Ah, yeah." He grinned at me, brown stains on his teeth. "This one's been locked up because of failure to pay the rental fees. Six months of back rent are due."

He stared at me expectantly. Did he want me to pull out my wallet and fork it over?

"Didn't they call you to tell you we'd be over?" My frustration was brimming. Why hadn't Jeffries taken care of this? Yet, as long as he took care of Lindsey, all else would be forgiven.

"Nope; no one called. You gonna pay the fees?" he asked.

"No, no, no. You don't understand. I'm not the owner or related to him. The owner, Mark Sills, and his wife, are dead. They were murdered. We need to get into their unit to search it. I'm investigating—"

"Oh, it's O.K., Officer." He winked. "I was kidding. You can get in. We're always ready to assist the police."

Impersonating a police officer is against the law, and I never do it by introducing myself as one or stating I am an officer; however, if the person I'm speaking with makes the assumption I usually let them go on believing that way. I tried correcting him once.

"I'm a private insurance investigator," I clarified. "Can I get in there?"

"Certainly, detective. I have to get the keys for you to unlock the doors, and then you can search all you like. But you can't take anything unless you got the right paperwork."

"Of course not. Are you coming with me?" I inquired.

"No. I gotta stay here to answer phones and in case anyone else comes in and needs me."

I headed back to unit 121. One of the keys opened the outside door, which led to a hallway filled with roll-up doors. The second key opened one of those. I pushed it up and back until it stayed put. The space was climate controlled but unlit inside. Only the hallway's fluorescent lights shone in dimly.

The light was enough for me to see the space was not being used as storage. Immediately evident was the lack of boxes and cartons. In fact, the room looked like a room, almost empty, except for a made-up double bed, an old dresser with a mirror, and a trash can arranged as if this were a seldom-used guest room. But judging from the condoms in the trash can by the bed, Mark Sills had been using the space as a little love nest. On top of the dresser were two large flashlight lanterns with several spare batteries. The second drawer was cracked open, and I peeked in to find some toiletries—perfume, deodorant, cologne. I wondered if the space had been used for one long-lasting affair or many short-flung trysts.

Secrets, betrayal, and lies—this tiny room with the worn blue bedspread and garage sale dresser revealed it all. It symbolized how far Mark Sills was willing to go, a chilling look at Mark Sills' life, deceptive and cunning, yet so sad and hopeless. I wondered if he or his lover had looked at themselves in the mirror and saw a side of themselves they never thought they'd become. In the back of my mind, I hoped if Lindsey ever felt that way, she'd divorce me rather than carry on in such a manner.

Two sources had told me Mark Sills had had an affair but it was over and he had reconciled with Nikki. Perhaps the reason why the rental space had gone unpaid for months. Mark would rather have all the contents go to auction than have to dispose of them in some way which might risk having to explain to his lovely wife.

I was about to pull open the top drawer by using my shirt over the knob when Jeffries appeared.

He gave a low whistle. "Crafty fellow."

I nodded.

"Sorry I'm late. I went ahead and got judge approval on opening this place up, just in case, and I brought Detective Henderson with me. He's observing, for the record. You haven't moved anything?"

"No. I peeked in the open drawer, but I didn't rummage through anything."

"Let's see what we've got."

Jeffries donned a pair of gloves, clicked on his pocket tape recorder, and opened the drawers one at a time.

"First drawer, size eight clothes, designer labels, for the lady. A spare polo shirt for our gentleman. A few panties." He held up a lacy, burgundy pair and offered them my way. "You haven't been getting into any of these lately."

"Not funny." But I couldn't help laugh.

"Lindsey is so ticked at you, and when she sees those cuts and bruises she's going to freak."

"You can't tell her," I said.

"I won't even ask how you got them. I figure you'll tell me in your own sweet time." Jeffries sighed, shook his head, and resumed his search.

"Second drawer, Degree deodorant, White Diamonds perfume, Old Spice cologne. Some K-Y lube and Trojan condoms."

"And more batteries," I added from over his shoulder.

"Third drawer, empty."

"Fourth drawer, empty. Top of dresser, two flashlights and eight batteries. Box of tissues."

I motioned to the trash. It was piled high, and I hoped full of some useful evidence. Jeffries wrinkled his nose at the used condoms on top.

"You want to take a turn? Get some practice?" he asked.

"No thanks. You're doing a great job. I'll just watch."

"Huh," he muttered as he lifted the first one aside. "Used condoms, three to be exact, and the empty wrappers. Some food napkins and a Wok-To-Go Chinese take-out box with chopsticks, and..."

"And what?"

"And a charge card receipt." He un-crinkled it. "To Neiman Marcus."

"Name or signature?" I leaned over and took a look.

"No."

"Keep digging," I urged.

"You're loving this a little too much, though." Jeffries gritted his teeth as he went through a pile of wadded up tissues with some kind of dried fluids on them.

"Can you DNA test that?" I asked.

"Yeah, but what good would it do? Unless the woman is already in the database nothing would match up, and we already know the man involved."

"We could match it up if we find a suspect."

"Any suggestions?" he asked suspiciously.

"Not yet, but I'm working on it. Keep looking."

Jeffries put the tissues aside and resumed his dig. "Empty McDonald's cup, chewing gum, two pieces, candy wrappers, and whoo—"

"What?"

Jeffries flattened out a piece of crumpled up notebook paper with writing on it.

"What is it?" I asked.

"It says: 1561 ATL 4:30 10/29."

"A plane flight," we both spoke at the same time.

"There's more," Jeffries added. "There was a connecting flight from Las Vegas to O'Hare, then coming into Atlanta at 4:30 on October 29th, but these flights were almost a year ago. And departure dates are here, too."

"Mark ended his affair, must have been six months ago because he hadn't paid his rental fee since January. Those might have been flights from the last time the woman came to see him."

"Do you know where she lived?"

"No. I thought she lived around here, but I guess not. Unless those flights weren't related to his affair."

"Worth looking in to."

"Anything more in there?" I indicated the can.

"Nope."

"I want to jot down a few notes before we go," I said. "If that's all right?"

"Knock yourself out." Jeffries eyes flashed briefly across my injuries and then averted.

I copied the flight dates and times, the charge card number, the receipt number and date, the brand names of the perfume and clothing, and the name of the Chinese take-out place.

"I ought to be able to find her based on this," I said.

"You think so?" Jeffries smirked.

"I do."

"Want to wager?"

"Depends on the wager."

"Oh, I don't know, how about loser buys the winner a new TV?"

"A new TV? I don't need a TV. I need this case solved. How about we see who finds her first and forget the rest?"

Jeffries shrugged.

"I'll see you later, man. I gotta get started." I indicated my notes and checked the time—5 P.M.

Lindsey's car wasn't in the garage, as I should have expected, but I hoped to see it anyway. She was somewhere else, being kept safe. Outside the summer sun still shone brightly, but inside the blinds were pulled shut to keep the cool air in, and it was dark throughout.

No messages on the answering machine. She didn't even call. I had to admit I had been neglecting her recently. I'd been spending most of the time on a case that wasn't even mine to work when I should have been focusing more on her. I won't proclaim to know much about women—merely enough to get myself in trouble. But I do know women, or even men for that matter, don't like to be left alone night after night. Every once in a while it's good to be on your own, but humans are social creatures needing company in one form or another. What she wasn't getting from me, she might try to find elsewhere. Mark Sills' sordid little storage room came back to mind. Selfish as it was, I suddenly felt lonely and wished she were home.

I couldn't sleep. I tried to watch TV. Usually I'm a senseless blob if the TV is on and I have a remote in my hand. But my fear and my guilty conscience held battles in my mind and wouldn't let me get absorbed by any program no matter how captivating it might have normally been. Mostly, I tried to figure out what I was going to do next and how I would apologize to Lindsey when I got the chance. A pointless endeavor. Anytime I've ever rehearsed a speech to give someone, I end up throwing it out the window when the time comes to use it and I say what fits the moment.

At 1 A.M. I wondered where Lindsey was. I wondered if she was

up thinking about me. Had she gone to Margie's or to a friend? Had
Jeffries gotten her a hotel? What if something had happened to her? A
horrible rush of thoughts ran through my head—train wrecks,
kidnappings, car wrecks, and car jackings.

*   *   *   *   *

The next morning I called Lindsey's friend and boss, attorney
Robert Mayson, to ask for a few favors.

"You realize it's Sunday?" Robert asked. "Most attorneys don't
work on weekends."

"I know, I'll pay for the time—or overtime. Do you know anyone
at Jackson, Bowden, and Morris? They are family law attorneys, wills and
stuff."

"I don't, but let me make a few calls. They say you can find anyone
with six calls. I'll check the theory. If I get someone, what exactly is it you
want?"

"I want to see the will of Mark Sills—today."

"It's Sunday."

"So you've said. But I need it today."

"All right, give me a little while, and I'll call you back if I have any
luck."

I had breakfast, showered and checked my wounds—very tender
and swollen. Decided a baseball cap was in order again. While I was
dressing, Robert Mayson called to say he had reached Carol Jackson, one
of the senior attorneys at the firm. She would meet me at the offices on
her way to late church services, if I could leave straight away and
wouldn't take long.

Their offices were located in Duluth, a suburb of Atlanta. Senior
attorney Carol Jackson didn't keep me waiting. Within minutes of my
arrival she pulled up in a sparkling silver Lexus. I introduced myself.

"Hello, Mr. Grey." She shook my hand and then unlocked the
office door. "If you'll follow me, we can discuss your needs in my
office."

"Yes, thank you."

She escorted me to a cozy office space including a sitting area. On
the side table were family photos of her husband and daughter jumping
in fall leaves and climbing trees. Her daughter had her same pale eyes and
ashen hair. She motioned for me to sit.

"How can I help you?" She took the seat opposite.

"I need to see the wills of Mark and Nikki Sills. I'm investigating a two-million-dollar insurance claim. Both are deceased"

Ms. Jackson leaned in. Her long, silky hair slipped off her shoulders and fell forward. "I know. I'm sorry to hear it. They were very nice people."

"Since they had their wills done through your offices, are you handling the estate?"

"Well, there isn't an estate to speak of. All of the property and funds in question will be held by the state until an heir can be found."

"What? Why?"

"Both Mark and Nikki Sills listed each other as primary beneficiary and neither had a secondary beneficiary. Neither had other family, so the estate—what's left of it after paying debts—will be held until an heir, however distant, is found. After a set time there is a remote possibility their funds would become the property of the state."

"Really? So far there's been no one to claim any of it?"

"No."

"Is this the original will or have there been revisions?"

"Well, I'm really only to speak of the current will. Previous versions become null and void."

"Do you keep previous versions on file?"

"Yes." She leaned back in her chair and crossed her legs. "And I know you'd like to see a copy."

"Yes, I would."

"There could be legal issues with me allowing you to see this information." She folded her arms over her chest. "Especially if someone were to decide to challenge the will based on the information."

"I won't tell anyone—strictly confidential. I know I have no right to see the information, but I'd like to find out what happened to Mark and Nikki Sills." I added with a wink, "Besides, I don't really want to see the state get two million dollars of insurance money. They get enough already."

She laughed.

"Seriously, don't wills become public knowledge when they are registered? This information would be in the public domain soon enough anyway?"

"Not if there were previous versions, but never mind it. You and I have never met, but I'll do this as a favor for Mr. Mayson. One lawyer helping another. I'm prepared for the consequences, if any."

"Great. Thank you very much." I nodded.

"I'll round them up for you. You may wait in the conference room. I'll show you the way."

She stood up and led me down narrow halls past soft drink and coffee vending machines to a room filled with hundreds of law books in every size, shape, and color on the shelves along the walls. A large wood table filled the room almost corner to corner with a tiny glass candy dish carefully centered on top and filled with fruit chews.

"You won't be able to take copies. You may look at them while you are here, and I ask you not to take notes."

"Perfectly fine with me. Thanks." I smiled. I was certain I'd be able to memorize any information I might find and need.

"No problem." She nodded and shut the door as she left.

I browsed the bookshelves while she was gone. She returned with a thick file folder and a cup of coffee with a sugar packet and creamer.

"I will actually be going over some papers in my office, since I'm here. I only have about ten minutes, then I must go."

"That will be fine. I will let you know when I'm finished."

I made myself comfortable at the table. Two previous versions existed, but only for Mark Sills. Both his oldest will and his newest will gave everything to Nikki. The in-between will listed another woman, Gianina DeSantis, and was created right around the time he had been having an affair. The newest version was written only two months ago, I assumed sometime after his affair had supposedly ended.

There was an assortment of other papers, including a sheet with the names and addresses of all beneficiaries and witnesses, I assumed in case they needed to track someone down. Gianina DeSantis' address was listed as 1775 Adobe Sunset Drive, Las Vegas, Nevada.

Jackpot, I thought. *Guess who's going to Vegas.*

CHAPTER 13

After leaving the law offices, I first called Mr. Moore to take off Monday and Tuesday as days of vacation. He wasn't too pleased since I'd just been away for the fourth of July, but I had to do it. I wasn't sure I could get to Vegas and back in twenty-four hours. Then I called Jeffries.

"Cha-ching! I found her."

"Who is she?" he asked.

"Gianina DeSantis, living in Las Vegas. Can you run a check on her? See if she still lives there."

"Yeah, I already did. I tracked her down with her credit card number, account now closed."

"Ugh, you beat me."

"Yeah, where's my TV?"

"Now you know you're not getting a TV set from me. Besides, it's not fair play. You have too many advantages being an officer. You can do things I can't."

"Quit whining. Anyhow, when I checked her address from the credit card company it wasn't any good."

"Can you find out where she is now?"

"We're working on it. If she hasn't changed her driver's license or registered her car, it may take a while. We can use a tax return if she's submitted one this year. We'll be in for a wait because we have to pull her federal taxpayer information. We don't have any real evidence to show we need it. We'd need a judge to—"

"Never mind. I'll do it on my own. I'm going to Vegas and see if I can track her down the old-fashioned way."

"Are you serious?"

"Yes, very. This case is serious, seriously dangerous. I can't sit around and do nothing."

"When will you go?"

"Next flight I can get. You'll keep a watch on Lindsey for me and tell her I'm O.K. and where I am? If she needs to go somewhere, can you get her an escort?"

"Yeah, sure thing."

"Do you know any mob characters with an arm tattoo, like a band around the upper arm?"

"Not off hand, but probably most of them have tattoos. I can check our database of previous arrests and our wanted men."

"Good deal. I'll call you when I get back."

I threw together a travel bag at home and then headed for the airport. The wait was minimal, the flight uneventful except for some turbulence which kept me awake. With the time change going back three hours I arrived in Las Vegas only two hours after leaving Atlanta, yet it had been a five-hour flight. It was almost midnight by my mind's clock, and by the time I got a rental car and a hotel room I was exhausted. Fully clothed I fell across the bed, pulled up the corner of a sheet, and slept.

I awoke to bright sunlight streaming through the cracks in the hotel room curtains. I flung off the sweat-drenched sheets. I had neglected to turn on the air conditioner. Already this morning outside temperatures soared. I decided to take a run around this strange city to collect my thoughts and make my plan. I emerged into the hot, dry Nevada air, which was like walking into a 400-degree oven, and ran a quick three miles. I returned to the hotel to shower, quickly pack, check out, and then go once again back out into the heat. They say it's better out West because it's a dry heat. Bullshit, I decided as I climbed into the rental car. The seats were so hot I felt they were going to melt into my skin.

The only way to find Gianina DeSantis would be to start with her last known address and follow her trail. A landlord or old neighbors might know where she went. A local street map showed the way.

The whole area was flat, not a hill in sight. Landscaping included less grass and water-needy plants than back home in Georgia. Cactus and yucca plants seemed popular. Heat waves created mirages on the blacktop as I pulled up to 1775 Adobe Sunset. I doubted Ms. DeSantis had a landlord. Upscale, stucco-and-tile roof homes lined the street.

The house in question was surrounded by a black wrought iron fence and an intricately designed gate. I rang the bell. No answer. The neighbor across the street observed me looking about and around the sides of the house and called to me. Every neighborhood has one—the lady who sees and knows everything.

"Can I help you?" she asked. "The Pritchetts aren't home right now."

I crossed the street to speak to her. "Actually, I'm looking for

Gianina DeSantis. I believe she used to live here."

"Oh, yes, Nina. A beautiful young lady. She moved." She bent and pulled some weeds from her flower bed.

"Yes, I know. Do you know where?"

"Are you an old beau of hers?" She barely looked up from her chore.

"Yes, yes, I'm an old beau."

"She had a lot of beaus—can't find the right guy. How did you meet her?"

"Uh, work."

"Oh, well." She stood upright and looked me up and down disapprovingly. Noticing my injuries, she added, "You're probably one of the wrong guys then."

I didn't know what to say. She could see my surprise.

"What? You think an old woman like me didn't know what she was up to?"

Up to? How I wished I knew. I wished I could ask.

"Well, do you know where she is?"

"I don't think she'd appreciate me sending the likes of you her way again."

"I'm sorry, but I'm not understanding. I'm a nice guy. Maybe you should let her decide."

"Humpfh." She folded her arms and looked me over once more.

I stood silently, taking the examination.

"You're not an old beau, are you? You don't even know her," she said, squinting. "I can see it in your eyes. And your moment of confusion."

"What do you mean?"

"I'm an old lady, been around a lot of people. You're good people. I can tell by your mannerisms and again those eyes. You look like you took a beating and you're still looking for her. You won't let anything bad happen to her. So tell me who you are, really, and why you're here."

I nodded and pulled out my ID. "I'm a Paul Grey, an investigator from Atlanta."

"I'm Faith Russell." She took the card I offered.

"Glad to make your acquaintance."

"And why do you need the poor girl so badly?" Faith put her hand above her brow and squinted into the sun, looking into my eyes.

"Her ex-lover has been murdered. I want to talk to her." I moved to her left, so she could see me better.

"She didn't do it?" Faith's hand dropped to her side.

"We don't know who did it. We won't know until we get to ask her some questions. Do you think she did it?"

"I don't know the man. It might depend." She shrugged. "Who is 'we' since you're here by yourself?"

"A police officer and myself. We work together sometimes."

"Do you think she is in some kind of trouble?"

"I think she might have been mixed up in some bad dealings."

"Bad dealings, yes. I'm sure that's why she left and why you're here."

"Did she tell you anything? Do you know any information at all?"

"No. She said she'd spare me the details. Details would have been trouble for me evidently. Do you know the details?" Her eyes twinkled with curiosity.

"Some, but I don't think they should be shared. I want to warn you to be careful."

"I'm an old lady. I'm always cautious. And like I said I can tell about people."

"Others may come looking for her, or you."

"I'll be O.K." She winked reassuringly.

"Can you tell me about the people she used to hang out with? You said she was with the wrong guys."

"Yes, very undesirable the whole lot. You can find one of them at the Luxor casino at night, Joe Pagliani. He'll be at the back of the Isis bar, jet black hair and beady eyes. You can't miss him. They dated a while."

"Do you think he could be part of her troubles?"

"Might be. Her plan was to go to Atlanta after they broke up. She left about Christmastime without saying good-bye."

"Atlanta?" Her statement sent chill-bumps up my arms.

"Yeah, isn't that where you are from?"

"Yes. Are you sure she moved there?"

"Well, it was the plan. I wasn't sure until today."

"What made you sure today?"

"Well, it's funny you came along asking about Nina. I got a letter from her in this morning's mail."

"What? You didn't tell me. May I see it?"

"I wasn't sure if I was to tell you. I had to pray about it a moment and see what God put in my heart. Give me a minute; I'll get it."

The lady disappeared into her house and returned a few minutes later.

"Not much to it," she explained. "She's telling me not to worry about her and saying sorry for leaving without saying good-bye. Post office box for her address if I wanted to write."

She handed over the letter and a photo. "Thought you could use the photo, too," she said. "I know you don't know the first thing about the girl. Probably didn't even know what she looks like."

"Thank you."

"It's not a great picture. She didn't have much in the way of family, at least as far as I know, so she joined mine for Thanksgiving last year. She's on the right with the dark hair."

"This will be fine. Would you like me to return it to you?"

"When you're through with it."

"I could take the envelope with Nina's and your addresses on it."

"That will be fine," she agreed.

"Well, thanks for your help. Please be careful who you speak to."

She smiled. "I always am."

My next stop was the local Post Office to try to obtain a physical street address. Perhaps she'd had her mail forwarded. But she had not left any tracks. Her mail delivery had been stopped, and no forwarding address had been left, not even the post office box. It seemed Nina had wanted to disappear. I called my information back to Jeffries in Atlanta, then killed time until nightfall.

The Vegas strip was crowded, cars bumper to bumper, as the evening shifted into high gear. The marquis announced gala shows and comedians, as well as musicians, with thousands of dancing lights. Even the fast food joints were lit up like daytime. There were so many lights, when I looked up into the night sky I couldn't see a single star.

I pulled my car up to the Luxor casino and got out. The Luxor is a giant black onyx pyramid, with a streaming bright xenon light shooting out from the point at the top into the night sky. Having never been to a casino before, I was utterly astonished. My mouth and eyes gave away my awe.

"First time here?" a valet asked.

I nodded as I handed him my keys.

"Inside, head to the right to get a room or take the escalator to get to the attractions level. You'll see the casino."

"Thanks."

I hadn't planned on staying two nights, but at this point if it got much later, I might need a room. I had qualms about getting one there since I was going to be doing some investigating and had a history of being kicked out of places. I decided to wait on the room and headed into the casino through the Sphinx entryway.

The inside of the complex could only be described as colossal. A life-size replica of the temple of Ramses II filled the atrium. Huge stone pillars and statues of Egyptians, both standing and seated, guarded both sides of the room. The entire walkway was lined with large stone rams on pedestals and palm trees. It was a clash of ancient world and technology as the sights and sounds of the casino beckoned beyond the doorway.

Thousands of colorful lights brightly decorated the various slot machines and game play areas. Everything in a gambler's dream—keno, roulette, slots, video poker, craps, and more. The slots carried on in stereo sound effects and the cranking sound of the levers; flashing lights on top signaled an occasional payout followed by clinking coins in metal trays or plastic cups.

I scanned the casino and surrounding areas—various lounges, clubs, eateries, and big screen TVs. I stopped an employee for directions to the Isis lounge.

"Over there on the right." He pointed.

I headed for the bar on the other side, looking for the back table where I would find Joe Pagliani. When I thought I had spotted him, I took a table a few spaces away, ordered a drink, and observed for a while. He sat and nursed a Cosmopolitan martini as beautiful women stopped by every so often to chat and give him a kiss. The wait staff all seemed to know him well. Two different men had come by and talked with him. He offered them seats, which he hadn't done with the ladies. He seemed to be conducting business with the men because they stayed longer and acted less jovial than the women. When the first male visitor approached, he'd sent the current lady companion away.

On my waitress' next pass I stopped her. "The man over there is Joe Pagliani?"

"Yes."

"He seems very popular. What does he do? Does he own the place?"

"Heavens, no." She laughed. "He doesn't have any relation to the casino. They put up with him, though."

"The casino owners don't want him here? Why?"

"They don't mind him. He racks up a food and drink bill every night and pays it. He sells insurance."

"Insurance? That's what line of work I'm in. He's awfully

popular."

She smiled. "He's cute and wealthy."

I pulled out Nina DeSantis' picture. "Have you ever seen this woman?"

"Well, yes, but not for a long time." The smile she'd been wearing disappeared.

"Did she used to hang out with Joe?"

"Yeah, she did."

"Were they dating?"

"I think you should ask him."

"One more thing about this girl—do you know where she is now?"

"No idea. She quit coming around. Listen, I'd stay and talk, but unless you're a cop or something, I've got other customers."

"Oh, yes, I'm sorry. Please, go."

The waitress went back to work, but she returned in a few moments with a drink.

"I didn't order—" I began.

"It's from Mr. Pagliani. He said you need to join him."

"I do?"

"You better."

I took my drink from her hand and moved to Joe Pagliani's table.

"Paul Grey, insurance investigator." I reached and shook his hand.

"Joe, but you know already. When you spoke to the waitress for so long but never ordered a drink, I knew you were here for more than drinking."

"True. I'm trying to track down Gianina DeSantis." I held out her picture.

"I don't need the picture. I know Nina. Why the sneakiness?"

"I wanted to know something about you first before I began asking questions about her. Do you know where she is?"

"Yes and no. I'm afraid when you find her, she may be six feet under. She's done some serious double-crossing of a few influential people in this town, including me."

"I was told you two dated for a time?"

"Yes, but she also worked for me."

"In insurance?"

"Insurance? Ha! Who told you that? Never mind, tell me what you want with her."

"I'm looking for her because she is the beneficiary of a large life insurance claim."

"You flew out here for an insurance claim? Why not make a few calls?"

"Wait," I said, thinking. "I never told you I flew here from out of town."

"You have to be from out of town if you don't know who I am or what I do. I had the waitress check with the valet who remembered you. You have a rental car."

"Fair enough." I liked this guy. He was good. "You don't work in insurance like the waitress told me, do you?"

"Well, not in the same line of work or way as you do." He grinned. "I have a multi-faceted job. I provide insurance to casino owners and local prostitutes."

"You mean insurance, like protection?"

"Yeah. I make sure the ladies are safe to do their work. A portion of their earnings goes to my bosses. The casinos, some are mob-owned and some aren't. Some are rivals. My insurance helps keep the peace. The ones that need it pay for my services. I don't come cheap."

"I don't need to know this." I shook my head thinking this could only be trouble to be privy to more information.

"Everyone knows it. It's no big secret I've just spilled."

"We're talking about the mob, right?"

"Yes."

"Oh, God."

"Don't worry they won't hurt me for telling you anything, and I can tell you more. I'm too valuable to all sides. I hold most of the money in private accounts. If I die, they all lose. If a side breaks the peace, they lose, you see?"

"I see."

"But you on the other hand, you don't have anything to keep you alive." His glance went to my recovering bruises. "I can tell you more, but is it worth the risk? I give you the choice, but know this, the one thing that may keep you alive is maybe you know the whereabouts of Nina or something they don't know."

"But I don't know where she is; that's why I'm here."

"If you find her first, then you will know and they won't, see?"

I thought for a moment while he sipped on his martini.

"So do you want to know it all or not?" he asked.

"You two dated?"

"I loved her. She really got me, but her plan all along was to get out. She wanted out of the mob."

"And they don't want to let her go?"

"She knows too much. She knows me and most of the others. She knows the schemes we're running. She's made a poor choice by running. She said if anything happened to her, someone knows to release the information."

"Who?"

"Don't know, but they'll find the someone and kill him or her and then they'll kill Nina. She thinks she's found protection in Atlanta from another mob. They won't protect her. She's sealed her death sentence."

"So she is in Atlanta? And alive?"

"For the time being."

"What did she do for you?"

"She was a bag lady. She did money pick-ups. Attractive women aren't watched as closely as the men in this business, not that her job wasn't dangerous. She'd been arrested. That's where I come in. I have the protection for the men and women in the ranks."

"You paid her way out of jail?"

"We've got our own lawyers, but in her case we didn't need them. I paid the cop off."

"So that's how you met?"

"Yes, and she fell in love with me. It was only love for her rescuer, her hero, not real love. But still she double-crossed me when she decided to split."

"So you think she was playing you, she wasn't really in love?"

"Not like I was in love with her. Maybe she loved me a short time and then realized it wasn't right. I'd save her again if I could, but I can't."

"How long ago was this?"

"December of last year."

"About the same time she was involved with the insurance client I represent in Atlanta. He left his millions to her."

"She loved the guy? She wanted to leave the mob to be with him, so she used me to buy herself some time? She knew I wouldn't turn her in?"

"You seem to have deduced the same thing. You know your involvement makes you a suspect."

"A suspect?"

"Oh, you know, you're a smart man. I don't have to spell it out."

"No, go on, spell it out for me," he demanded.

"You may have killed the new boyfriend because you were

jealous."

"Jealous? I'm not jealous. I thought she loved me, but if she didn't—" He slammed back the rest of his martini. "Screw her."

"She probably did," I reassured him. I didn't want him drinking himself into a lovesick stupor before I was finished. "He was a mob affiliate as well. Maybe it was the money."

"I have money." he signaled for a new drink.

"Well, I don't know then. Where were you Friday night and Saturday morning of last week?"

"Where was I? Where I always am. I'm here."

"I see, and I suppose there would be witnesses?"

"Ah, yes, here's one now." He grabbed the passing waitress around the waist and pulled her towards him. "I need a refill."

She giggled and took his martini glass. "Yes, sir."

"And while you're here, will you please tell our enterprising detective who was sitting in this seat two Friday nights ago and every Friday night?"

"You were, of course."

"And for how long?"

"Until very late, about two or three?"

"And when I left, did I go alone?"

"No." She giggled again.

"Thanks, sweetheart. Now go get my drink." He winked and she smiled.

"You probably pay her to say the right things," I commented.

"She doesn't know the questions." He shrugged.

"Maybe. How long did you and Nina date?"

"About four months."

"Dated anyone seriously since?"

"No."

"You say she has evidence someone would release if she was killed? The person with the information would be in danger."

"Oh, hell, yes. They'll find whomever's been told before they go after Nina."

My thoughts flashed to the old lady, Nina's neighbor, and then to Mark Sills. The old lady would be an unlikely person to hold such information since she didn't know where Nina was, much less if she were alive or not. Mark Sills on the other hand, was a logical repository. He was intimate with her and would know if anything happened to her. What information had he been given?

"This evidence Nina has, is it tangible, like documents, or is it all in her head?"

"All up there." Joe tapped his temple with his forefinger and then paused. "You think you know who she told, don't you? Her lover, the one who left her millions?"

"Yes, I think so. The problem is, he's dead. Murdered. They'll be after Nina next."

"If you are right, you can't stop it. I pray you're wrong because I loved that one, I really did. If she's still alive, she'll be using a new name. She's smart."

I nodded, wondering what name Nina was now using. "You don't happen to know the new name, do you?"

He shook his head.

"Thanks."

I left Joe at the bar. Glancing over my shoulder, I watched him take a big swig of his new drink then slap the waitress on the butt. He would make adjustments, drink himself silly, sleep with someone tonight, all in an effort to forget all about her.

My thoughts switched to Lindsey. How I wished I could be with her. I wondered how she felt about having to remain out of sight, how she must hate it. I picked up a thimble for her collection from the casino gift shop then headed for the airport to see if I could catch a flight back home.

Fortunately I was able to get on a late flight on stand-by. However, severe weather made for an unpleasant trip and my arrival in Atlanta was delayed because of the storms. As I finally drove away from the airport parking lot in the pounding rain, I wondered what to do next. Nina DeSantis was somewhere in Atlanta under a false name, and all I had to go on was a post office box, and it would have to wait.

CHAPTER 14

My two flights across country in two days had left me dead tired. I felt I would need duct tape to keep my eyes open, and here I was heading to a hypnotism appointment, no less. *You are getting sleepy, very sleepy...*heck, I was that tenfold already.

Forensic hypnotist Dr. Jan Kosiak was expecting Davy Kimble, Martin Jeffries, and me. She had the room set up with two cameras—one closed circuit with video and one with just videotape. Dr. Kosiak and Davy sat opposite each other. Detective Jeffries sat off in the corner. I waited and observed in a separate room over the closed circuit television.

Dr. Kosiak began her session by dimming the lights, a relaxing ambiance. She turned on the recordings, introduced all those present, both in and out of the room, and noted the date and time. She and Davy discussed things of no consequence like sports and a few jokes, as the doctor built up a comfort level and rapport with Davy. Then she explained the process and countered some stage hypnosis misconceptions and some Hollywood myths.

"I cannot make you do anything against your will; for example, I cannot get you to give up your secrets," she explained.

"I have no secrets," Davy joked.

"Nor can I make you tell the truth if you are inclined to lie."

"I'm not lying. I have no secrets, and that's the truth." He smiled up at the camera.

"I have to explain these things so you will feel more comfortable. Do you have any questions?"

"No."

Davy signed consent forms as the doctor went down some questions and her checklist. Then she began the inducement of hypnosis.

I had to really concentrate on staying awake myself as the doctor instructed Davy to close his eyes and focus on his breathing and took him progressively further into relaxation. When Davy appeared to be in hypnotized state, even from our vantage point, Dr. Kosiak counted down backwards slowly from ten and then tried to elicit information.

"Now Davy," she said. "Today we are going to review a special film, a documentary, of the sequence of events as they occurred on Saturday, July 4th, the day in question. This film is like all films. It can be stopped, reversed, fast-forwarded, freeze-framed, and put into slow motion. Even though the event was traumatic, or even perhaps scary or leaving you fearful, you are watching the event as a documentary and can remain calm and relaxed and report objectively. You will be able to answer questions and give details. Now, I want you to think of a happy memory, event, or place. Are you thinking of one?"

"Yes," Davy replied quietly.

"Can you describe it?"

"Yes, it's my childhood tree house when I was twelve. It's where I got my first kiss."

Davy smiled a giddy, boyish smile.

"Good. Now if at any point you become agitated or uncomfortable I will send you to that memory. If I tell you to go to that memory, you must go immediately. Do you understand?"

"Yes."

"Good, now I want you to visualize the movie theater where we will see this documentary. You are standing in the doorway of a small, private theater room with large, cozy chairs. I want you to go inside and sit down and get comfortable in your seat." She paused for a moment and then continued. "Are you sitting down?"

"Yes."

"Can you see the theater around you?"

"Yes."

"O.K., good. Now the lights are dimming. The film is starting. Tell me what you see," she instructed.

Davy's first-hand narration of the events began with his waking, eating breakfast, and getting to his post at the race. Dr. Kosiak was careful not to make any suggestions or lead Davy to conclusions. She prodded with neutral open-ended or compound questioning. At this point, she directed Davy to fast forward to the point of the race where he started seeing runners.

"I was watching all the runners coming down the hill. They were a trickle at first, then so many bobbing up and down I felt sea-sick. I was hot and queasy."

"Did you try to get rid of the queasiness?"

"Yes, I looked for something to drink. Usually there are tables with cups of water, but not this time. Or sprinklers, but there were none.

I couldn't watch. I had to look away."

"In your police report, you reported looking up after Nikki Sills fell. I want you to go there in the film and freeze the film. Tell me what you see."

"I see people everywhere, the whole crowd."

"Look up, now what do you see?"

"I see three women looking down at me from a balcony."

"Which balcony?"

"The one on the far right, on the ninth floor."

"What are they doing?"

"Two are crying. The other has her face covered; I can't tell."

"Can you see up farther? What do you see?"

"Yes, I see more people, all sad or shocked. Some I can't see their faces."

"Tell me about them and where they are."

"There are people, five people, on the thirteenth, well, actually the fourteenth floor. There's a man alone on the twelfth floor and a couple on the balcony beside him. The balcony on the seventeenth floor....there's an open door."

"Do you see anything else?"

"No, that's it."

"Now let's back up to a time before Nikki Sills fell. You looked up when the music changed. Rewind to that time and pause. Can you see it?"

"Yes."

"Tell me is everything the same or are things different?"

"The people are happy and smiling. The group of five are sitting, not standing. But now I see the woman on the seventeenth floor, too. It's the woman who falls."

"Can you describe her?"

"Blonde flowing hair. She's cheering. I can't tell much else; it's too far. She appears to be slender."

"What is she doing?"

"Clapping, cheering."

"Do you notice any other details?"

"No."

"Let's go forward again now. Go in slow motion. Tell me what you see and when you see the woman who falls again."

Davy described a helicopter, a nearby skyscraper, and a small boy. He explained how as he knelt to have his picture taken with the boy he glanced up at the apartments again.

"Freeze there," Dr. Kosiak commanded. "Look around again, what do you see?"

"I'm looking around, and I see..."

"What do you see?"

"Oh, no. Oh, God." Davy's hand flinched.

"You have nothing to fear. Remember Davy, this is a movie. Now tell me what you see."

"I see her. Her arms flailing. Someone has her over the rail."

"Who is flailing?"

"The blonde girl, the one who fell." Davy's breathing grew more rapid. I could see his chest rise and fall.

"Who has her over the rail?"

"I don't know."

"Take the film forward a little at a time, very slowly, can you see who has her over the rail?"

"No. I don't know."

"What does the person look like?"

"I don't know. Oh, God." Davy stiffened.

"Is it a male or female?"

"I don't know. She'd going to fall, she's going—oh, God, there she goes."

"Can you see anyone?"

"No, no. Oh!"

"I want you to go to your safe place now, Davy. I want you to go to your safe place and stay there."

"O.K., I am."

"I am going to bring you out of your hypnotized state. I am going to count from one to ten. When I get to ten, you will come out of the hypnosis and you will feel rested, alert, and refreshed. You will be able to remember the events we have discussed with full detail and clarity. Are you ready?"

"Yes."

"One...two...three. You are feeling more awake. You can move and sense your muscles again."

Davy twitched slightly.

"Four...five...six," she continued. "Your breathing is returning to normal, but you still feel relaxed. Seven...eight. You feel clear-headed. Nine...ten. Open your eyes feeling refreshed and relaxed."

"Wow," Davy said as he shook himself off as a dog would do with water. "That was weird."

"How do you feel?"

"Great. That was some weird shit."

"So you've said." Dr. Kosiak spoke a little abruptly. "Do you know where you are?"

"Yes; your office."

"And today's date?"

"July, uh, July 14th."

Dr. Kosiak proceeded through some post-hypnosis questions and then added, "If you recall additional information in the future you should report it to Detective Jeffries."

"Yes, I will."

"This concludes our session on July 14th. The time is 10:12 A.M."

"Wow, it's been an hour? I can't believe it."

"Mr. Grey, you may come in now."

When I entered the room, Dr. Kosiak was handing over one tape of the session.

"We'll take this copy to Chief Blumberg to see if he'll want to reopen the Nikki Sills case based on new evidence," Detective Jeffries said. "Dr. Kosiak will keep the other tape in case we need it for a trial."

"I'm going to take off the rest of the day," Davy said. "Can you and Mr. Grey take the tape?"

"Are you not feeling well?" Dr. Kosiak asked.

"I'm feeling fine, great actually." Davy smiled sheepishly at our questioning looks. "Normally I wouldn't like knowing how the woman was killed, walking around now with a vivid memory of it, but I think it may help solve the case, and that's good. But what I really need to thank you for, Doctor, is giving me back a memory I had lost. Remember when I had to pick a 'happy' place? Well, it was my tree house from when I was a kid. My wife, Mayvel, and I were both twelve when she gave me my first kiss there. She was my sweetheart from seventh grade all the way through high school, and then we married. The memory reminds me why I love her so much. I want to take off the rest of the day just to be with her."

"Uh-huh," Jeffries said. "Just to be with her. Feeling a little romantic?"

"Yeah, you could say that."

We all chuckled knowingly.

"Fine." Jeffries looked at me for confirmation, and I nodded. "Paul and I will take the tape to the station."

"Thanks guys, and thanks again, Doctor."

"My pleasure." She smiled and they shook hands.

Davy dashed out as we gave our thanks and good-byes to the doctor. I arranged to meet Jeffries at the station right away.

As I drove I thought about Davy and his wife. I longed to know the new love feeling again. Was there a way to get it back, to get back the tingle, the flutter-in-the-heart feeling? A way to feel so in the moment each second seems to last forever? Jealous of Davy's rekindled love for his wife, I wished I could have some spark in my relationship with Lindsey. Not that I didn't love her; I certainly loved her, but our relationship had been so tense recently. Maybe we needed to try some hypnosis to help solve our problems. Maybe we could revisit those moments of our youth, those moments made us love each other all this time. I sighed deeply. I missed Lindsey. Perhaps the old adage "absence makes the heart grow fonder" would hold true in this case and not work the opposite making Lindsey realize what a schmuck I truly am.

I drove slowly to allow Jeffries time to arrive first and get Chief Blumberg's attention. After managing to find a parking space, I went in to find them in Chief Blumberg's office.

"We've already discussed re-opening the case as far as the police are concerned," Jeffries said. "Davy's evidence, plus the fact Mark Sills has also been murdered warrants more investigation on the case."

"We certainly will need to find out what the connection is, why both husband and wife were killed within a week of each other," the Chief said.

"If the police re-open the case and discuss changing the cause of death with the medical examiner's office, do you think Morehouse Insurance will follow suit and allow further investigation as well?" Jeffries asked.

"I certainly hope so. I will present the information to them tomorrow morning." I shrugged. "I can't say for sure what they'll do, but if there is a chance it will save them money, I'm thinking they'll allow it."

"I always knew it! Insurance, in it for the money, I say." Chief Blumberg huffed. "That's why they argue every last claim down to the pennies. My wife's family's summer home in Florida was damaged by a hurricane or tropical storm or something. Anyhow, the insurance never paid anything near what the costs were to repair it."

"Uh, Chief," Jeffries tilted his head towards me, indicating my presence. Jeffries appeared concerned the Chief's comment would insult me.

"Oh, I don't mean you." Chief Blumberg vaguely pointed in my direction. "You're a fine fellow. I mean the bosses, you know."

"Yes, I know." I smiled to show no harm done. "Well, I have to be going."

"Dismissed," said Chief Blumberg.

Jeffries escorted me out. "By the way, the tip you gave us about Houghton Lofton was a dud."

"What? They do all the money laundering there." I stopped dead.

"Not anymore. The place was completely closed up. No furniture, no nothing by the time we got our search warrant."

"Nothing?"

"Not even a hair."

"Wow. The mob moves fast. That's not good." I shook my head.

"And nix on the guy with tattoo. We've got lots of tattoos on fellows, but would need more to go on."

"Younger than me, dark hair and eyes?" I suggested.

"No, that's not going to do it. You'd need to come look at photos to identify him."

"I can't." I shrugged. "I never actually saw him. I got the description from a by-stander."

"Can't help you much then. What are you going to do next?"

"I don't know, but I'll keep you posted," I explained to Jeffries as we walked down the hall. "Lindsey is still all right? You'll tell her I'm all right?"

"Yes, she's fine, and I'll talk with her later. When can I tell her she can go out and about again? What can I tell her?"

"I don't know yet. I can't even tell you yet. Explain I'm working on the problem and making progress."

"Your bruises and cuts are fading. Hold out a couple more days and you won't even have to tell her about those."

"Ha, ha." I laughed sarcastically. "By the way, where is she?"

"We have her at a hotel. If you think she'd be all right at Margie's, we can take her there."

"I don't know yet. Give me another twenty-four hours, and I'll let you know. I've got some loose ends to work on first."

"I've got you covered."

I placed a quick call to the Peachtree race photographers to see if they had located a picture of Mark Sills. The girl claimed to have found it and would put it in the mail to me. This meant Mark had started the race. Had he in fact run fast enough to arrive at the apartments with enough time to kill Nikki? Or was there someone else?

I left the station and drove immediately to a gas station where I purchased a large map of Atlanta and surrounding areas and took it home. I changed out of my suit and into some comfortable shorts and a T-shirt. I tended to my abduction injuries and then got a cold Coke and some chips.

With the large map sprawled across the coffee table I marked the spot of the Magnolia Apartments where I had been picked up and thrown in the van. My abductors had warned me not to try to discover where they had taken me or their identities, although I had a pretty good idea who they worked for—Vincent Artello. The journey taking me to the building took about ten minutes, and I remembered feeling the van stopping and starting at traffic lights. Calculating they couldn't have driven more than ten miles in ten minutes, I drew a circle in a ten mile radius around the Apartments. This circle ran from Sandy Springs clockwise through Chamblee, Clarkston, Patherville, Hapeville, Six Flags, and Cumberland Mall.

I knew as most people in Atlanta know, one cannot travel ten miles in ten minutes in the city. And my measurement radius was as the crow flies, not taking into consideration turns, right angles, traffic lights, or one-way streets. In all actuality, my abductors probably couldn't have taken me more than five or six miles from the Magnolia Apartments.

Using a dotted line, I drew a new circumference inside my first one. The new circle had a five-and-a-half-mile radius as the maximum distance able to travel if going in a straight line.

Then I marked my drop-off point, where I'd been released in Porterdale. The trip had taken about thirty minutes. So calculating thirty minutes to be about thirty miles, maybe a little more if traveling over sixty miles per hour, I drew a third larger circle from the release point. The resulting thirty mile radius overlapped my first two circles in a narrow sliver. The intersection began around Northlake Mall at Interstate 285 and concluded southwest of Grant Park near Hapeville. That sliver had to contain the building where they had taken me. It included parts of North Decatur, Decatur, and East Atlanta, areas around Glenwood Avenue, Memorial Drive, Moreland Avenue, and Interstate 20.

On the map it appeared a narrow sliver, but in actuality it was a large region to cover. I was going to need help.

Fortunately, my wife worked in politics and knew tons of connections in all areas of state and local government. Problem was I didn't know them, and Lindsey was hiding out, making it difficult for me to ask her. I could call Jeffries and have him put me through to her in some way or another. But the whole idea sounded like trouble. Best not to allow Lindsey the opportunity to ask questions or get upset. I decided my only solution would be to find Jodi Barrett, Lindsey's right hand, and ask her.

I headed over to Jodi's house. She arrived at the door, pleasantly surprised to see me.

"Hi, Paul!" She beamed. "What are you doing here? Where's Lindsey?"

"She's not here. I'm working on a case. I think you can help me."

"You know I'd help you any way you'd want me to." She smiled and invited me inside.

Her words always had a hint of allure, like she was testing me, waiting to see if I'd make a move on her. She was beautiful—slim and petite, with shiny blonde hair. She was always cheery, with oozing, honey speech. And in another lifetime if she and I weren't both married, who knows? Perhaps if I were single the fantasy would be ruined for her; I'd somehow be less desirable.

"Well..." I cleared my throat. "I need to know who I can go to with some questions about construction. Is there a way to get a list of current construction projects or permits for the Atlanta area?"

"Gee, don't want much, do you? Let's see who we know." She took me to her office, turned on her computer, and logged into her database. "Our contacts include constituents, contributors, government officials. I'll try to find someone who'll be willing to help us."

"Great. How long should I give you?"

"I'm not sure. If I find someone, I'll have to get on the phone, then the time for any reports they need to run. Do you need a search of the whole Atlanta area or can it be narrower?"

I pulled out my map and pointed to the overlap. "I need to know about this area, and I don't need residential construction."

"We can probably use zip codes more easily. I have a zip code map, I can cross reference. What information do you need from the search?" She took out a notepad.

"Company, company owner or superintendent, the address, the type of construction, and what stage the projects are in."

"For what time period?"

"Six months ago to current, I guess." I shrugged.

"You only want construction completed in that time frame, or in any stage?"

"Any stage." I appreciated her intelligence. She knew how to narrow down and winnow out facts.

"O.K., I've got it. How about you go get lunch for us both and bring it back here?" she suggested.

I agreed, after all, it wasn't a date or anything. So I drove out and picked up some sub sandwiches and chips from a local deli—ham and turkey with Swiss for us both. I figured she could pick off what she didn't want.

Too bad people aren't more like sandwiches, where you can easily get rid of what you don't like. I knew how Lindsey would order me—extra romance and hold the suspense.

Upon arriving back her house, Jodi stood over the fax machine, which spat out one page after another.

"This is the short list," she explained. "The condensed information on 115 current construction projects in your search area. I had them email the complete details as a file to you in case you needed them. This list should get you started."

She handed over the first couple of pages. I made myself comfortable for the wait and began looking down the list. I immediately eliminated single story structures and those far from completion. If those criteria were met, I starred the project for special consideration if it included a parking deck or garage.

The last of the eight pages came off the fax, and Jodi approached, holding them. "Oh, my gosh, Paul. What happened to your head? I didn't notice before."

"It's fine, really. I've been wearing a baseball cap." I warded off her hand as she reached out.

"Poor baby," she cooed. "Are you sure you're all right?"

"Yes, let's get back to this." I indicated the papers.

"Oh, well, what are you looking for?"

I explained my parameters.

"I'm a hands-on kind of girl," she said. "Can I help?"

"Sure, knock yourself out."

She took a pen off the desk and began crossing off incompatible job sites. "Why are you looking at all these buildings?"

"I'm not. I'm looking for one in particular."

"Why?"

"I can't tell you."

Jodi appeared a little perturbed, or taken aback, by my secrecy, my refusal to tell her since she was so dutifully helping me. She snapped the papers in her hands twice.

"I really can't say. It's for your own good. I haven't even told Lindsey because of the potential danger."

She shrugged. "Oh, well. You are going to have to narrow this search some other way or you have a lot of driving around to do."

"You're right. There are two left on this page and three on here, plus another five on this one makes ten."

Jodi picked up my previous two pages to add to her three. "Let's see, I've got four plus eight and five."

"Twenty-seven in all," I computed. "The names of the companies are listed here, but I'll need superintendents' or owners' names to narrow the list further. Will those be on the email?"

"Yes."

"And who do I owe thanks to for all this?"

"Well, me." She batted her eyes, "and Nick Ballantine, a constituent and friend who works for the permit and construction licensing department."

"My biggest thanks to you both, then. I've got to run. I have someone else I need to go see."

"Oh, well. Glad I could help." She watched me gather all the papers and the map together.

I thanked her again and went looking for a bookstore. At best my judgments of time elapsed and distance were only best guesses, but my only clues and starting point. I had decided I would need a more detailed road map of the city area within the intersection points so I bought an expensive street map. I transferred my radius lines onto it while having a coffee in the bookstore's café. Then I looked at my remaining twenty-seven job sites. Using the detailed street names I was able to remove about another ten construction sites off the list. Since Jodi had pulled the reports by zip code, some sites were within the same area according to their zip code, but the address actually fell outside my intersection zone.

I felt certain I needed to stick close to Interstate 20 in my search because I remembered quite a long time of highway-type travel, and my drop-off location point had been close to this highway. I felt certain the best candidates for further investigation would be those close to this highway around small sections of Glenwood Avenue, Moreland Avenue, and Memorial Drive.

My next stop was going to be to visit someone I wasn't sure would want visitors. In fact, last time I saw him, he told me never to come back.

CHAPTER 15

And who could blame Stuart Newsome for feeling that way? I had incorrectly accused him of murder and broke into his shooting range to look for evidence. But Stuart Newsome had the connections and perhaps the insider information I needed to get some answers. He was *not* happy to see me.

"I should have you tossed out on your ass," he threatened, lifting his short but bulky frame halfway from his chair.

"Now, if you were going to toss me, you would have done it already and not allowed your staff to bring me back here to your office in the first place."

Stuart Newsome folded his arms and sighed, his bluff called. "True. I'm curious what possibly could be so important you would dare show your face in here. No one else in your family has been killed. I'm guessin' you're here on some other business."

"Well, it is a murder, but no one in my family. Mob family, I believe."

"Mob? Are you asking me to inform you on the mob? Are you tryin' to get me killed?"

"Yes and no, respectively. You've got your ear to the ground, so to speak. You might be able to help."

"Let's hear it." He waved his hand. "Does it have anything to do with your gettin' hurt? I couldn't help but notice."

"Not really. Do you know a Mark Sills, Nikki Sills, or Nina DeSantis?"

"Nope. I don't know 'em, but somehow the Nikki name sounds familiar, but I can't place it."

"Nikki Sills was on the news—fell from her balcony last week," I said.

"Ah, yes, that was it."

"How about Vincent Artello or Saul Dedmon?"

"Yep. Saul's dead. Vinnie's been on ice."

"Does Vincent Artello have any land development companies or construction companies, or does he do any contract work?"

"Possibly. I don't know; he's got lots of businesses."

"Who would know?"

"I've got someone I could ask next time he's in."

"You trust him?"

"What do you mean, trust him? Trust isn't a word used much by the mob. If you mean, do I trust him not to run to Vinnie about my askin'?"

"Yes."

"Yeah."

"Do you know any loan sharks by the name of Eddie?"

"Nope, but again, I can find him."

I stopped and thought for a moment. "Why are you being so cooperative? Why are you willing to help me out?"

"A little suspicious, are we? A little paranoid?"

"Well, this doesn't strike me as you acting like yourself."

"And exactly how do I act? How much do you really know about me?"

"Not much. Don't change the subject. Why are you helping me?"

"Don't worry so much. There's something in all this for me. I won't bullshit. This isn't selfless heroics on my part."

"What do you want?"

"We'll get to what I want when you're done. Any more questions?"

"Yes. Have you heard of any ordered hits recently?"

"Hits aren't usually discussed in front of the likes of me. I know too many cops."

"Discussed or not, do you know of any?"

"Nope."

"Have you heard anything interesting from anyone even remotely connected with the mob?"

"You'll have to be more specific. You have something in mind?"

"Anything about a girl—trying to find her or wanting her killed?"

"Actually, yeah. There is talk about a girl they're tryin' to find. Seen her picture, but don't remember her name."

"Nina DeSantis?" I tried again.

"No, someone else."

I pulled out my wallet and the folded photo of Nina at Thanksgiving dinner and held it out to him. "Her?"

"Yes, that's her, but her name's not whatever it was you said."

"Why are they looking for her?"

"Don't know for sure, but I think they are tryin' to rein her in.

She's got dreams of freedom, but she knows too much."

"Any idea if they've found her?"

"No, but—"

My cell phone rang. Stuart Newsome waited patiently as I answered.

"Hello, Paul Grey."

"Hello, this is Vincent Artello."

Stuart Newsome had to see the color wash completely away from my face. I had to sit down. It's not everyday I get a phone call from a Mafia leader.

What's wrong? Who is it? Stuart Newsome mouthed.

I grabbed a pen and shakily wrote M-O-B upside down on his desk blotter.

"Jesus!" he muttered.

"How did you get my cell phone number?" I asked.

"Don't worry about it," he said. "Know this, if I'd wanted you dead you woulda blown up just now when you answered your phone. So you can rest easy. I'm not gonna kill you, and I didn't kill Mark Sills or his pretty wife neither. Someone else wanted them dead—a woman."

"Who? What woman and why?"

"You're the detective. You figure it out."

Click. Silence. Silence on the phone. Dumbfounded silence between Stuart Newsome and me.

Finally I broke it. "They know I'm here. They know what I'm doing," I said, panicked.

"Now don't go getting all paranoid again. Did anyone follow you?"

"Not that I know of."

"Were you looking?"

"Yes, well, no. I'm always watching. It's become automatic, but I don't really remember on the way over here. Could your office be bugged?"

"No way. Who was it? What did the person say?"

"It's almost like they knew I was here and what I was asking about."

"What did the person say?" Stuart demanded again.

"Vincent Artello. He gave me a clue. I think he was trying to tell me Nina DeSantis killed Mark and Nikki Sills."

"Is she a suspect? You think she killed him so you are looking for her?"

"Yes, but I don't know if she did it. I think the mob may have been involved or done it."

"Maybe they are using you, tryin' to mislead you."

"You think it's a coincidence we were talking about her and he called?"

Stuart shrugged.

"Find out anything you can for me, will you?" I asked, almost begged.

Stuart looked hesitant. Maybe he sensed my neediness and would refuse as some kind of revenge. "What's in it for me?"

"I asked you already. I won't ever bother you again."

"A glass promise, easily broken the next time someone starts throwing stones."

"Tell me what you want."

"I'll give you information whenever you need it, but if or when I ever need your investigative services, you'll be there for me at no charge and no questions asked."

"You anticipating a murder around here?"

"No. Deal or not?"

"Deal." We shook on it.

"I'll get on it right away, and I'll be in touch soon," he said as I handed him my business card with my cell number.

I wondered as I departed, *How soon was soon?* Could it be soon enough? Did he mean a few hours or a few days? I was at a stopping block. What else could I do?

I pulled out my file and looked at the list of evidence from the storage unit. White Diamonds perfume, size 8, Neiman Marcus, and Wok-To-Go. Wok-To-Go would be easiest to investigate. I called information for the number and then got their address. There was only one in Atlanta, so I made the drive.

When I entered Wok-To-Go, I found myself surrounded by wonderful smells. Before I left I would have to order something to eat, I promised myself.

"Hello, may I take your order?" The Asian girl spoke with only a slight accent.

"I'm a private investigator." I had my card and Nina DeSantis' picture out. "I'd like to know if this woman is a customer of yours?"

"A P.I.?" She smiled and took the picture. "I like detective shows."

She studied the photo for a moment.

"Do you recognize her?" I asked.

"Uh, no, but let me ask the others."

She walked through a small doorway, and I could hear the higher-pitched, excited talk of several people in the back all conversing in their native tongue, which I presumed to be a Chinese dialect.

Two people came out with the girl I had originally introduced myself to.

"He knows her," she said.

The third person, a girl, must have been a curious observer.

"Who is she? Do you know where she lives?" I inquired.

"Her name, I can find out. She lives in the Magnolia Apartments. I'm the delivery driver. I go there."

"What?" I was shocked. "The Magnolia? Are you sure?"

"Yes, I'm sure. I look it up." He moved over to the computer. He typed a few things and then used the up and down arrows.

I waited patiently, but at the same time my heart was pounding. This could explain so many things.

"Ah, here she is. Cynthia Norris, Number 15C at the Magnolia Apartments. Sometimes she order take-out, sometimes she order delivery. I deliver. Nice lady and tips good. I always take her an extra egg roll and fortune cookie."

"Cynthia Norris? Do you have her phone number?"

He nodded.

"I need your help. I want you to call her and tell her she won the monthly drawing for a free dinner."

"We don't have a drawing." The girl shook her head, confused.

"No, I know. I'll buy the food. Tell her she won it. Don't tell her about me. Ask her if she wants it delivered tonight."

"Ah, O.K."

"If she wants the dinner tonight, I'll deliver it to her, but you don't tell her who I am," I repeated for clarification. "Do you understand?"

The girl nodded and made the call. I could hear Nina's excited voice on the phone. She said something about never winning anything in her whole life and how nice because she was hungry. She ordered some stir-fry with chicken and pasta and extra snap peas.

"I will need a delivery hat or bag or something, however you would normally take her the food," I said to the young man. "I'll return them."

He handed me his hat. In a few minutes the food was prepared, put into take-out boxes, and handed over to me.

"Good luck." The boy gave me a thumbs up.

"Yes, thanks."

At the Magnolia, the security desk buzzed me in and then called up to Nina, a.k.a. Cynthia Norris, to confirm the delivery. Having been there before, I pulled the hat low on my head and avoided eye contact. However, it was the red-headed one, not Sue whom I had spent time talking with before. I was sent up to the fifteenth floor, where I knocked three times.

Nina opened the door. A tidal wave of her perfume overcame me, causing my eyes to burn, yet I could still see she was flawlessly attractive. Interracial yellow-brown skin defied pinpointing to one skin color group or another.

"Oh, hello. I thought it would be Steve delivering." Her voice was soothing.

"Not tonight," I said. "I'm Paul Grey, and I'm not actually a delivery person for Wok-To-Go. I do have your food, though."

Nina moved to shut the door. I stuck my foot in the jam.

"I'm not here to harm you," I added. "I'm an investigator. If you'll let me get a card for you, you'll see."

I tried to balance the food and get a card out of my wallet at the same time, still keeping my foot lodged firmly in the door. The juggling act must have been comic enough Nina lost her fear. She opened the door and took the food from me. I produced the card.

"I wanted to ask you some questions about the mob. I know you work for them. And I also need to ask about Mark and Nikki Sills, whom I know you knew."

"I don't know anything."

"I disagree. Nina, you know too much, which is why the mob is a problem for you. You're running?"

"No, you must have me confused. I'm Cynthia Norris. Now, if you'll excuse me, my food is getting cold."

"All right, Cynthia, if that's what you want to go by. I spoke to Faith. She's worried about you."

"Faith? You leave her out of this."

"I am. I met her in Las Vegas while trying to track you down. She gave me the letter you sent with your Post Office box."

"What do you want?"

"You and Mark Sills used to date. When did you last see Mark Sills?"

"I don't remember." Cynthia had set the food down and reached into her umbrella stand. As if unsheathing a sword, she withdrew an umbrella and aimed its point threateningly at my stomach. "Now if you'll kindly remove your foot from my doorway?"

I debated. She aimed the point a little lower.

"Whoa." I moved my foot.

The door promptly slammed in my face.

"Do you remember the day of the Peachtree Road Race when Nikki Sills was killed?" I yelled through the door.

"I am not going to talk to you. Now go away, or I'll have to call the police."

"Do you remember?" I repeated. After a few seconds of silence I added, "If I can find you, the mob will find you, too. It's just a matter of time."

I got no response. Damn. I should have kept my foot in the door. But, small consolation prize, I now knew her alias, her address, a partial layout of her apartment, her phone number, and exactly how she looks—enough to conduct some serious surveillance. I made a quick run to return the Wok hat and insulated bag. On impulse I bought enough food for myself and one other person.

CHAPTER 16

I placed a call to Martin Jeffries.

"Found Gianina DeSantis yet?" I asked.

"She's in Georgia and she has a previous arrest record."

"Oh, Jeffries, you're holding out on me. You know where she is, don't you?"

"Yeah, but the boss said not to tell you. Sorry, man. We're trying to protect you."

"I found her anyway, under the alias Cynthia Norris, at the Magnolia Apartments."

"Weird coincidence, huh?"

"Is it? I'm not sure. I got into her building and tried to talk to her but couldn't get her to let me in her apartment."

"Bravo for getting in the building. We'll be over there tomorrow with a search warrant and some questions of our own. Anything I need to know beforehand?"

"Beware of the umbrella. What about the evidence you found at the park? Anything on Mark Sills' murder you can tell me?"

"I can't share most of it. I can tell you the footprint was a male or male-size shoe. Probably tall. And dark hair."

"Oh, that helps. You could be describing me, for God's sake."

"I know it leaves lots of options. It can take weeks to get things back from the lab."

"Cynthia Norris is tall and has dark hair. Joe Pagliani in Vegas did. Maybe Eddie does, too."

"Yeah, we know Cynthia. We're checking all the angles," he explained. "Who's Joe and who's Eddie?"

"Joe and Eddie, oh. Joe's a mobster. He's in love with Cynthia. Not a bad suspect for Mark's killing, but not Nikki's. He's tall and dark-haired, but it's doubtful he'd do something personally. He's the type to find a hired hand. Eddie is a loan shark here in Atlanta, African-American. I don't know his height. I've only seen his arm, from a car window."

"I won't ask. And his connection to Mark, let me guess, he had a loan out to him?"

"Yeah, but it wasn't overdue or anything. I don't think he killed him, but he might know who would."

"We'll check him out. Got a last name?"

"No, sorry."

"You're not holding out on me?"

"No."

"Anything else?" Jeffries asked as much to probe as to be sure I was all right.

"Yes. I'll need a parking space at the Magnolia again. This time I'd like to park in the drive instead of across the street. Can you work it out?"

"Not a problem. Just park and if anyone questions—"

"I'll call," I said.

"What about Lindsey? Did you decide where you want her to stay and what I should tell her?"

"Where is she staying? I'm going to go pick her up."

"You sure?"

"Yes, positive."

"She's at the Embassy Suites on Peachtree."

"Am I footing the bill?"

"It's where she wanted to go, and, frankly, she wasn't in the mood to negotiate anything less."

"I understand. I owe you big time for arranging it all."

"No problem."

We wrapped up our call. It was getting late. If I was going to pick up Lindsey, I'd need to get a move on. I figured, she was as safe with me as she was at the hotel. Besides, on surveillance she'd be stuck with me and we'd have a chance to talk—to really talk.

"Give me one good reason why I should let you in," Lindsey demanded through the cracked door.

I held up the bag of Chinese food.

"A bribe?" She laughed and let me in.

"Sort of, I want to take you with me on surveillance."

"Surveillance? You're kidding, right?" she asked.

"Well, no. I was thinking it would give us some time alone."

"Alone, but on the job."

"I doubt there will be much work. I'll be sitting in the car all night."

I tucked the small thimble into Lindsey's hand. She glanced down at it, rolling it over in her palm to see the words, *Las Vegas.*

"You've been busy. You'll explain? And will there be snacks?" Lindsey added, "I'm tired of ordering room service."

"Yes. I've already got this Chinese stir fry for us both."

"Speaking of stir, I am stir crazy. You realize I haven't been anywhere for like three days? I can't even keep track it's been so long."

"Yes, I know. And yes, I can explain it all."

"You better."

She packed her things quickly, not at all to my liking. She didn't fold anything or sort the dirty and clean. "Don't say anything," she warned after noticing my looks.

"I wasn't." I shrugged innocently. I knew I was in enough hot water already. I didn't need to pick a battle over something so unimportant as organizational skills.

"You were about to," she challenged.

O.K., quick, change the subject. "Was the food here good?"

"Yeah, but I want some things that aren't on their menu." She shrugged and continued to toss things randomly into her suitcase.

"You name it and we'll go get whatever it is you want."

"How long are we going to be on surveillance?"

"At least twelve hours, maybe longer."

"O.K. I've got three things. I want a chocolate shake from Checkers, Swiss Cake Rolls from the grocery, and some chips—sour cream and onion."

"What a combination," I commented. "On top of Chinese?"

"Well, I'm not going to eat them all at once," she replied. "You said we'd be all night or longer."

"All right, are you packed? Let's eat this and then let's go."

We ate quickly then settled our bill. We stopped for all the various munchies and some soft drinks, and headed over to the Magnolia Apartments. I parked the car under the shadows of some tall trees in the circular drive behind the tenants' parking entrance and called up to Cynthia's apartment. When she answered, I knew she was at home. Now we had to sit and wait.

For the first two hours I explained everything that had happened and the facts on the case in detail. I left nothing out. Lindsey wasn't pleased, especially about my injuries, but she wasn't surprised either.

"You have a way of finding trouble, don't you?" She summed it all up.

"Yes, I guess so. I don't really go looking for it." I unwrapped a pair of Swiss Cake Rolls.

"Your unsuspecting nature is what bothers me, I guess. You don't think you're looking for it, or you don't sense the danger, and by then it's too late."

"I do sense danger. Precisely the reason why I had you sent to a hotel."

"Ugh." Lindsey flopped back into her seat and the whole car wobbled. "You didn't *sense* it, you goofus. You were already in it at that point. That's what I mean about too late."

I studied my treat for disassembly, peeling the chocolate from around the outside, and thought about how to reply. "You're right, of course, as usual."

"What?"

"I said, you are right. I should listen to you more often."

"Can I get your confession in writing?" She laughed and motioned for me to pass one of my rolls to her. "I could frame it."

"I don't know how to solve the problem. Do you?"

"Well, you could not take cases involving murders. That would be a start." Lindsey bit into her roll.

"But in life insurance, all death claims could be potential murders. The vast majority are not, but they always could be. How am I supposed to know which ones to take and which ones to avoid?"

She shrugged. "I don't know. But something has to change. Maybe you could switch with Glenn or Shawn?"

"I agree something has to change, but even their departments could be dangerous. Anyone faking a claim for thousands or even hundreds of thousands might be dangerous to the investigator."

"Yeah, like the guy who used to work there who got hit with a bat."

"Exactly. So I'm not sure what to do." With my Swiss Cake Roll's chocolate exterior peeled and consumed, I bit into the remaining cake and icing.

"You know how we've talked about having kids, starting a family? I wouldn't even want to think about it with you working at a job that could get you killed."

"Starting a family?"

"You want to have kids, right?"

"I did; I do. I didn't think we were in any hurry."

"We've been married a long time. I wouldn't call anything a hurry at this point."

"No, well anyway, I'm not arguing timing. My work can get dangerous, but let's face it. I could get killed doing anything. I could work in a factory making these." I waved the roll. "And drown in a vat of melted chocolate. I think when your time comes, it comes."

"I think so too, in some degree. I think we all have a time, but—"

"If you believe in fate of some kind then job choice won't alter it."

"Don't debate me philosophically. I got an A in philosophy and debate; I'll win," Lindsey half-teased and half-threatened. "Even if you believe in predestination, you believe in free will. You choose something less dangerous and God knows you were going to make that choice. You should avoid dangerous activities, like skydiving and rock climbing."

"And private investigating." I finished her thought. "But look at your parents. They didn't do anything hazardous and they died in a car wreck. Death can happen anywhere at any time."

"True. We don't know when. I don't want anything tragic to happen in the lives of our future children."

"But you can't protect them from everything."

"Paul, I'm afraid. After my parents died, it was the hardest thing." She stopped and wiped a tear.

"I know."

"No, you don't. It was too much to have to handle. There were so many doubts and 'ifs.' What if they hadn't driven that route? What if they had had a better car? If you died while working on a case, I would feel that was something entirely preventable."

"Too many doubts and 'ifs.' Almost like guilt?"

"Yes. I know how hard it was to lose both my parents. I can't even imagine what it would be like to be the surviving parent and have to explain your death to my own child."

"Well, not to worry. We don't have kids."

"Yes, but what about my own loss? I might die of a broken heart. I've lost all those I love; I can't lose you, too."

"You won't. Things will change. I promise." I took her hand and caressed it. "As soon as this case is over, I can look for a different job."

"You haven't been too good about keeping your promises lately. If you recall you were supposed to be telling me everything. And today is the first I learn anything about why I've been kept locked away and what happened to you."

"I was afraid they would hurt you."

"So you think it is safe to tell me now?"

"I don't know." I shrugged.

"Oh, wonderful! You're the Greatest American Hero and going to protect me?"

"Actually, I was hoping you would turn into Wonder Woman and protect me. You could help me fend off attackers or save me with those deflector arm things."

"Or, I could use my truth lasso on you." She put her arms around me. "There. Now about what you said, something like making changes as soon as this case is over. You promised. Is that the truth?"

"It is the God's-honest truth. And speaking of truth, I love you so very much."

"Really, how do you love me?"

"When we're together I want every second to last forever."

"And?"

"And, when I see you after having been away for a while, my heart flutters, and I want to be alone with you."

"You've been away from me for a while. You want to be alone with me now?"

"Yes." I took a strand of her hair and traced it alongside her face to her shoulder—so baby soft and shimmery. "Your hair looks really nice. You're beautiful," I said low and deep, stroking its length again. I inhaled slowly.

She turned sideways in her seat and leaned in, putting her lips to my ear. Breathing heavily, she doused it with heat and then brushed her lips along my ear and down my neck, whispering, "We are alone."

I plunged my face and nose into her silken hair and the back of her neck and took in her smell.

"Do I smell good?" she asked coyly.

"You do. You smell sexy. New perfume?"

She shook her head then held her left hand out to my cheek, cupped my chin a moment, and looked deep into my eyes before slipping her right hand into my shirt and rubbing it across my chest. I closed my eyes and let my head fall back to the seat. She leaned across and kissed my ear and neck again.

"I do want you alone." I gritted my teeth. I sat up quickly at the sound of her car door opening, putting my hand to my gun.

"It's just me," she said. "Let's get in the backseat."

"What? Backseat?" She caught me totally by surprise. I'd never have thought I would hear that from her. "Are you sure?"

"I'm sure. We won't do anything to get ourselves arrested."

I opened my door, and we both stood outside, looking up through

the trees into the dark night. A street light at the roadside tried to light
our location, but it stood at a distance. This corner of the driveway was
edged by thick tree branches and very dark. I'd chosen it for surveillance
for that reason. Only spotted and faded, filtered light made its way over
to where we were.

Lindsey lifted the latch to move the seat up and climbed into the
rear. She motioned, "come on," and, after a quick look around to make
sure no one was watching, I obliged. I soon found myself awkwardly, yet
in a strange way also comfortably, lying somewhat across the backseat.
My head rested along the backseat on one side and my legs extended to
the floor on the other side. Lindsey straddled my hips and pushed my
shoulders down into the seat. I reached up to touch her with one hand.
She playfully slapped it away.

"Uh, uh, uh," she said. "You don't move or do anything unless I
tell you to. You've been a bad boy."

I nodded in agreement. I had the game made, and I was liking it.

She bent over and again kissed my ear and neck slightly, all the
while running her fingers around in my hair. I could feel her chest rise
and fall against mine. My heartbeat soon rose from my chest into my
throat. I could hear the thump-thump in my mouth as I opened it to
receive her kiss. She pressed to my lips; her tongue softly glanced my
upper lip and teeth. She was setting me on fire. The pressure of her hips
on mine, her kisses, her everything—oh, God. I reached to touch her
again.

"O.K.," she murmured.

I ran my hands over her shoulders, down her sides, and to her hips
and pulled her tighter to me. Then I ran my hands back up her sides but
under her blouse.

A pair of headlights swept into the parking lot startling us both.

"It's dark, lie still," I said. "No one will see us."

Lindsey giggled. "I feel like we're back in high school."

I smiled at her beautiful face, half-lit, half in darkness. It did feel
like long ago—that fluttery feeling, the one I wanted to feel again. "Yes,
it does."

I kissed her long and hard. She returned the favor. We exchanged
kisses for a while. Then Lindsey sat up when the coast was clear and
commented," I never knew surveillance could be this much fun."

"Usually it's not." I grinned.

"It better not be." She looked around and out all the windows.
"Problem is you could lose your prey this way."

"Most definitely, but I don't think Cynthia's going anywhere at this time. It's the middle of the night."

Lindsey shrugged. "You never know."

"True." I sat upright a little too, and Lindsey slid into the seat next to me. "Thanks for the make out session."

"No problem." She climbed over the console and into the front seat. She pulled down the lighted mirror and straightened her hair.

"Too bad we didn't know each other when we were in high school. We missed out on all those teenage love memories."

"You, maybe. I was making out with other boys," she teased.

"Ah, I see. Well, anyway, now I have a good memory, and it reminds me of when we were dating."

"We never made out in the car," she countered.

I attempted to crawl into the front like Lindsey had, and it simply wasn't working. "Yeah, but we made out."

She giggled and sighed. "It's good to feel like that again, huh?"

"Yes." I nodded and awkwardly pulled my contorted legs out from under me. "If I had to do it all over again, even with hindsight being twenty-twenty, I'd love you and marry you. In fact, I would have done it sooner."

"Me, too," she replied, yawning.

"Are you tired?" I asked.

"Yeah." She nodded sleepily, her eyes droopy.

"Why don't you rest?"

"I was going to try to help keep you awake."

"I'll be fine. Go ahead and get some sleep."

She tilted the seat back and stretched out. "I wish I had a pillow." She yawned the words out.

"Sorry, no pillows. I'll wake you if anything exciting happens, but I doubt anything—"

I looked over at Lindsey. Her eyes were closed peacefully. She was probably already asleep. The hours crept by slowly. Only once did anyone come along to question our presence. The security man rapped on the window, asked who we were and why we were there. One phone call and we quickly had it resolved. Lindsey awoke periodically to adjust her positioning. At the crack of dawn, she sat bolt upright.

"Uh, what a horrible dream I was having," she said. "I was shot between the eyes!"

"I didn't think you could dream your own death."

"Oh, I didn't die. I survived, so I was walking around with this hole between my eyes and had to solve my own murder."

"Who did it?"

"I don't know. I didn't solve it."

"No stress on your shoulders. Your dream carries no meaning for your life," I teased.

"Ironic, huh? It was a bad dream."

"I'm sorry."

"It's O.K. I'm all right. So what about breakfast?"

I knew we couldn't go too long without thinking about food. Lindsey loved to eat, but she had a high metabolism, and it never stuck around on her body for long. Lucky her.

"Well, let's see." I rummaged through the grocery bag. "We've got doughnuts and some soft drinks."

"Yuck, not for me."

"No doughnuts?"

"No, too sweet. You know, I'm used to cereal or toast and juice."

"Well, here's a plan. The Colony Square has a great breakfast. We can take turns keeping watch. Let me go run and then you can get breakfast. We can both keep our cell phones and call in case Cynthia moves."

"Go run? Why?"

"To stretch my legs. To think. I don't know; it feels good."

"Why can't I get breakfast first? I might miss out if it gets later and Cynthia comes out."

"Then you go eat first."

"Do you want me to bring you anything?"

"No, the doughnuts will be fine for me."

She wrinkled her nose to say "Eeww" and popped out of the car. Flashing a smile over her shoulder, she disappeared at the dip to cross the street and then reappeared going up the hill to the hotel. I watched carefully to make sure no one appeared to be following her. She called me a few moments later, happily getting a table.

"I'm inside. They have an all-you-can-eat buffet." I could hear the excitement in her voice. "I'll be about twenty minutes."

"Take your time. Enjoy it," I said.

"Oh, I will."

A little more than twenty-five minutes later, she emerged, grinning.

"Was it good?"

"Yes." She rubbed her full belly. "Now you can go run. I'll call if I see anything."

"Or if you need me."

"I'll be fine," she said. "Leave me the keys, and I'll lock myself in."

I took my gun and my holster with me and set off toward the park gates. It was an uneventful run. I thought mostly about what Lindsey and I had discussed and not so much the case. One thing I did know—I had to talk to Cynthia Norris. She was key. She lived in the building. It would have been easy for her to kill Nikki Sills, and she had motive—she loved Mark. She might have killed Mark in anger, when he didn't return her love. It seemed to me to be case solved, if only I could get something to back it up. I wondered if and when the police would talk to her.

My wonderment was answered by the time I returned to the car. Two police cars had joined us in the driveway.

"Hey, the police went up," Lindsey said. "I didn't call because I knew you'd be back soon. She's not going anywhere."

"You sure they've gone to see Cynthia?"

"Pretty sure. They didn't arrive with blue lights flashing or anything. They were carrying papers."

"Probably a search warrant or something. They'll be a while. Let's go over to my office. I've got to talk to Cynthia, but this waiting around for the police to finish up isn't going to do me much good."

"Whatever you think is best to get it resolved." Lindsey shrugged.

Feeling quite stinky from my run, we traveled home so I could shower and change, then I drove us over to Morehouse Insurance. Lindsey sat quietly in the corner painting her nails. Meanwhile I was doing paperwork when Glenn and Shawn arrived.

"Ooh-wee is Mr. Moore mad at you." Glenn shook his head. "What'd you do? He's been spitting fire."

Lindsey looked up, interested.

"I took off two days of work," I replied.

"Well, it's a good thing you're here today."

Shawn chuckled. "He makes me laugh when he gets mad. He looks like one of the little people from the Wizard of Oz, and then add red-faced and angry and I crack up."

"Listen to you, Miss Politically Correct. Shouldn't that be 'height-challenged'?" Glenn ribbed.

"Well, it's a good thing he only gets mad at me then," I said.

"So he's mad about two days off? Does he still know you're working on the Nikki Sills thing?"

"If he doesn't, he'll know shortly. I'm about to go talk to him about that." I stood up and stepped forward.

"Whoa, Cowboy." Shawn jumped in front of me. "Not a good idea."

"Yeah, ix-nay. Remember those old fake commercials on Saturday Night Live reruns?"

"Yes?" I didn't get where he was going.

"Well, 'Bad Idea Jeans.' Ring any bells?"

Lindsey laughed. "He's always wearing those."

"Ha, ha. Sorry, guys. He's going to find out sooner or later. I'd prefer he hear it straight from me."

"Suit yourself." Shawn stepped aside. "We'll get some boxes so Lindsey can start packing your desk."

Glenn shrugged and turned back to his desk, all the while humming the funeral Taps.

I heard Lindsey whisper to Shawn, who sat down by her, "Is he really going to get fired?"

I couldn't tell if her question was out of eagerness or anxiety, and I didn't hear the response. I took the elevator up to Mr. Moore's office. His Highness the Busy One kept me waiting for nearly thirty minutes. At least I was getting paid to sit and flip through Reader's Digest magazines. I was reading a fascinating article about a man who'd been stranded in the New England mountain wilderness in winter and how he'd survived. It was educational and included lists of edible plants and drawings of simple snares. But I wondered if the writers of the article really thought those were things anybody would ever need to know or get to use? My brain, a storehouse of useless trivia and information, took it all in; however, I didn't get to finish before Mr. Moore called for me. Better hope I don't get stuck in the wilderness, unprepared and all.

"You can't keep taking vacation days left and right. We have to schedule these things in a company this size."

"Respectfully, sir, I don't see the problem. I earned the days off. Would you rather I lie next time and call in sick?"

Mr. Moore's face seemed to puff up, and the red on his cheeks and neck deepened. I could begin to see Shawn's impression of him as he warmed up for a rant. I felt it best to cut him off and get everything out on the table at once and then let him be mad at me.

"Mr. Moore, my attendance aside, I want to speak to you about a much more important matter concerning millions of dollars."

"Millions?" Mr. Moore's fist poised to pound, fell almost soundlessly.

I had hit where it counted—dollars—so I continued. "The police have re-opened the Nikki Sills case and are now declaring it a murder. There's a chance her husband, the beneficiary, had her killed for the insurance. In which case, we won't pay."

"Fabulous."

"In fact, I've also discovered a loophole in our life insurance policy procedures I'd like to discuss later, but, as part and parcel to that, I did discover 1.5 million in claims were actually forged or fraudulent documents and therefore not valid."

"Fantastic."

"In addition, I have been working on the Nikki Sills case closely with the police to try to find her murderer. I know you took me off the case; however, I believe my time was well spent since it has saved the company 1.5 million dollars already."

I kept throwing out the dollar signs, knowing money would be the hear all, end all of the conversation, not my transgressions, not my frivolous use of vacation days, nor my disobedience of company policy.

"Yes, yes. Well done."

"I'm well aware my job is not to find the murderer, but with your permission in order to save the company additional money, I'd like to continue to work that angle. Investigating this case, I've angered some people, and I feel myself and my family are threatened. I would like to continue to work towards finding the killer so my life can return to normal more quickly. You know as well as I, the police do not always have the manpower to resolve such things in a timely manner. I'll work on my new cases as well, of course."

"Of course," Mr. Moore said, almost mesmerized. Then, shaking out of it, he added, "Mr. Grey, you have directly gone against me. You are not paid to think or make decisions; that is what I am paid for. Nevertheless, I am glad to see you are not such cattle like so many other folks going blindly where it makes no sense to go."

"Thank you, sir."

"In addition, it is not your job to further investigate at this point, but since you appear to believe there is a clear and present danger to yourself and your wife, I'm sure you must be on the right track. You angered the right persons and must be close to solving the case. It would be senseless to stop you at this point, not that you would."

"Yes, sir. I agree."

"Now, about this loophole?"

"Oh, yes, sir. It is a definite problem but easy to correct. You could make some simple suggestions to the higher-ups."

"Ah! We could get a promotion for such a thing. Will it save the company money?" He rubbed his fingers together like a greedy Midas.

"Potentially, but I'm not interested in a promotion. You don't even need to mention me."

"Really?" Mr. Moore's eyes widened, a child in a toy store with no credit limit.

"Really. Now here it is..."

*   *   *   *   *

What kind of person says "fabulous" and "clear and present danger"? Mr. Moore must feel himself to be powerful, like a president, but at least he was still compassionate enough to help me out. After all, I'd probably handed him a promotion up the corporate ladder. Myra would be so displeased.

"Back to pack your things?" Glenn asked, half teasing, half serious.

"No. It went over well."

"Oh, good," said Lindsey.

"What did you do? Blackmail him?" Shawn asked.

"Let's just say I had some ammunition I'd saved up," I mused. "I can't tell you all my secrets."

I sat down to gather my things so Lindsey and I could get back on surveillance. With Mr. Moore's approval, I didn't need time off to work on the case.

We picked up an early lunch, and when we arrived back at Cynthia's apartment, the police were still there.

"I figured they'd be a while."

"What would they be searching for?" Lindsey asked.

"Well, in Nikki's murder there was no weapon. Perhaps a house key to their apartment. Or in the case of Mark's murder, a knife. Maybe documents to support the claim she was having an affair with Mark, to establish they knew each other."

"Oh. Well, I could see where it could take a while to look for a key. It could be hidden anywhere."

We sat and sat. We talked a little more about the risks of investigation, but the resolution to the problem still appeared to be the same. I was going to have to change jobs, as much as I hated it. I could always go back to computer work.

The police concluded their business around three o'clock, and shortly after they left, Cynthia left. We followed her to an assortment of places—the dry cleaners, the coffee shop, a movie rental store, where she checked out three movies. All a true challenge to my skills at tailing.

"Looks like another long, boring night on the job," I said to Lindsey as we watched Cynthia emerge from the movie store. "She has a whole night's worth of films."

"Not from the backseat." Lindsey smiled.

Maybe we should go home tonight, just for a while. We followed Cynthia to a shopping mall.

"She knows what you look like. Let me follow her around inside," Lindsey suggested. "I can talk to you on the cell the whole time."

I didn't want to agree to it, but it did seem to be the best option other than both of us sitting in the car having no idea where she was or who she might be talking to.

Lindsey followed her to the bookstore, several clothing stores, including the lingerie store, and finally to the Food Court, where Cynthia ate dinner. Lindsey grabbed two subs for us. When Cynthia left the mall, Lindsey and I followed her by car to a local dance club.

"Not very busy here," Lindsey said. "You think she'll notice me and recognize me from the mall if I go in?"

"I'm not sure. How close to her did you get? Did she see you?"

"Well, I'm not experienced at this, but I kept a distance. I don't think she knew I was there."

I mulled it over. "I really need to talk to her. Maybe I should go in. This might be the best chance I'll have. She can't slam any doors in my face or call the cops."

"Maybe," Lindsey agreed. "She might leave or tell the bouncer."

"I'm going."

I opened my door and was about to step from the car when Lindsey grabbed my arm and squeezed it tight. "Wait," she hissed and pulled me back in.

"What? What's wrong?" I noticed her frozen stare at a man crossing the parking lot a short distance from us.

CHAPTER 17

"That man—I've seen him already today," Lindsey pulled me back into the center of the car.

"You have?"

"Yes—at the mall, when I was following Cynthia."

"Are you sure?"

Lindsey nodded. "I'm absolutely positive."

"Do you think he's following Cynthia, too?"

"Why else would he be around her at both places? He's following her, like us."

I shrugged. "Maybe Jeffries put a tail on her, a plain clothes cop."

"Call him," Lindsey pleaded. "I don't like the way he looks. He doesn't look like a cop. He looks creepy."

"They aren't supposed to look like cops when they're tailing someone," I explained as I dialed.

But, as Lindsey suspected, the man was not a cop. Jeffries denied assigning a man to Cynthia and swore he wasn't holding out on me.

"So who is he, then?" Lindsey asked.

"Mob?" I suggested.

"Of course; that makes sense," she agreed.

"Now I'm not sure I should go in."

"Me either. Let's eat and think about it for a minute."

I opened my sub, but I could barely eat. Anxiety tied my stomach in knots. I needed to talk to Cynthia, but the possible mob presence scared me. But hadn't Vincent called me himself to tell me about a woman suspect? They wanted me there. They wanted me to find her. I decided to go inside. Lindsey accepted my rationale, but not without misgivings.

I concealed my gun before approaching the club. I paid my Wednesday half-price cover charge and entered the building. Not too busy. After all, it was mid-week and still fairly early in the evening, but nonetheless the music was thump-thumping, shaking my rib cage. I wondered how it could be affecting my heart to be shaken around so, not to mention my eardrums. Still, the techno beat droned on, the same continuous background beat no matter what song or how many times the song was changed.

The bar was in a prime cental location from which I could look for Cynthia amongst the small crowd. Clusters of people hung together and singular or paired people moved about. Getting a good look at anyone was difficult in the semi-darkness punctuated by flashing lasers. The lighting of the club, what small amount there was, had an overall green hue making everyone look a bit monstrous. Dating—that was the monster. Thank goodness I didn't have to go through dating again, but hooking up, finding a partner or a one night stand, was what the club was for. I could see it in their eyes. Their eyes were like those of wolves looking to devour someone. The sexual content and energy of the room was high.

I ordered a plain Coke and swivelled on my stool this way and that, looking for Cynthia or the man we'd seen follow her inside. Presently, a couple approached and behind them the man. He took a bar stool to my right, skipping two seats between us, and looked out into the club past me. If he truly was following Cynthia, he'd be watching her. Tracking his gaze to the left, I spotted her sitting alone behind a group of standing girls. A difficult-to-see area off in the dark corner.

The man at the bar looked nervous. He bit his nails and ordered a shot, which he promptly downed. His eyes were narrow, with slightly darkened circles under them as if he suffered allergies or lack of sleep. If he'd been on surveillance, he could be lacking sleep. I wondered what my own self looked like. I stole a glance into the mirror facade of the bar. *Ugh; awful.* Upon more examination of the man I noticed he was also sweating, more than normal or what would be normal for the temperature of the room. He was anxious about something. Maybe he'd been sent by the mob, not to watch Cynthia but to kill her? Would he commit a murder in such a public place? I had no way to know.

The man ordered two more shots of Tequila and then made his move. I prepared to have to stop him, tackle him, whatever it would take. I had my gun. I could use it, I reassured myself. I moved in behind him.

He approached Cynthia and said, "Hello. I'm Grant. I don't use corny pick-up lines. I was wondering if I could buy you a drink?"

I ducked into the booth catty-corner but behind them both.

"I'm not drinking," she said without looking up.

"Well, a Coke, a juice, whatever." He shrugged.

"I'm not drinking anything," she clarified, raising her cobalt blue eyes to meet his.

"Oh, well, O.K. then. Can I sit down?"

"There are lots of seats around here. You don't need my permission to sit." She had a velvety, breathy voice that even when dismissing someone seemed inviting all the same.

"I meant I'd like to sit and talk with you. Are you waiting for someone or something?" He smiled, a nice smile.

"No and no." She smiled in return.

Despite all her exotic looks, long chocolate-colored hair in tight corkscrew curls, sleek legs, manicured hands and toes, her smile was horrible with pursed lips and closed mouth like she had tasted something bad.

"Jeez, what is your problem? I was trying to get to know you a little bit."

"I'm not here to get a date. I don't want to get to know anyone," she replied apologetically, not gruffly. "I'm sorry. I lost someone. He died, and I'm really not interested. Sorry."

"Oh, no. I understand. I'm sorry. I shouldn't have intruded."

"That's O.K. I mean, I am sitting alone at a club. What should a guy think, right?" She laughed, a fake falsetto laugh. "Why don't you sit down? We can talk, and you can still buy me a drink, as long as you know it's not going anywhere."

"Yeah, all right." He slid into the booth. "I'm Grant, and you are?"

"Cynthia."

"Cynthia. What will you have to drink?"

"A Diet Coke."

And so their conversation continued on trivial matters for about fifteen minutes. I learned Cynthia was working as a pet store obedience trainer and groomer even though she had no experience at either and hated dogs. She's a firm believer in horoscopes, astrology, numerology, and fortune-telling, which explains the fortune cookies. She did a quick astrological assessment of his and her potential compatibility.

"Sorry, we wouldn't be a match even if I was looking." She smiled her sour smile again.

"Oh, well. I guess I better keep my eye out then. The night is still young. I enjoyed talking with you."

"Me, too. Thanks for the drink."

"No problem." He waved his nothing-to-it hand. "But here, let me give you my number, just in case you change your mind or something."

He pulled out a pen and wrote something, presumably a phone number on a napkin.

"Thanks."

Then the man, Grant, disappeared into the darkness of elsewhere in the club. I took a tour around to see if he was still somewhere watching and did not see him, although I was certain he was there. I had a "watched" feeling as I approached Cynthia's booth.

"Hello," I said.

"I'm not looking to hook-up. I got rid of some other guy and now—" She looked up and the glimmer of recognition crossed her eyes. "You. I know you."

"Yes, Paul Grey. I'm the private investigator who tried to speak with you at your apartment."

"Go away. Leave me alone."

"I'm afraid I can't. I must talk to you about the murders of Mark and Nikki Sills." I sat down across from her. I noted Grant's phone number on the napkin and quickly rehearsed it several times to try to memorize it.

"I can't talk to you."

"Look, you're number one suspect at this point. You have two mobs after you. Your best bet is to turn yourself in to the police. They can protect you, maybe get you some leniency from the courts."

"What? Are you saying admit I'm guilty?" Her bright blue eyes flew wide with shock.

"Are you guilty?"

"Hell, no. And if you think the police can protect me, you are sadly mistaken."

"You were having an affair with Mark Sills. He broke it off, so you killed his wife. When he still didn't return to you, you killed him. You have access to the building; you know his routines. It fits perfectly."

"Perfect, except I didn't do any of it."

"You deny the affair? We found your love nest."

"My love nest? You really don't know anything. Now if you'll excuse me, I'm going to the ladies' room."

She got up and I followed.

"I have questions."

"Are you planning on following me in here?" She paused at the door.

"No." I glanced in through the door which she held wide. There were no windows. "But you can't hide out in there forever, and I'll be waiting right here when you come out."

She huffed, entered, and let the door swing shut. She must have decided to test my resolve, because she stayed in the restroom a very long time. I wrote down Grant's number before I forgot it. When she finally emerged, I was right at her side.

"I know you don't want to talk to me—"

"That's right. Exactly why I'm leaving."

"Wait." I grabbed her elbow lightly. "If you won't talk to me, at least listen to what I have to say."

"You've got about thirty seconds." She folded her arms and stuck one long leg out to the side and tapped her foot.

"There is a man following you. Grant, the one who sat and talked with you. He followed you from the mall to here and that may not be all. The mob may have sent him to kill you."

"What? The mousy guy? Sounds like you're the one following me. And so what? Maybe he saw me at the mall and liked me and that's why he followed me."

"Sounds like stalker material. Be careful. You have information I want and need, and I'll get it eventually. I don't want the mob killing you off before I get my chance."

"Ha, the mob. I've got them in my pocket." She started off again at a brisk pace, purse swinging and heels clicking. "They won't harm me."

"Really? What does your horoscope say?" I followed behind, dodging other folks.

"Never mind my horoscope; perhaps you should be checking yours."

"Are you threatening me?"

Stopping with her hand on the exit door, she turned and faced me. "No, I am not threatening you. But if you really think that man is from the mob and he's following me, then he now knows you are following me, too. If he kills me, he'll have to kill you."

"Actually, a personal call from Vincent Artello is what put me on your trail."

"Really?" She faked interest. "What a news headline. 'Mafia Kills Husband and Wife, Attempts Cover-up, Blames Mistress.' I'm not interested in what you are telling me. I've been through a lot, I've seen a lot, and I know a lot. Not much you can say will have any effect."

"What about the police? They were at your place today."

"Yeah? So. They didn't find anything because there isn't anything."

"How did you end up living in the same building as Mark Sills?"

"We both worked for the same people. Now, if you'll excuse me."

She swung the door open wide.

I followed her out to her car. She unlocked it and climbed in with me standing nearly over her.

"Watch your feet when I pull out," she warned and shut her door.

I moved away. She started the car and then unrolled the window.

"On second thought," she said. "I don't want to talk to you, but here's some food for thought, so to speak. I know you think I killed Nikki to get Mark for myself. Fact is, Mark killed her for the money."

"So who killed Mark then, and why? You. For the money. You were in his will."

"Where did you hear that? I haven't been on his will since he decided to cut things off with me."

"Who was it then? No one else had a motive to kill them both."

"No one? And who says one person had to kill them both? You're not a very good detective then if the thought hasn't crossed your mind."

"The thought, what thought? You're not making any sense."

"You found the love nest, right? You think I was the only one?"

I nodded.

"Wrong," she snapped, rolled up her window, and left.

"Come on," Lindsey hollered from our car. She already had it started and she was ready to drive. "You'll lose her."

"She's probably going home." I jumped in.

"Look, there's that guy."

He was already in his car and we watched as he pulled out and followed Cynthia.

"Stay behind him," I directed.

"What did you and she talk about?" Lindsey asked.

"She suggested Mark may have had more than one affair."

"Is it possible?"

"Well, yes, but we don't have any names or evidence to support it. Cynthia is still my best suspect because of her location in the building. Another mistress may have wanted to kill Nikki but wouldn't have had any access."

"Unless he had affairs with other women who lived in his building. Once a cheater, always a cheater."

"Ah... good point. We'll look into it."

"How? Who would we ask?"

"Maybe the loan shark, Eddie. Or even the security at the front desk of the apartments. There were several pieces of evidence at the storage unit, but I'm fairly certain they all point to Cynthia and no one else."

We followed Grant who followed Cynthia, right back to her apartment. Grant parked in the parking deck and emerged out onto the sidewalk a little while later. He sat on a ledge across the street and smoked a cigarette.

"Could be another long night." Lindsey put her hand on my thigh.

My heart jumped into sexual overdrive at the thoughts I was having.

"Yes, could be a long night." I swallowed hard as my throat already was getting dry.

She leaned over and kissed me, hard, then sat upright as if a sudden thought or problem had occurred to her.

"What? What's wrong?" I asked.

"We don't have any food, do we?"

"Not really, but once we're sure she's settled in for the night, we might be able to go get something quickly." I tried to coax her back to me, but she resisted.

"Don't get me wrong, I appreciate your affection, but I can't believe there's nothing else we can do but sit around and watch her. Don't you have any other clues you need to pursue?"

"Well," I said slowly, debating on whether a "no" answer would gain more making out or not or if she would detect the truth. "I can go in and ask about Mark and his romantic escapades. Would you like me to do that?"

She nodded. "I hate feeling helpless with nothing to do. Well, not nothing to do...there's always that." She indicated by rubbing my leg again. "But you know what I mean. Don't you want to get this case resolved? So we can go home to, you know."

"Yes, I do. Do you want to come in with me? Cynthia knows we're following her and so does the other fellow. There's no need to hide we're here."

"No. I can stay here."

"Are you worried it might be dangerous for you to stay outside alone?"

"Yes, the other fellow makes me nervous. He's creepy looking. But you might need a pair of eyes out here. And I can clearly see him."

"We'll use our cell phones. You can call mine now, and I'll keep the line open. If you need me, yell loudly, and I'll hear you."

She dialed, and we tested the connection.

I got out and crossed to the entrance. I buzzed the desk, and the girl let me in.

"Who are you here to see? Someone is expecting you?" she asked.

"No. Actually, I was hoping to ask you a few questions." I showed her my card. "I'm Paul Grey. I've been here a few times with the police, working on the Mark and Nikki Sills case."

She nodded. "I'm Joyce. How can I help?"

"I was wondering if you ever saw Mark Sills with a woman or women other than his wife, and, if so, what type of relationship did it seem to be?"

The girl shifted as if she were suddenly uncomfortable. "Um, well, I don't really like gossip about other people," she explained.

"No, not gossip. Only what you've seen or what you know for fact."

"I'm not sure I know anything." She folded her arms in retreat.

"Did you ever see him with other women?"

"Sometimes, on the elevator or outside by the parking garage."

"Were these casual meetings? For instance, they both happened to come in at the same time or both be on the elevator at the same time? Or did they seem to be together, meeting? Do you think it was more than casual coincidence?"

"I guess casual." She shrugged.

"Can you tell me who he was with?"

She shook her head. "I wouldn't want to tell you. It wouldn't be keeping our tenant's privacy."

"But they were tenants?"

"Yes."

"How many different ones? Did any of them ever seem more than casual?"

"I don't know. I don't keep up with the love lives around here." She stomped her foot defiantly.

"Paul, Paul—" I heard Lindsey's voice and my heart jumped.

"Excuse me," I said to the girl and turned to talk. "What is it? Are you all right?"

"I'm fine. I could hear the conversation. I think you should ask her if she was ever attracted to Mark Sills. Ask her if she ever talked to him or spent time with him more than casually."

Lindsey had a good intuitive sense about people. Perhaps she was sensing the girl's reluctance as admission of guilt.

"O.K., I will. Now quit scaring me, and don't call me unless there's a problem."

I turned back to the girl. "Miss...I'm sorry, Joyce. I really need your help."

Her eyes wouldn't meet mine.

"I want to respect privacy as well, but everything in Mark Sills' past is going to be dug up by the police, people like me—or worse, news reporters," I explained.

Her head snapped up and her eyes widened. "I don't want information being twisted by news reporters. They'll make it look really bad."

"I need you to tell me what you know."

"I think he was more than casual sometimes, a lot of times."

"Did you feel Mr. Sills was an attractive man?"

She blushed, a light red like her curly hair, but enough to be telling. "Yes."

"So he flirted with you or other women in the building?"

"Yes.

"Did it ever go beyond flirting for you or anyone else, as far as you know?"

Joyce clamped her lips shut. Her eyes squinted. She opened her mouth as if to speak but then clamped it shut again.

"You don't know what to say or how to say it. You don't want to lose your job or your reputation. You're afraid you'll be treated as a suspect."

"Yes, yes." She nodded and her coffee brown eyes glossed. "How do you know this?"

"Well—" I hesitated, trying to come up with a better answer than woman's intuition, but I couldn't find one. "Well, it doesn't matter. If you want to be treated like a suspect, then keep hiding the facts. When the police find you've been hiding information, they'll want to know why."

"Like you said. I don't want to risk my job or be treated like I might have had something to do with their murders. I thought I should distance myself from them."

"So, were you having an affair with Mark Sills?"

"No. It never got that far. Well, we messed around a little, but I never slept with him."

"Where was this?"

"I met him in the storage locker area one time and once in the stairs."

He had a thing for storage areas. And pretty girls. I wonder what it was about

Nikki that couldn't hold his interest.

"Did he ever tell you why he wanted to have an affair? Was there a problem in his marriage?"

"No. I think he had an ego thing, like he deserved more than one girl, but we don't deserve him. At first I was attracted to the cockiness, but then later I found it obnoxious, so I refused to sleep with him."

"When was this?"

"About two months ago. It only lasted for about a week, then he moved on when he realized pressuring me wouldn't work."

"Moved on? To who?"

"I've seen him with other ladies who live here, but I don't know what if anything he did with them."

"You realize, this does make you suspicious. You were romantically involved with him, even if briefly. You say it didn't go anywhere, but we only have your word."

"I know." She shrugged.

"You knew the wife, too?"

"Um, yes."

"Other than in your line of work?" I asked.

"Yes. She invited me up for coffee one day, insisted actually. Then I figured out what she wanted—to know if I'd had sex with him."

"She knew?"

"She knew he'd had his eye on me, but she didn't know how far it had gone."

"She told me to leave him alone, and I assured her I had already intended to, even before talking with her."

"And then what?" I asked.

"That was it. I think I was a game between them. I almost believe he told her about me and expected her to talk to me."

"You don't think she figured it out on her own?"

"No. How could she? She never saw us together, and I told no one. Believe me, I could get fired for what I did. I heard a rumor she was pregnant. Maybe she wanted to make sure the competition was gone."

"Did she talk to anyone else? Invite them up the way she did for you?"

"I think she might have, anyone Mark might have had his eye on, but I don't know for sure. She was always very pleasant to me, even afterwards. She was a really nice person."

"Where were you on the fourth of July? Were you on duty?"

"No. It was the other girl. I was at home. And here's where you ask for my alibi, which I have none."

"Paul, Paul, Paul—" I heard Lindsey again.

"I've got to go," I said to the girl and then into the phone, "Yes? You O.K.?"

"The man, Grant. He went back into the garage; he's leaving. What do you want to do?"

"Start the car. I'm on my way out." I threw the door open.

CHAPTER 18

Lindsey had the car running, lights on, and she pulled up to the door of the apartments. She slid over as I jumped in.

"Which way?" I asked.

"That way." She pointed up the hill toward Peachtree Street.

"Do you see him? Do you see him?" I repeated, looking every which way for our quarry. "What could be so important he would leave his post?"

"Hunger?" Lindsey joked. "Ah, there he is."

We took a quick right on Peachtree and closed in a short distance behind him.

"We're good. I think we'll be able to follow him from here."

"This is so exciting," Lindsey raved. "I had no idea, the adrenaline rush."

"Yeah, until you lose someone. Losing a tail is a real let down."

"Well, don't lose him then."

We followed him to the highway, Interstate 20 and headed out of town going east. It all seemed very familiar, the turns, the road sounds, the distance. And soon I could see why. We pulled up to a building construction site that looked like it was within days of being open for business. I was sure it was where I had been taken only a few days before. A large sign for Aries Engineering and BancTrust indicated the contractor and financing for the project.

"Now what?" Lindsey asked as we stopped a safe distance from the building and watched Grant park his car.

"I'm going in," I said.

"What? Are you crazy? You can't go in there."

"Yes, I can. I've been there before."

"You'll be caught for sure. I won't let you do it."

"We have to know what is going on. I have to go. I can find my way around." I unlocked my door and moved to get out.

Lindsey reached over and grabbed my arm, a gentle restraint. "No. Even if this the same place, you were blindfolded and carried around."

"I've got to go now. He's going in. If I don't follow him, I definitely won't find my way." I opened the car door and slid out.

"No, Paul."

"Shhh. I'll be fine. If I'm not back out in about fifteen minutes, you can call the police."

"Oh, Paul, don't."

Sneaking along the darkened side of the street, I approached the building and peeked around the corner to glance inside. I saw no lights, no one. The door Grant used was still unlocked. I slipped in and held the door with some resistance to let it glide shut with only a slight click.

Inside was the lobby in near darkness, the elevator buttons glowing. I was certain Grant had not gone up. Both elevators were at the lobby and not moving. The building smelled of fresh paint, a newness. I was now certain this was where I had been taken. I stood still, stopped breathing, and listened. Ah, very faint murmurs from off to the right. I crept along the wall to try to get close enough to listen yet be far enough away to get hidden should the conversation conclude and someone come out.

I remained completely still and breathed very little. The voices at first were undistinguishable. Then I could begin to decipher two distinct voices.

"How's surveillance, buddy?" a man's voice asked.

"It's fine. Why did you beep me? I had to leave my tail."

"Boss wants to know if she is still out of line? Or has she straightened up?" the man asked.

I recognized the man's voice and inflection as one of those who had helped abduct me.

"She's straight," Grant replied.

"About damn time," the man said. "She better tow the line. The boss says if she does anything wrong, you have permission to kill her."

"I think she'll behave. She seems to have realized—" Grant began.

"Don't give me your bullshit. She hasn't realized anything. She's still playing, biding her time." The man cut him off.

"No, I don't think so," Grant denied. "She's done everything they've asked her to do. She killed Mark, just like the boss wanted her to."

"I know, I know. Buddy, if I didn't know any better, I'd think you had the hots for the broad. You're always singin' her praises."

"She's a good person. I think it's wrong he told her to do that and then stuck a private eye on her tail. He might as well have told the guy she did it," Grant complained.

"Well, he didn't beat around the bush much. What'd you expect? She hasn't been doing her job; she's caused a lot of trouble for us. She should have stayed in Vegas. They're after her, too. So far the boss won't tell them where she is. But if they find her, stay out of the way."

"But, the boss agreed to protect her."

"An exchange in which she hasn't kept up her end of the deal."

"She left Vegas for good reason. She must have a good reason for not keeping the deal, too." Grant's voice took on a defensive tone.

"Yeah? How would you know? You talk to her? If you did, the boss won't like it much."

"No, I haven't talked to her. I just know."

"I'd keep my mouth shut if I was you. He may want rid of her any day now, and if you're tangled up with her, he may sign your death sentence, too."

"I'm not tangled. Everything will be fine if he would wait and see."

"Look, man. He can't wait and see. If she makes any wrong moves, it could mean prison for all of us. She knows way too much about us; the people in Vegas want her for the same reason. She's trouble."

"I don't believe it."

"Do I need to take you off this duty? 'Cause I have serious doubts you'd be able to put a bullet in her head if you need to."

"I won't need to."

"Keep an eye on her, and if she even so much as breathes the wrong way, you kill her. Got it?"

"O.K., I got it. What about the private eye?"

"Let him do his work. He'll figure out Cynthia's guilty and bring the police down on her."

"What if she tries to turn evidence on us?"

"She'll be killed. Long arms reach into prison, my friend."

"What if she tries to run? Tries to leave?"

"Kill her."

"So, she's pretty much dead either way then?"

"Unless she keeps her mouth shut, which would demonstrate some allegiances, and does her time for the crime. If she behaves, our lawyers and our cops can help her. We can make evidence disappear. Right now, the boss wants to make sure she knows her place and pays a little for her being such a pain in the ass."

"So keep an eye on her and forget the private investigator?"

"Yeah, unless you've got to kill her. Then you'll have to get rid of him first. Can you do that?"

"Yeah."

"You can make it look like she did it."

"Yeah."

"Well, then get back to work," he demanded.

I quickly backed out into the lobby and moved across it to the adjacent hallway. Here I hid in complete darkness and watched as Grant quietly left through the same door we had entered.

Then I waited to see what the other man would do. If he came down the hall I was in, I was in trouble. But he did not. He went to the front door, locked it, and then took the elevator up to the fifth floor. When I was certain the coast was clear, I left my blanket of darkness and snuck over to the front door. Thankfully, it still opened from the inside, even though it was locked from the outside.

I checked to see if the coast was clear then crossed the street with speed and jumped into the car with Lindsey.

"So?" she asked.

"Well, we're safe for now. The mob is leaving us alone."

"That's good. They talked about us?"

"They talked about me, briefly. Mostly they talked about how Cynthia has made a rope and pretty much hung herself. She's a problem for them, but they didn't really say how or why. They could kill her at any time, but because she killed Mark they feel she's back in line for now."

"How will we know if they decide to kill her?"

"When they come after me, it means they need me out of the way so they can get to her."

"But a moment ago you said we were safe?"

"We are until they change their minds and need her dead."

"Aren't they afraid you'll see it or know?"

"Sweetie, that's what I said. They would have to get rid of me first."

"Oh, yeah. Mental deficiency caused by lack of food," she smarted.

Mmm...food...my stomach rumbled. I hadn't felt my hunger until that moment.

"What do you want? Name it and we'll get it."

"Really?"

"Well, take-out."

"Better than nothing. How about rotisserie chicken and salad?"

"Sounds good."

We picked up some chicken, salad, fries, and drinks and reported back to Cynthia's to watch and wait. Grant was already there, back on post.

"We could make our own little bit of fun again," Lindsey suggested.

"I would, but it bothers me to have to sit here and I can't do anything. I can't tell Jeffries about the building or that they might kill Cynthia at any time."

"I don't like the part about them having to dispose of you first, forget her." Lindsey folded her arms over her chest.

"Now, you're not being very nice."

"She's a killer, a murderer."

"We don't know for sure."

"Grant reported Cynthia killed Mark." She leaned forward earnestly.

"That's what he said, yes." I shrugged.

"But you don't believe it?" Lindsey flopped back in her seat so quickly the whole car jiggled.

"It's possible it was someone else. Mark was a philanderer. Another girlfriend could have killed Nikki or him or both."

"Once a cheater, always a cheater," Lindsey commented.

"Time will tell, and hopefully some evidence."

I looked up at the side of the apartment building, some windows lit, some dark. That's how this case felt to me, sometimes lit up, like I knew exactly what I was doing, and sometimes in total pitch black, without a clue.

In the morning, Lindsey went to eat and by the time she returned, Cynthia had left for work at her dog grooming job. So this time as I went to run, Lindsey, tired of being cooped up in the car, came down to the park with me. She sat on a bench to listen to the birds and "people watch." There were several people in the park at the time, a mom with a baby and stroller, a businessman reading his paper, and other runners.

The light of the sun scattered through the trees, starting off low and pink, an unassuming day that could turn out cool or hot—too early to tell. For now the coolness was appreciated as I trekked around the park. A few early morning squirrels looking panicked scattered before my steps. *Dumb squirrels; I'm not chasing you.* I slowed my pace when I heard cracking twigs in the bushes to my right, perhaps a stray dog or a cat. Too big to be a squirrel. I took a step closer.

A figure, wrapped in black, like death itself, jumped out and grabbed my right arm. Holding it, the figure pierced it with a knife then swung to get around behind me. The cut was so sharp, I knew it happened, but it didn't hurt until a few seconds later, late enough I had time to react to the attacker and not the pain. I twisted away, blocking an attempt to take my gun from its' holster.

"Help me," I shouted as I turned heel and accelerated down the path, out of the clearing. "Help!"

I wanted to find witnesses, find Lindsey, and be clear to defend myself. With my arm held tight to my side, I ran stiffly. With my good arm I drew my gun. Next thing I knew, I felt hands clasping around my calves and felt the thud of the person's body as he landed behind me in a tackling move. The gun left my grasp. I groped for something, anything to prevent my fall, but clasped nothing but air. I attempted to curl to relax my descent, the attacker, still grasping my heels tightly, pulling me taut. I fell to the pavement, rounded shoulder first, rolling onto my front. I felt the dig of tiny rough pieces of concrete tearing through my shirt. My cheek and nose burned, but my feet were free. I kicked and rolled onto my back.

The attacker came from my left side and lunged on top of me. I caught him in mid-fling, but not before his knife caught the side of one of my fingers.

"Shit," I yelled as I threw him off of me with my good arm. He tumbled into the grass and dirt.

I could hear Lindsey on the other side of the park screaming. "Somebody help him!"

Unbearable pain in my finger, blood streaking down my arm, I scanned the ground frantically for my gun. The gun was nowhere to be seen. Then both of us were up and facing off. He or she had dark eyes under the dark mask and a tall, strong build. The clothing, all dark brown and black, was non-descript, unisex looking with black gloves.

"Who are you and what do you want?" I demanded.

The reply came as a quick lunge forward. I dodged. The attacker stumbled and recovered, turned quickly, and hacked at me several more times, viciously and with lightning speed. I jumped back and back again, hands out in defense ready to catch the wrist with the knife if possible. On the next lunge, I dodged only with my top half, grabbed my assailant's arm on the way past, and swept my leg under his legs. With a heavy thud my attacker was down but rolled quickly away. The knife lay at the pavement. I picked it up. I wasn't good at knife fighting, but I would certainly try.

My hand throbbed at holding the knife so tightly. I waggled it in front of me. The attacker must have twisted an ankle on the way down and stood lightly on the one foot, a small hole in the side of the pant leg, some blood. I looked at my own blood-streaked hands and arms. *I've had enough of this bastard; he's dead.*

Either the injury or the look on my face or the distant sirens was enough to send the assailant running, or rather limping off, disappearing into the more wooded area. I sank to the ground on my knees and then down to my side.

A few moments later, Lindsey was looking down at me.

"I saw the whole thing. Oh, my God." She held her hand over my bleeding arm and rolled me onto my back carefully.

Now the pain came on full force, adrenaline subsided. I dropped the knife.

"I'm hurt," I said. "He's getting away."

"Don't worry," she said. "I've got you."

The world seemed dark, my peripheral vision failing. Only through narrow slits or tunnels could I see Lindsey's concerned face hovering over mine. One of her tears fell from her cheek into my eye. I blinked it away, then my eyes shut but didn't open.

CHAPTER 19

I opened my eyes. *Oh, this was all too familiar a scene.* A hospital bed, beeping equipment, tubes, and me, sore, in the bed. This time it was darker in the room, curtains drawn shut. I felt my right arm—stitches. My arm was secured so it wouldn't move. I looked down at my finger. *Thank goodness, still there.* Stitches in it as well. The blood had been cleaned off and my clothes had been changed.

Then I saw Lindsey, sleeping quietly in a chair in a corner of the room.

"Lindsey," I whispered.

She stirred and sat up.

"Lindsey, hey. How long have I been out?"

"A couple hours. They did some repair on your arm and finger."

"What's going on with these?" I indicated the wires and tubes.

"IV. You had some painkillers."

"What did the doctor say about my arm?"

"You shouldn't move it. You have some major damage. He said you were lucky the cut went straight in and not across the muscle or into the major artery."

"Will it need to be restrained like this all the time?"

"A sling, yes, all the time until it heals. Also, you will need some therapy to get back all your movement and flexibility."

"Medicines for pain?"

"Yes. The painkiller they gave you here will have to clear your system before you can go. They'll prescribe something for pain and to keep away infection."

"So we can go?"

"Shortly. And then we have to talk to Jeffries."

"I can't give much of a description. Dark eyes, that's about it. Can't even say if it was male or female. Have you heard anything?"

"The knife. It could match the one used to kill Mark. They're looking for prints."

"What about the park? Anyone searching there?"

"Yes. They're investigating right now. Jeffries still wants to talk to you. He thinks you may know who it was."

"Now how am I supposed to know that?"

She shrugged.

"Well, we're going to meet Jeffries, and then you're going back into protective custody."

"Ugh, no. Paul—"

"Lindsey, you know it's best."

She nodded in agreement, even though her hung head showed she hated to admit it. We checked out of the hospital after a long discussion with the doctor, including a prognosis, instructions on how to treat the injury, and when to come back in. Then we drove over to the park with police escort to meet up with Jeffries.

"This is familiar, huh?" He indicated the crime scene tape and crew at work.

"Better weather," I said.

"Yes. If you are ever killed, I'll thank you for doing it on a nice sunny day."

"If I have any say about it, I don't want to be killed on any type of day. Got anything yet?"

"No. We have a man tracker on the case, followed some footprints, lost the suspect on the pavement outside the park."

"Same footprints as in Mark's case?"

"Possibly."

"May I see the trail?"

"Yeah, let me get my guy." Jeffries whistled.

A bulky, Hispanic fellow looked up and came over at his beckon.

"This is Detective Carlos Nunez. He's our tracker. Carlos, show him the trail and tell him what you know."

"Certainly, boss. Follow me." Lindsey hung out by Jeffries while Carlos took me to the spot where the attack began. "We've got tracks both coming and going. We're working on shoe make and size right now. A boot, average size."

"Where do the tracks come from?"

"Well, we can trace them back to the pavement. The ground is fairly dry, but the boots made enough of a disruption on the soil and vegetation we can see he or she entered the park on that side over there." He pointed.

"And after the attack?"

"After the attack, there's a trace of limping in the gait. Found blood all around, but won't know if it was yours until testing is done.

Some of it could be from the attacker. Then over here we find the same prints." Carlos pointed. "But we lose the trail outside the park. We've set up a perimeter about a mile out, but that's a lot of ground and no description to go on."

"I haven't had a chance to give the description yet. It's all but worthless. The mask and gloves were no doubt removed. He or she could be anybody—even you." I peered into his dark eyes.

"We'll keep looking. If those items were discarded, we'll find them and hopefully some clues, too."

I meandered back over to Jeffries. "Not much to go on."

"No," he agreed. "Not unless you can give me some direction, a hint."

"You think I know who did this?"

"Maybe," he said. "You've held out on me before."

"Well, I don't know. As for a description: dark eyes, I think, medium skin, probably Caucasian, but I can't be sure. Average to tall height and strong build. Of course, shorter than I am."

"Male or female?" He jotted down some notes.

"Can't say. I want to say male, but it could have been a strong woman."

"Paul," Lindsey interrupted. "Don't you think those people you followed last night deserve mention?"

"No," I replied sternly and then to Jeffries, " I'm going to need a favor. Can you help me out?"

"I won't know until you tell me what it is."

"I need you to put Lindsey up somewhere again, keep an eye on her."

"No, Paul, I don't want to," Lindsey complained.

"There's no other choice. You can't stay with me; it's too dangerous to be around me."

"How about getting a little help? Sometimes you don't have to go it alone."

"And sometimes I do," I replied. "So, Jeffries, how about it? Can you do it?"

"I can handle it. Same place or somewhere else?"

"I'm thinking something a little more secure."

"No problem." He reached into his jacket and pulled out my gun. "Here, this was found. It's yours? Yes?"

"Yes, thanks."

I took Lindsey aside, reassured her, kissed her, and then left her to

Jeffries' care. I wondered if she would tell him everything while I was gone, even though she knew I wouldn't want her to. Fact was, I didn't know who had done it. It could have been the mob, or specifically Grant. If Cynthia felt I was getting too close, it could have been her. Or maybe someone I hadn't discovered or thought of yet. My only starting point would still be to keep an eye on Cynthia, so I was heading up the street to her apartment when my cell phone rang, startling me. I was going to be jumpy until this case was over, maybe longer. I looked around for cars and cautiously answered.

"Hello?"

"Hey, it's Stuart Newsome."

"Oh, hey. Did you find out something for me?"

"Yeah. Can you meet? The food court at Perimeter Mall?"

"Sounds good. When?"

"About forty minutes from now?"

"Yeah, I can make it there by then. I'll head over right away."

I wondered if I should have asked Stuart to come to me. What if something happened at Cynthia's and I missed it? But I didn't call him back. Instead I took a taxi.

Stuart Newsome must have had a reason to want to meet at the food court. It was crowded and busy, lots of noise. I wondered if what Stuart had found out was what made him want so much cover noise, the only possible reason for wanting to meet someplace so public. Stuart approached my table, sat down, and looked over his shoulder.

"Were you followed?" he asked me.

"I don't think so. You?"

"No. What's with the arm?" He indicated the sling.

"Running accident."

"Uh-huh." He sat back and assessed my scratched face, all the while grinning, disbelieving. "Well, may I suggest you be more careful? You seem to be havin' a lot of accidents these days."

"Tell me what you found out."

"Here's the scoop." Stuart hunched forward, his large torso a wall encompassing us as he spoke in hushed tones. "The girl you asked about, Gianina DeSantis, is using the name Cynthia Norris. The Las Vegas mob has been looking for her, but Atlanta folks know where she's been all along."

"Did you find out why they are looking for her?"

"She held an information-sensitive position in Vegas. I found out she'd made a deal with some Atlanta figures to get protection from Vegas which is why Atlanta mob won't spill where she is. Unfortunately for her, they are about done with her. She seems to have no allegiances, and they aren't gonna let it pass. They have her tabbed 24/7, and those days are numbered. They will probably order a hit."

"They are going to kill her? When?"

"Don't know, they may or they may not. She may redeem herself and be spared or they may kill her today or a week from now. It may already be too late."

"Anything else?"

"Nothing more about her or the Sills people."

"What about Eddie, the loan shark?"

"Oh, yeah. Eddie Cannon. He operates somewhere over in Decatur, but rumor has it he actually lives out in North Gwinnett or Barrow county somewhere."

"And what about the construction business and Vincent Artello?"

"As far as construction businesses, Vincent himself doesn't have any, but his main man does. Dan Sigarro has a company called Aries Engineering and Construction. Don't know how they use the business in their scheme of things, but there you have it."

I knew how they used it—empty buildings for torture, questioning, or killing, and poured cement for hiding bodies. I'd been at one of their sites the night before while following Grant.

"Thanks, Stuart. If or when you ever need me, just give me a call."

"I will."

I got up to leave.

"Hey." He stopped me by my good arm. "Come by and practice at my range sometime. It's the best in Atlanta."

I nodded agreement, not sure if that was an invitation or an order and further stipulation to our arrangement in exchange for his help.

I went by the information desk of the mall to ask for a phone book, but they didn't have one. I dialed information on my cell phone, but there was no listing for an Eddie Cannon anywhere in Atlanta. Perhaps he was too far outside the city. I decided I could have the taxi drive me around town, and I would start asking for him. A few street corners, a few bars, a couple of pool halls and I could find him I was certain. I looked at my watch—but what did the time matter? What else did I have to do?

But instead of looking for him by asking around the gritty streets, I decided to try a different route. I could use a phone book and look him up. I needed an address, and as Lindsey had pointed out to me previously, sometimes there are easy ways to find someone. I was going to have a huge taxi fee as the fare soared as we began the drive out toward Gwinnett, traveling north on Interstate 85. When I got far enough out, I had the taxi stop at a gas station, and I asked for a local phone book. Eddie hadn't been in the Atlanta directory, but he was in the local book, and I got an address—1081 Brown Thrasher Circle, Brazelton. I could call ahead, but a surprise visit seemed to make more sense. I usually don't want to give my suspects or witnesses opportunities to make things up or try to cover up.

It was another twenty-minute drive from the gas station. Around six o'clock the taxi pulled up the short drive to Eddie's brick ranch home. Houses along this street had older styles or looks, brown-stained roofs, and grown-up trees. Eddie's house in particular was probably nearly thirty years old but was still well kept with neat edged lawn, newly painted shutters and trim, and a bowl of daisies on the steps.

I asked the cab to wait. Then, careful not to bump my arm, I eased myself from the car and began up the walkway to the front but paused in my tracks. I heard voices and hammering from the backyard. The houses sat on ample-sized lots close to the street but with about a hundred feet of backyard, which in this case was fenced. I stood up on tiptoe and peered over the six-foot fence to see who I presumed to be Eddie, his wife, and two children.

Eddie was kneeling over some wood beams with a hammer in his right hand. His body language spoke of agitation; perhaps the project wasn't going well. Then I heard the sharp pitch of his wife's voice.

"Are you sure you should be doing it that way?" she asked.

"Just let me do this," he said. His voice was the same deep mellow tone I'd heard when he'd spoken with Mark. "I can't do this with you standing over me."

"Sorrr-rree," she said sarcastically, hands on hips, and she didn't back off.

I knocked vigorously on the gate and called loudly. This moved her to action. She came my way. One of her boys ran across her path, stick in hand. In one swoop she'd snagged it from his grasp and laid a wallop across his buttocks with it and never lost a step.

"I've told you not to play with sticks," she hollered over her shoulder, no sympathy to his crocodile cries.

"May I help you?" She squinted one eye and one brow raised suspiciously. Her glance flitted to my arm and then back to my eyes.

"Yes. I'm Paul Grey, a private investigator. Are you Eddie's wife?"

"Damn straight. You think I'd be havin' younguns with that man without a ring on this finger?" She waggled her hand before my face.

"Uh, no, that's not what I meant."

"I'm tired of you sorry-ass white trash always showing up at my place looking for money to pay for gambling or bills or whatever—"

I interrupted before she could further elaborate. "I'm sorry. That's not why I'm here—"

"Well then, why are you here?" She placed her hands on her hips and assessed me with a hair-to-toes scan, lingering again on the arm sling.

"I'm a private investigator. I'm here to ask Eddie some questions." I handed her my business card.

"Eddie, my Eddie? Is he in trouble? What did he do?" She unlatched the gate and let me in.

"Yes, your Eddie, but I'm not here about him really. I want to ask him about a client."

"A client? Lowlifes all of them. I'm so quick to judge 'cause they're always judging me. They think black, five kids, and assume I'm uneducated, illiterate, poor, and on welfare. You probably thought it, too."

"Actually, no. But I am guilty of judging people too quickly sometimes. Don't we all?"

"The ones coming to see Eddie are the worst. They judge, and they're the good-for-nothing ones. Hypocrites."

"Hypocrites, I agree," I said, thinking about her initial assumption about me.

"Now, don't play with me. Being downright agreeable to everything ain't gonna get you any closer than this to my Eddie."

She was a sturdy woman, and she was in my way. I smiled amicably.

"Don't give me a smile. I don't like the way you look," she said.

"Now wait a minute. You looked at me and saw middle-class, well-dressed white male, and at first you thought I was clientele for Eddie. Since you've been corrected, you now think I must be a cop or someone here to bust him. Either way, you've judged me in the same manner you hate to be judged. Doesn't that make you the hypocrite?"

"Huh." She huffed, but at least she didn't throw me out.

"Do unto others?" I suggested.

She folded her arms. "You're right. I didn't make you out to be smart either."

When I didn't laugh at her attempt to break the tension with humor she added, "I'm not sure now is the best time. He's in a very foul mood. This project has gotten to him."

My glance over her shoulder to Eddie revealed him steadfast at work. From the parts and pieces, including lattice, it appeared to be a gazebo.

"I can see that. A gazebo, is it?"

She nodded.

"I know a little about gazebo-building. Perhaps I could help him work while I talk to him? Make the work go faster and distract him?"

"Oh, Jesus, thank you. I'm not sure he's doin' it right. He needs the help. He's not much of a do-it-yourselfer."

We approached the work site.

"Eddie?" she called.

"What!?" He threw down his hammer and then turned to see me.

"You have a guest," she said. "And he can help you."

The look on his face was anything but the look of a man wanting help.

CHAPTER 20

"I don't need anybody's help, you devil of a woman. Now go away, both of you," Eddie sputtered.

"Eddie!" she chastised.

"What?" He looked up to see a very cross expression on his wife's face which I guess he understood from past experience. "Oh, O.K."

He stood up. "Eddie Cannon, and you are?"

"Paul Grey, a private investigator. I'm here to talk to you about Mark Sills."

"Hmm, Mark Sills? I don't think I know him."

"Yes, you do. He was a client, owed you a lot of money. And I believe he was killed before he could pay it back. "

"I don't have to talk to you. You're not a cop. Now get off my property before I call them."

"I need some answers first, if you don't mind."

"I do mind." He stepped forward.

"Now, Eddie," his wife cautioned.

I stepped back. "I'm not here to challenge you. If you don't talk to me, the cops will be here next, and it won't be to remove me. They'll be here with all the same questions I've got."

Eddie shifted to a less aggressive stance and thought a moment. "If what you say is true, they'll be here anyway, even if I do talk to you."

"True." I nodded. "But none of them will help you build your gazebo while they talk."

"What do you know about carpentry? How can you help? You have a lame arm."

"Well, my wife says I'm a fountain of useless knowledge and trivia. I may not be good labor, but I'm a good supervisor, and I can tell by looking here your first problem is your layout isn't squared up."

"Uh-huh, exactly what I said." Eddie's wife nodded excitedly.

"Shut-up, Corrianne," Eddie demanded. "And get the kids out of here. All their racket is giving me a headache."

"All right," she said and yelled, "Boys, come inside. Daddy's in a bad mood."

"I am not—" he began, but since he was already talking to her backside, he gave up.

"Hand me a tape measure," I said.

Eddie passed it over.

"The first thing we need is to use a long board and mark a five-foot span on it. Then we measure from one corner of the gazebo layout square. Measure three feet on one side and four on the other." I marked as I spoke. "Then we lay the five-foot piece across on a diagonal and move the pieces until the marks match up to make a 3-4-5 triangle, a right triangle."

"Pythagorean theorem," he said.

I nodded as I held the pieces together with my good arm while he hammered and then explained, "Once you've squared the corners you can use this same piece and three others like it to make the diagonal facets of the octagon."

Eddie got down on the ground to measure and mark the next corner.

"What will the overall size be?" I asked. "Ten or twelve foot?"

"Twelve."

"Easy. Five-foot facets will be perfect. Now, about Mark Sills, did he pay you back before he died? You knew he was killed?"

"Word travels fast in my business, so yes, I knew he was dead. And no, he didn't pay me."

"About your business, I know he was in financial trouble; he owed money to the mob, and his wife was murdered. Could her murder or Mark's be related to his financial problems?"

"Now, wait a minute. I have to scare 'em up a bit, even rough them up sometimes to get payment, but I haven't ever killed anyone for it." Eddie hammered a squared corner into place.

While he hammered I slowly measured and marked the next sides using my good arm.

"But you threaten them?" I asked.

"Well, yes. I've even broken some bones, but I won't have the death of a man on my list of sins at Judgment Day." He shook his head.

"I see."

"You don't believe me? I don't tell them that, of course. Fear of death is what motivates some of them. Besides, Mark's debt wasn't overdue."

I knew from the conversation I'd overheard between Eddie and Mark this was true, but I didn't say as much.

"What I believe doesn't matter," I said. "I'm simply after the truth. Any idea who would want Mark and his wife killed or why? You're the only one he owed money to."

"No, not true. He owed another loan, he owed the mob, and he probably owed his bookie for gambling."

"He'd paid the mob, and he'd paid the other loan with your loan."

"He told you that? You take his word, but not mine?"

"I didn't say that. Who was the other loan from? Do you know his name?"

"Her, actually. Her name is Desiree."

"No last name?"

"Nope. And him saying he paid her doesn't make it true."

"Do you believe Desiree, the mob, or the bookie would have killed Mark or his wife?"

"Desiree, no way. Mob, maybe. Bookie, I doubt it."

Eddie continued squaring and hammering his corners together.

"Why do you say that?"

"Well, I know Desiree's street rep, and she's tough, but it's tough love, not killing. She can sure as hell break a leg or bust a nose; she a tough mother trying to show them they need to do the right thing."

"The right thing being to pay up?"

"Yes. As for the bookie, most bookies keep a buffer. You send the money to an account, and they pay winnings in and draw losses out. I'm sure whatever Mark owed would be covered. Bookies make good money so they would be foolish to commit two murders. Not worth the risk the police would figure it out, don't you think?"

"Maybe. I hadn't found anything about a bookie. I knew he gambled."

"I think it's the mob."

"But why the mob? Why would they risk murder and the others wouldn't?"

"Why do they ever risk a murder, or gangs for that matter? The mob is a grown-up gang. You gotta keep them all in line. Mark was way out of line—he stole a lot of money from them. Maybe they killed him and his wife as a demonstration? And they have ways of keeping distance, keeping clean."

Eddie's sides were all finished. "Now what?"

On a scratch piece of paper I did some calculations.

"Now measure forty-two inches from each corner on both sides, and align your boards marked for five feet on the diagonal. Then screw them together." I took the board from his hands and demonstrated. "You'll need three more like this."

He nodded and went to his saw. I waited for the power-sawing to stop before I asked anything else. He marked his five-foot spans and began aligning them.

"This is working out great." He admired his even sides and screwed the first board into place.

"Ever heard of Vincent Artello?" I inquired.

"Yeah, of course. He's mob."

"Do you think he could be the one who had Mark killed?"

"Possible, I guess. The whole reason Mark needed money from me, was to pay him. But if he did pay, I don't know why they'd do him in unless it was to make an example." Eddie stopped the electric screwdriver and added, "Wait, unless he knew something, something they didn't want him to know."

"Like what?"

"I don't know. He worked for them, and he'd gotten greedy. I know he did things the mob considered out of line. Maybe he discovered something he shouldn't have." Eddie moved to the second board and secured it in place.

I thought of Cynthia Norris and whatever information it was she might possess. "Ever heard of Cynthia Norris?"

"Nope." Eddie still in a squat, scooted over to the next corner, and continued work.

"You know all these mob names, all the loan sharks, but never heard of Cynthia Norris? What about Gianina DeSantis?"

"Nope."

"Eddie, I know you're connected. You must know something."

"I don't know anything. Why are you accusing me of hiding something? I've got nothing to hide. I've told you everything I know."

"Exactly what I'd expect to hear from someone who's got something to hide." I shrugged. "Oh well, I guess you won't be needing my help then."

I watched as Eddie's eyes did a quick assessment of the work left to be done—holes to dig, lumber to cut, angles to measure.

"O.K., O.K. Give me a minute."

Eddie disappeared into the house and emerged a few minutes later with a boom box. He plugged it in on the deck and turned it up loud enough the rap came rumbling out and the speaker rattled. I worried about the neighbors.

Eddie sidled up close to me and whispered, his deep voice dropping even deeper, "You can't be too careful."

"Yeah, true," I agreed.

He knelt down to secure his last board. I crouched down beside him.

"I know who you're talking about. She was having an affair with Mark, and she's all trouble. She's got affiliations with two mobs, one here and one elsewhere."

"Las Vegas, I know. Tell me something I don't know."

"I will, it's just..."

"What?"

"I've got my wife and kids to think about. I shouldn't be talking to you. They may not like it." Eddie stood up to get the post hole digger.

"They won't ever know," I assured him, moving closer to continue our clandestine conversation.

"Yeah, right," Eddie said sarcastically as he began to pound the post hole digger into the unforgiving earth. "Anyway, she was a key player in Vegas. She has some important numbers in her head—overseas bank accounts. She picked up money and made deposits. She has access to their accounts. Enough money to make oneself disappear for good, buy a private island somewhere, you know. But, I think she's smart enough not to try to do it, though. And she supposedly knows lots of names—people in the government that have been bought. Lots of high-powered people who want to keep her quiet. She brokered a deal to come to Atlanta, but she didn't honor her end. She's got no allegiances, and she'd going to end up dead. It's a question of which mob is going to get to her first."

Eddie paused, out of breath from pounding the ground and talking at the same time.

"Well, the Las Vegas ones don't know where she is."

"Or maybe they do, and they want to make sure she hasn't given the information to anyone else, like Mark. She probably thought having all that information would protect her, and maybe it has to some degree."

"Would she kill Mark or his wife?" I asked as Eddie began digging his hole again.

"I could see where she might kill the wife to get her out of the way, but not Mark. I believe she told Mark everything. She probably made him commit the names and numbers to heart so if anything happened to her he could turn the information over to the cops. She needed him alive."

"He told you this?"

"Well, not in so many words. Let's say I like to know a lot about my clients and all their risk factors before I make a loan. We had some in-depth conversations before I loaned him money the first time. And I checked him out, a little investigation I did myself." Eddie grimaced, a proud smile combined with hard labor.

"And you loaned him the money? You didn't see a risk the mob might kill him?"

"Well, the affair with Cynthia was over. I wasn't sure the mob even knew about it. It was her job to be close to him. I thought if he paid the mob what he'd stolen from their accounts, he'd be all right."

"What? Her job to be close to him?"

"Yeah, I think that's how I understood it. She was keeping watch on him. She was getting close because the mob wanted her to."

"Really? Huh."

Eddie had finished digging the first hole. He took the tool to work on the second hole while I prepared the post and hand-shoveled in cement about the pole. I wasn't sure what to ask him next, if anything. He'd confirmed my information about Cynthia and my suspicion she might have killed Nikki.

Yelling from the direction of the fence gate startled us both. Eddie shut off the music.

"I know him," I said to Eddie. "Police Detective Martin Jeffries."

"Oh, great." He sighed. "I guess I have to let him in."

"I'd make him do some work while you talk," I suggested under my breath as I followed him over to the gate. "I've got what I wanted. Tell him only what you need to."

Eddie nodded and handed me the post hole digger.

"Hello, Martin." I smiled from inside the gate. "This is Eddie Cannon. Eddie this is Detective Martin Jeffries."

"I'm here to ask you some questions about Mark Sills, a client of yours," Jeffries said.

Eddie unlocked the gate. "Come on in."

"You're just in time." I handed Jeffries the post hole digger. "We've started digging the holes, and I was about to leave."

Jeffries took the tool, a confused look upon his face. "Yeah, O.K."

"Thanks, Eddie, for your help. Good luck with your project." I shut the gate as I departed, feeling a little smug at having gotten to Eddie first and giving Jeffries a little extra work to do. Then I remembered—the taxi.

CHAPTER 21

I arrived back at Cynthia's apartment tired and not ready to stay up all night on surveillance. On a quick tour on foot through the apartment parking lot, it didn't appear she was home. I returned to wait in my car, which I had parked in my usual position in the driveway. I noticed Grant wasn't in his usual spot and assumed he was out following Cynthia, wherever she was. I *had* to make her talk, but how? She could easily have killed Nikki since she lived in the building. I'd have to come up with a plan.

Then I noticed Grant had arrived, but walked past his usual post and was approaching the building on foot. What was he up to?

He disappeared inside and didn't come back out. How was it he was able to get inside and remain there if he wasn't a tenant? I got out of my car. I crept by the lobby window and looked for him, but he was not there. I went to the door and was promptly buzzed in.

"Hello," I said, approaching the red-haired girl.

"It's you again." She held back none of her disappointment. "I told you everything I know."

"Joyce, the man who came in before me. Do you know him?"

"No."

"Where did he go? Why did you let him in?"

"He's a cop. He went up to do some work in Mr. Sills' apartment."

I glanced over at the elevators. The one elevator was on its way down; the other stopped at the fifteenth floor—Cynthia's floor.

"Did he show you identification?" I asked.

"Yes, of course. I am doing my job here," she said defensively.

"Yes, I know. What did his identification say?"

"He's with the police, like I said."

This wasn't going to lead anywhere I could see. She didn't know anything. As far as she knew, he really was a cop. He must have had some fake badge to flash at her.

Then it began to make sense to me. The mob had ordered a hit on Cynthia. He was going up to wait for her and then kill her in her own apartment. My attacker in the park had probably been him, trying to get me out of the way. Of course, my car had been left there while I was in the hospital and taken the taxi around to do my investigating, so it hadn't moved all day. He probably assumed I was still hospitalized or otherwise off the case and he was free to do his dirty work.

Luckily, I'd seen him go inside. Now the trick would be to catch Cynthia and not allow her to go up to her apartment.

"I'm going to have to wait here until Cynthia Norris comes back."

"Cynthia Norris? Why?"

"It has to do with the same case; trust me. I'll stay out of the way. Is there somewhere I can sit?"

She motioned to a small chair around the corner, which I took. I watched the small television on her desk while I passed the time. Tenants came and went fairly regularly.

Around ten o'clock, Cynthia came in. I jumped up to catch her.

"Cynthia, Cynthia." I grabbed her arm as she approached the elevator. "We have to talk. Now. And not here."

"What are you talking about? I already told you I'm not talking to you." She shook my hand loose and looked down at my sling. "What happened to you?"

"Listen, you can't go up to your apartment. Your time is up, if you know what I mean."

"No, I don't." She tapped her foot in an agitated manner.

"Ma'am, is everything O.K.?" The security girl asked.

"Yes, everything is fine," Cynthia replied and pressed the elevator button again.

Thankfully, both elevators were up and taking their time coming back down, giving me a chance to persuade her.

"Joe Pagliani said you didn't have much time left until they found you. Well, they found you." I pointed up towards her apartment.

"Ah." She nodded, finally understanding. "What do you propose?"

"We need to get out of here, quickly," I explained and then said to the girl at the counter, "Call Martin Jeffries at the police department. Tell him to send cars here and to Colony Square. And this is important, tell him not to let any of the men go inside either place until they see either a signal from me or trouble of some kind. Also important, tell him to send the cars silent, no sirens. Got it?"

The girl nodded, a serious look to her face.

Cynthia and I scooted out the door, and I whisked her across the street to the Colony Square Hotel. We went up to the dining area and got a table.

"You have worn out your welcome here in Atlanta," I explained.

"I thought you said it was Joe and his guys that found me."

"Either way." I shrugged. "Your only chance is to go to the police now."

"No way. I can leave now, even without packing, and go to another city."

"I can't let you go. I know you killed Nikki Sills. An officer under hypnosis reported seeing her being thrown over the balcony."

"By me?"

"Then you killed Mark. I heard the mob report on it."

"You believe them?"

"Look, why don't you start at the beginning at be honest about it. That's the only way anyone is going to be able to help you out of this."

"Or I can go out on my own and take my chances."

"And eventually the mob will find and kill you. I've heard you know a lot, enough to put some major players away. Why not use it? Why not plea-bargain to help yourself and give them some major payback?"

"Plea-bargain? Again, you're assuming I am guilty of something. How do I know this isn't a set-up? Maybe you've been sent to kill me. Maybe there's not even anyone in my apartment."

"We can go and find out," I suggested and swept my good arm in a motion saying, "After you."

She shook her head. "No, I do actually believe you. My taro reading a while back told me I'd have to trust a stranger, I just didn't understand what it meant until today. It was a matter of time until the mob found me. And I have no protection now."

"Your protection was Mark Sills? He knew what you know and was supposed to turn it over if anything happened to you, right?"

"Yes, that's why I didn't kill him. I needed him."

"How did you end up with needing protection from not one but two mobs in the first place?"

"It's a long story."

"I've got time. And you need to take the time to tell me. You know running at this point won't make any difference."

She shrugged. "It might for me."

"If you really want to make a difference, tell me who killed Mark and Nikki Sills. Make the people responsible pay for it. And I'm sure whatever information you have could reveal other crimes, other things deserving punishment."

"Yes."

"If you don't clear things up, all the evidence makes it appear you are the guilty party. Even the profile of the murderer for Mark Sills fit you perfectly."

"How so?"

"You were disgruntled. He'd dumped you, and you were angry at him for it. The police psychologist said someone who loved him killed him."

"Or someone trying to set me up."

"And who is that? You will have to tell me or the police or both. You want it to be over, otherwise you wouldn't have come with me to talk here, knowing the police were on their way."

"Well, I wanted to see what you had planned. See if you had anything up your sleeve."

"I don't. I want some answers."

"Jeez, where would I even start?"

"I don't care. Explain it all. Start at the beginning."

"What do you already know?"

"Tell me everything, and I'll let you know if it can be skipped."

She took a deep breath and sighed. "Can I get some coffee?"

"Certainly." I motioned to a waitress and placed an order for coffee and dessert.

"Let's start with Las Vegas. In Vegas, I was a bag woman, not in the street sense. A bag woman was a money transfer from one place to another for the mob. I handled large money laundering transfers and deposits into all the bank accounts locally and offshore. I wasn't married to or connected to the mob in any way when I started, so I was above suspicion for the police. I got in a full two years before they took notice. Meanwhile, I had all the account numbers and security information all up here." She pointed to her head.

"So you could drain a financial account very easily."

"Yes, I could have taken millions, probably enough to disappear with, but the more you take the less willing the mob is to *let* you disappear. They would have found me and killed me for sure."

"Why did you want to leave?"

"Well, I got arrested once, and it scared me. I spent a week in jail and decided it wasn't worth the risk. What if I got convicted of something and had to spend a long time in jail? I couldn't do it."

"So you asked to be let go?"

"Sort of. I made friends with a guy. You mentioned him—Joe.

He's in a protectionary role. I met him when they got me out of jail and off the hook. Anyhow, I got cozy with him, hoping when I wanted to go, he'd help me."

"But he wouldn't?"

"No. Whenever I brought up the idea, he'd dismiss it as crazy. 'Suicide' was his exact word." Cynthia accepted her cup of coffee from the waitress.

"So then what?" I prodded.

"So I decided I'd have to make the move on my own." She shrugged and opened two sugar packets, dumping them in her coffee. "I figured if I could get work with another mob, in a role where they needed me, they'd protect me from the guys in Vegas. If Vegas people killed me, it'd be like an act of war on the other mob."

"So you came to Atlanta?"

"Not right away. I found who I needed to find and got an assignment. My job was to watch Mark Sills."

"Watch Mark? I thought you loved him."

"An unintentional by-product. I was taken in by the Atlanta mob because they knew they could use me. I was the right person at the right time. They thought my looks were exotic enough to capture Mark's attention and hold it. Then I was supposed to find out how much money he'd taken and how he'd done it. Mark evidently had previous affairs, and they were certain he'd go for me."

"And he did."

"The proverbial hook, line, and sinker." She took a small sip. "We started having our little 'get togethers' last year at a storage place—sordid yet a turn-on at the same time." She paused and licked her lips. "Anyhow, I didn't realize at first he was also looking for a way out of the mob. We were two of a kind. He gave me all the information I was looking for and some I wasn't. He gave me names and connections and methods. Sooner than I knew it, I had sensitive information again. Then they couldn't let me go."

"So now you're in deep with both." I took a drink.

"Yes. Mark was giving the information to me as a way of protecting himself."

"So did you tell him about your assignment?"

"Hell, no. He'd have turned and run and gotten us both killed. Besides, by that point we both really liked each other. I know for me it was no longer a job to be with him. But I did tell him about Vegas and my problems with them. So then he got an earful of my information."

"You both became lifesavers for the other, so to speak."

"Yes, we both committed to memory what the other knew. We knew the risk. If one of us got killed..." She stopped, cupped her mug, and stared down into its murky brown as if looking into a crystal ball. "We never intended for it to happen."

"What?"

"Death. We thought we'd cheated it and we'd get out scot-free." Cynthia's eyes developed a faraway look, staring right through her drink.

"So how did it happen? Who killed him?" I tried to get her back.

"I'm getting there, O.K.?" Hands still cupped securely around the mug, her head snapped up and her eyes narrowed. "Let me take my time telling this. In December, when Atlanta offered to get me an apartment in the same building as Mark, I decided I was valuable enough and could make the move from Vegas safely. I arranged for a name change, and the Atlanta mob promised to keep my location a secret and not inform on me as long as I did what they told me to."

"So you left Vegas and came here."

"Mark was extremely happy. We were making plans. He put me as primary beneficiary in his will, so if anything happened to him I'd get the money. We were in love."

"What about Nikki? You killed her to get her out of the way?" I took a bite of the cheesecake placed in front of me.

Cynthia did the same and answered with her mouth full. "No, we could have run off, but it was Mark's idea to stay. It was his idea to kill Nikki for the insurance. Her money would come to him and then if he died it would come to me."

"So you killed him, too. Because you thought you'd get all the money."

"No. We planned it together, to kill her. Then we'd take all the money and disappear together into some small, dink town in the middle of nowhere. We were going to open up a pizza place."

"So what happened? Mark changed his mind and decided not to kill her?"

"It's not so simple. I was assigned to watch Mark. I had already begun reporting on him before I realized I was in love with him, before I moved here. Then it was too late. Once they had the information I'd gotten, they wanted him killed—as a warning to others. I was supposed to do it."

"And did you?"

"No! Of course not. I had to tell him the truth. I had to tell him everything, hoping he'd leave with me, skip town. But he refused."

"When was this?"

"About two months ago. But instead of leaving, he bargained with them, said he'd pay the money back in ten days. He thought they'd let him live. He was angry I hadn't told him sooner. He told me he was going back to Nikki. He said he couldn't believe he'd been brainwashed by me into nearly killing his wife. It didn't help she'd told him she was pregnant either. He was feeling guilty, too."

"So why didn't you leave without him?" I continued to pick at my dessert between sips of coffee.

"My horoscope told me a loved one would come around, if I would stick by him. I thought I could convince him. I'd give it a while and see. I kept telling my boss Mark had more information, if they'd let me keep working on him. I kept putting off the need to kill him. I told them they'd get their money back and Mark was good for his word. He paid it back, but it didn't matter."

"They were going to kill him either way?"

"Yes, and I tried to tell him." She shrugged then licked her dessert fork and got another bite. "Meanwhile, I needed him and my position to protect myself. I'd made the switch to Atlanta, which was risky. I tried talking some sense into Mark, but he was convinced he needed to do the right thing and go back to Nikki."

Things were starting to come together. I realized when the affair had appeared to end, it was really just when she moved to Atlanta. Once she was here the affair continued until very recently.

Cynthia continued, "So, I decided I had to approach it from the other side. I went to see Nikki to see if I could get her to understand. If Mark stuck around it would put her and her baby at risk. It would be better if he left."

"How did you tell her? Did you tell her about your affair?"

"I didn't come right out with it, but she pretty much already knew. She was a smart lady. Anyhow, the day of the race, I was at her place. I knew Mark wouldn't be there."

"Did he know you were there?"

"No. I came around to talk to her. When she opened the door, she had a towel on her head; she'd been in the shower. I told her bluntly who I was and asked to talk. It started out civilized; she made me some tea. We sat in the living room to talk. She invited me to stay to watch the race."

"What made it turn uncivilized?"

"Me. I was sitting out on the balcony with her. We'd brought two chairs out to sit on, and I was looking at her. She was beautiful—lush blonde hair, and her eyes, a man could get lost in them, I could see it. Her skin, everything, the perfection of her. And the baby, his baby. I felt this terrible rush of jealousy."

"So you killed her in a jealous rage?"

"No. Who's telling the story?" She stopped angrily.

"You. Sorry. Go ahead."

Cynthia took her time getting started again. She took a bite of cake, sat silently chewing, then washed it down with her coffee. "I need a refill," she said.

"No problem." I got the attention of our waitress again, who promptly brought a new cup.

Cynthia again added sugars while I waited for her to continue. She cleared her throat. "I told Nikki about Mark and me and the mob. I told her about the danger for her and her child if she remained involved with him. She told me she wasn't involved, she was married to him. I was the one who involved him in all this mess, she accused. She said he wouldn't have stolen from the mob unless I'd driven him to do it, which wasn't true."

"She didn't accept any responsibility for their financial problems?"

"No." She blew on her coffee to cool it.

"Why didn't you tell her about the insurance policies and Mark's plot to kill her?"

"Oh, I did. She didn't believe me. I kept getting more and more angry. There was a lot of commotion, music, and noise. I felt so flustered, my heart and mind. I was so angry at her selfishness. She would get them both killed. Mark was dead if he stuck around, she didn't see it. She thought I wanted her out of the way so I could have him. I wanted him to live, with or without me, it didn't matter." Cynthia slammed down her coffee mug. Some of the dark brew sloshed onto the tablecloth. "She wouldn't listen. I began to see. She would have to be out of the picture. She'd never let him go; she was killing him. I could see, if she was gone, it would all work out. Mark would be safe; I'd be safe. He'd come back to me, and we'd be together."

"You thought if you killed his wife, he'd change his mind and be with you?"

"Well, when you put it that way, no. I was saving him, don't you see?"

"So how did you do it?"

"We were sitting. She could see I was getting angry, but she wouldn't bend. She asked me to leave. She stood up to show me out. I assessed it, and I knew I could take her. I hit her, hard, to try to knock her out. I wasn't trying to make it look like a suicide. I wasn't planning on staying around. I was getting rid of her. She fell, almost unconscious, but she wasn't out long. She was totally disoriented and I quickly picked her up over my shoulder and was lifting her to put her over the rail, when she grabbed the pot and plant and held on to them. With the leverage, I couldn't get her over. When I tried to move her and re-grasp, the plant and pot were lifted off the hook and she dropped them. She yelled, but the music and the chopper were so loud, her screams were drowned out. She tried to get her hands on the rail, but she couldn't. I had her by the torso and her legs. I flipped her over, and she went. I didn't stick around."

"No. Why would you? You went back to your place downstairs, locking the door behind you."

"Yes. I set up the one chair which had been knocked over and I put the other chair back in the bathroom first, to make sure it looked like only one person had been there. And I had a key; I was supposed to kill Mark. I'd lifted Mark's keys from him one time when we were together and passed them off so the mob could get a key made for me. I locked the deadbolt from the outside and that was it."

"But you left behind a glass with fingerprints?"

"I did? Oh, yes, I did. My mistake."

"Mark knew you did it. You killed her."

"Yes, he knew."

"Why didn't he turn you in? Why didn't he tell me about you when I came around asking, or tell the police?"

"I don't know. I think it was because he still had feelings for me, even though he didn't want to. Plus I still had his information, and he had mine. We still each served as a protection for the other."

"So who killed Mark? The mob?"

"It must have been. It wasn't me. The mob here realized I loved Mark and would never kill him. I guess they put two and two together, and they knew I had no allegiances to them or Nevada, only to Mark. They ordered me one last time to kill him, probably to see if I'd come around to my 'senses' as they would put it."

"Why would Grant, who's waiting in your apartment, tell them you killed Mark? I heard him."

"I have no idea. We can go ask him."

"Uh, risky."

"Yeah, story of my life thus far. Well, Mark wouldn't come near me. He wanted nothing to do with me because he suspected I killed Nikki. I was angry with him for not seeing what sacrifices I'd made for him. I was risking everything every second I stuck around, but I wanted to make sure."

"Make sure?"

"Make sure he'd be all right, make sure he didn't change his mind and want to come with me. I did confront him, trying to force him to see my side. I was angry when he didn't want to be with me, but I didn't kill him."

"You fit the profile. Everything you said fits perfectly."

"Well, I guess I was set up then. The mob killed him; they got two birds with one stone. They got rid of him. He knew too much, and he'd stolen from them. And me, either they'd kill me later, which it looks like that's the case, or, if I got arrested, I'd be locked up for two murders and who would listen to my story? Maybe they'd even have me killed in prison so I couldn't plea-bargain or testify against any of them."

"But I'm telling you, the mob thinks you killed Mark. I heard them. So why would they kill you now?"

"I don't know, but if they are turning on me, I can turn on them. I guess I'd be willing to give you my evidence and information on both Nevada and Atlanta if you think it would get me a reduced sentence. I know we're surrounded by now, and I won't be leaving except in a body bag or a police car."

"Why the change of heart?"

"It's not really a change of heart. I guess it's my destiny. My horoscope told me I must give up a dream today to make amends, but everything will be okay."

"You follow your horoscope that closely? You believe it?"

"Yes, and I can't believe a jury wouldn't see this my way. I'm a victim, too. I'll serve my time, and when I get out I can turn my life around."

"Assuming the mob will let you alone."

"As much as I hated jail when I was in, I'd rather go to jail than die."

"But, they could kill you in jail."

"Not if I had witness protection. With the right security measures, they wouldn't find me."

"The mob seems to have their ways. They got someone into your apartment building. They have cops on their side."

"True. Even if I did get killed by the mob, at least I'll know I made some things right. I can't deny my fate, to make amends. I can help put some major players behind bars if I turn evidence over. Do you think I could get a reduced sentence?"

"I can't guarantee anything. I don't do law."

"I want some assurances."

"I'm sorry. I can't assure you of anything. I think a prison term for voluntary manslaughter is about ten years, getting out at six years for good behavior or for a deal."

"I would want to be in the witness protection program and relocated."

"I don't—"

"I know, I know. Call someone who can make me a deal."

I called the police station and asked them to put me through to Detective Jeffries.

"Hey, man, where are you?" Jeffries asked.

"Inside the Colony Square Hotel restaurant. Cynthia wants to cut a deal. In exchange for information she has on the mob, she wants a reduced term and witness protection."

"I can't authorize anything. I'll have to get back to you."

"He'll have to get back to us. Is that O.K.?" I asked Cynthia.

"Yeah, fine." She nodded.

"She's good with that. Call me on this cell number," I replied. "Where are you?"

"Outside your position."

"Good deal."

Cynthia and I discussed her plan further, working through all the possibilities.

"What if they say no deal or no to the witness protection?" I asked.

"No deal is no deal. If I'm going to give myself up, that's one thing. If I'm going to give up more than myself, then I need something in return."

"What about making amends? You'll still go to jail either way."

"Ah, yes, but hopefully for a shorter time and securing my safety as well. Without the witness protection, I'd rather die now than go to jail only to wait around for it later. I'd never be safe, I'd live every day wondering when death would come."

"But one never knows when they will die. How is this different?"

"Most of us aren't murdered, as will be the case with me. Most people don't worry about death because they assume they'll live to a natural old age. I won't have that luxury."

"You said everything would be fine according to your horoscope."

"True, but it doesn't say what I need to do to make that happen. I need to look out for myself, too."

"So you'd rather die now, even today?"

"Pretty much. Maybe I have to die to make amends."

I leaned back into my seat in disbelief. I could believe she killed Nikki, even Mark, but I couldn't believe anyone would be willing to give up their own life so easily.

"Am I that difficult to understand? You don't seem to respect any of my decisions, the way I do things."

"I don't agree with your choices, no. You have killed someone. You have lived a life a crime, working for the mob. You're selfish. You won't turn over evidence to help the police unless you get something out of it. I'm the opposite."

"Yah, yah. You fight crime; you help the police. You put people like me away."

"Exactly. But at the same time, I do want to understand. It would help me."

"Help you become a better detective?" She scoffed.

My cell phone rang and with anxiety I answered, hoping it was Jeffries and we'd have a deal.

"It's Jeffries," he said. "Here's the deal. First off, we don't know if she really knows anything or not, so we can't make promises until we hear what she has. If she has something good, we can cut her time served. Second, she would have to surrender and turn herself in as her first act of good faith. She can surrender through you or a lawyer."

"What about witness protection?"

"No deal. Not until she comes in first and we find out what she has. There's a chance we won't be able to do anything for her. She might want to seek out legal counsel for help on all this."

"I'll relay the message. I don't think this will go well."

Cynthia eyes lifted quickly to meet mine. "No deal? I'm shocked."

"Well, a deal is tentative. You would have to surrender first and give your information. Then they would decide on working a sentencing deal and witness protection."

"That's ludicrous. Who in their right mind would give away all their cards they have to bargain with?"

"Jeffries suggested you get a lawyer."

"Screw this. I'm getting out of here, that's what I'm doing." She stood up.

"Where are you going?" I stood up to follow her.

"To my apartment, to take my chances."

"You'll be killed." I quickly tossed some cash out on the table, more than covering the bill. But I didn't have time to wait for change as she took off.

"Not necessarily. Even if, it will satisfy me. I'll be dead; I've lost everything, so why not? The police will be able to get my murderer, since they are right outside. Maybe he'll turn over evidence for them. Maybe this is how I make amends."

"Don't do this." I lightly took her arm near the elbow to try to slow her.

"Do what?" She stopped and turned to face me. "At least this way maybe I can get some answers, find out who killed Mark. I'm going to ask the guy in my apartment for some answers. They owe me that before I go."

"How do you know he won't shoot you as you open the door?"

"I don't, but usually the standard operating procedures are a little more discreet."

I followed her out. "Would you like an officer to go up with you? I'm sure they would agree to go."

"I don't think so."

"What about me? Would you allow me to go?"

"You have a death wish?" She chortled, an ugly sound like a snorting boar.

"No, I think he'll find it harder to get rid of both of us."

"I don't care if I die. You do. That's the problem." She took off again.

"So can I come?" I asked.

"No." She shook her head without even turning around.

I followed only a pace behind her all the way out of the hotel, into the street, and up the walk to her apartment, the entire while trying to change her mind.

"This is where I leave you." She stood before the front desk.

"What's the problem, ma'am?" the security girl asked. "Why did you have me call the police before you left earlier?"

"It's nothing. Everything's fine," she replied curtly.

"No, it's not. She's lying," I said. Two glares, one shocked and one angry, pierced me.

"He no longer needs to be in the building. He does not have my permission to come up." She waggled a finger at me. Then she jumped on an elevator before I could argue further.

I pushed the button to try to reopen the doors.

"Sir, you can't go up," the security girl warned.

"Joyce, she's in danger. That's why I had you call the police."

"There's a police officer in here already, remember?"

"No. He's not a cop. Don't you think it's strange an officer went up, yet I had you call the police? Wouldn't they know an officer was already here?"

Her expression changed from stern to worried, thoughtful.

"So who is that guy?"

"An imposter. He's here to kill her. He's not a cop." I watched as the elevator reached fifteen, then urgently said, "I need a key—a master key so I can get in."

She unlocked and pulled open a drawer and began to dig around. Then she paused, her hand still inside. "How do I know you're not the one trying to kill her?"

"Oh, for God's sake. I wouldn't have brought her back if I wanted her dead. Call the cops again. Repeat what I've told you. They need to send men up. They're right outside. A key, I need a key." I pointed to the drawer.

She continued stirring the contents of the drawer with her hand. Producing a large set of keys, she said, "It's one of these."

She flipped one by one. "Ah, fifteen, this one."

I grabbed it from her and worked at un-threading it from the chain while she picked up the phone and dialed.

"I'm going up," I said.

The phone wedged between her shoulder and her ear, she nodded. I was in the elevator before I knew if she got through to the police or not. I tried Jeffries' number myself and got a busy signal. Damn. I tried to visualize Cynthia's floor plan, remembering only the little I had seen of it when I'd delivered food to her door. From what I could piece together, I was certain it was similar to the Sills' apartment, only mirror imaged.

The elevator opened on floor fifteen, and I approached Cynthia's apartment door tenaciously. I pulled out my cell phone and dialed the number I had for Grant. Then, standing at the door, I listened carefully for his phone ringing inside. Where was he?

I heard the distinct tones of the William Tell Overture and muffled voices, enough for me to know my suspect wasn't right inside the door. This gave me a few seconds. I wasn't trained in SWAT procedures. Could I get in and get him in my sights before he got me? Did I have the element of surprise on my side? Was he busy taking care of Cynthia? I pulled out my gun and readied it. Then realized I had big problems. With my injury and my sling I couldn't hold my gun and unlock the door at the same time. I really couldn't even handle the gun. I wasn't much of a one-armed shot. I was going to have to unlock the door and hope I could do it quietly enough I wouldn't be discovered. And then I would have to enter and use my one hand for the gun. Why weren't the police here yet? Why couldn't they do this?

I took the key and gently, ever so slightly, slipped it bit by bit into the lock. I put my ear up to the door. I could still hear muffled voices, so I twisted the key, hoping the turning and unlocking of the door wouldn't be heard over the conversation. Then I slowly and gently withdrew the key and pocketed it.

In order to have my gun ready I was going to have to turn the knob and open the door with my bum arm. I took a deep breath and prepared for the rush in. My palms sweated, the gun feeling slick in my hand, unsteady. I licked my dry lips, and as I swallowed hard I could feel my pulse rise in my throat.

CHAPTER 22

Just as I was about to go barging in, I decided maybe I could wait. I didn't have to be the hero. There didn't seem to be any pressing need for me to go in right then. The muffled voices continued, without elevation of pitch or any sign of anxiety. I stood and listened. The voices were almost conversational, no, almost jovial.

Had the two of them been in this together all along? Were they working together? Were they working to thwart me, to throw me off? As long as there didn't seem to be a problem, I was content to wait outside, although I did want to know what was being said. I stuck my ear so hard on the door it felt suctioned. I heard a laugh, then an angry voice. Then something smashed from where I assumed would be the kitchen area.

Time to go in. Anger and smashing things wasn't good; time for some heroics. I twisted the knob on the door and it opened, quickly and with moderate noise. I had my gun up and ready. I scanned the foyer and what I could see of the living room and kitchen. No one.

Then the voices again. It was the kitchen. They were both bent down, picking something up. That's why I couldn't see them. I could hear them, and it was opportunity knocking—they couldn't see me. They were so distracted I was busy sneaking around to the doorway to take aim.

About halfway there, while crouched under the pass-through window to the living room, my ankle popped. I froze. I held my breath. The two of them seemed not to have noticed. Their conversation continued. I remained crouched and listened. The discussion, almost friendly,amicable it seemed. The whole situation didn't feel right.

Inching slowly around the corner, I pulled myself more upright and took aim. Both persons were clearly in my sights. Grant appeared startled to see me, Cythnia not so much. They were picking up shards of glass from the kitchen floor. Something had broken. My gun was pointed at them, and they stood up slowly, Cynthia in front of Grant.

"Put your hands where I can see them," I demanded.

Cynthia raised her hands, palms extended and open. Grant was doing the same, but then, in a frenzied rush, threw his arm around

Cynthia's neck and put a sharp piece of glass to her throat, pulling her back into his chest and holding her there.

Cynthia's eyes bulged in fear. In her stiffened posture, she nearly fell backwards. Grant stumbled a little, but held her securely.

"I told you to stay out of this, I can handle it," Cynthia fumed. "Look now and see what you've done."

"I heard breaking glass and loud voices. I thought he was going to kill you," I explained.

"Huh. In case you hadn't noticed, I wasn't in this situation until you came barging in." She moved her arm up and down, displaying herself.

"She's right." I addressed Grant. "You weren't trying to kill her a minute ago. Were you biding your time, waiting for the right moment?"

"No," he explained. "You have it all wrong. I don't want to kill her."

"I think he's telling the truth. He wasn't holding anything like this." She motioned to her neck. "Until you arrived waving around a gun."

"You startled me," Grant explained. "I, we, didn't know who you were or what you plan on doing."

"I plan on holding you here until the police arrive. If you don't want to kill her, then let her go," I said.

"Yeah, let me go," she demanded.

"No, sorry. She's my collateral now. I don't want to kill her, but I will if I have to, so back off."

"What is it you want? Why are you here?" I asked.

"Well, I was supposed to be keeping an eye on her for the mob while they figured out a way to get rid of her. You're very complicated, you know," he said to her. "Having come from Las Vegas spared you a while. They couldn't dispose of you until both sides were sure you hadn't given any information to anyone else."

"But I did," she said.

"Yes, I know you did. That was what I told them. So then they needed to find out who knew and how much. They had to assess; would they need to kill those persons?"

"So they determined Mark had to die?" I asked.

"Yes, and then Cynthia, too. But the more I got to see of her, the more I knew I couldn't do it."

"So you were supposed to kill her?" I asked, but to myself I wondered, *Where is Jeffries? What is taking so long for them to get up here?*

"At first, no. But now, yes."

"What? Kill me?" Cynthia interrupted.

"Is that why you came after me yesterday morning?" I ignored Cynthia's query and lifted my arm and sling to show my injury. "This way, I'd be out of the way, no witnesses."

"I wasn't trying to kill you," Grant explained. "I needed to get you out of the way. I needed you gone, no witnesses."

"You were trying to kill me."

"What are you talking about? You were going to kill him then come for me?" Cynthia asked.

"No. I wasn't going to kill you either. I wanted to make you an offer, like I was telling you, to get away. But if we made a getaway, no one could know where we went. Including him." Grant indicated me.

"He's made an offer?" I asked.

"He was waiting outside. He said he was with the mob, not some lonely guy looking for a date, and needed to talk to me."

"And you let him in?"

"Well, he wasn't trying to kill me," she explained. "We were talking and he was getting around to the offer, so to speak."

"So what's the offer?"

"He'd help me get away."

"Yes. I'd help you get away. We'd both get away, and we'd be together," Grant explained.

"Together?" Cynthia seemed shocked.

"Yes, you and me. I love you."

"Now wait." Cynthia's eyes widened. "Oh, oh. It was you. You killed Mark."

She struggled briefly to break Grant's choke hold around her neck, but the shard of glass pressed tighter to her neck, and she let her arms flop. "You can't love me; you barely know me."

"I know everything about you," he explained. "It's been my job to watch you and study you. I know your favorite food, your favorite perfume, shit, I know you better than you do in some ways."

"What the hell are you talking about? You're blabbering." Cynthia reached up and took hold of Grant's arm around her neck and tried again to break free.

"Cynthia, shut up," I demanded. I could see and understand the whole picture now. I could see the story on Grant's face. Rejection or denial wouldn't be Cynthia's best move. Jeffries had better hurry up. "Don't say anything else. Let the man speak."

"Who are you to tell me to be quiet, you—" she began, but a tightened grip from Grant cut her off.

"Shut up," he said. "He's right. Let me talk."

"You're the boss," she said. Grant's grip loosened a smidgen with her agreement.

"Everything I've done has been for you." He stroked the side of her face, still holding the sharp piece of glass. "You were supposed to do it, but you didn't, so I've given up everything for you."

"What are you talking about?" she demanded.

"Two of a kind," I commented. What was it with these people and surveillance? Everyone falling in love with each other. It was a good thing I didn't have that problem. I added, "Maybe you two deserve each other."

Cynthia clenched her jaw and her fists. If she were loose, she may have hit me, but she was effectively restrained.

"I've tried so hard to put off your death sentence. I've done all I could. I told them you were coming around. Then I killed Mark, but I told them you did it, you'd followed through on your orders. I tried to make it look like you killed him."

"You did a good job," I said. "I'm surprised she hasn't been arrested for it yet."

"I hoped with Mark gone, they'd think you'd reformed your allegiances, and we could have time to get away. It would give us some time before they figured out you hadn't killed him. I thought with Mark gone, you might love me. I'd give up the mob; we'd be together."

"Love you? Why would I want to be with you?" Cynthia asked. She wasn't getting the idea. She laughed. "How could I love you?"

I shot her a stern look that said, *Shhhh, you idiot*, and *Stop* at the same time. Grant's fingers pressed the glass a little more stiffly against her skin.

"Ow, ow, ohhhh," she complained.

"Perhaps if we'd gotten to discuss this without him barging in—" He indicated me, the gun. "I was going to get us both away."

"I thought you were telling *me* how to get away, not for us to be together," Cynthia said.

"Something for nothing?" I asked. "You had to be wondering."

"I hadn't gotten to telling her any of this other stuff," Grant explained. "And I really would have liked to have been able to tell her under better circumstances."

"Better circumstances?" Cynthia huffed. "When exactly would

have been a better time to tell me you killed my boyfriend?"

"A private time, not with a gun pointed at us and glass at your throat."

"So when would we have had a private time? Today?"

"Oh, no, after we'd gotten away."

"Look, you've made it clear you aren't going to kill her. Put the glass down, and I'll put the gun down. The police have the place surrounded. You won't be leaving according to your plan." At least I hoped.

"No." He shook his head.

"I can't believe you're doing this or that you actually thought I could love you. You're nothing compared to Mark. I loved him and you killed him. You're an asshole, a fool, you're—"

I was shaking my head, trying to indicate to Cynthia she should be quiet, hold back, but she didn't care. Her verbally abusive tirade continued.

"You're low-life scum. You are such a freakin' loser to think you could possibly deserve someone like me."

"I do deserve you. I did everything for you." Grant's words came out haltingly, filled with anger. "I should slit your throat right now."

"No," I protested and stepped forward, aiming my gun at his head.

But Cynthia egged him on, "Go ahead, you coward. I'd rather die than be with you. You must be insane if you think—" were the last words from Cynthia's mouth.

In a movement almost dance-like as if releasing her for a twirl, Grant pulled his hand from lower left to upper right, a drawing of the sword motion. Only not to defend a poor maiden, but to slit her throat instead. The motion freed her, spinning, toppling to the floor. Her hands flew up, grasping at her throat, blood spilling before her body hit the ground, hands unable to catch her fall. In the next split second, Grant quickly lunged toward me. With Cynthia clear, I took my shot, hitting his thigh. My goal to maim, not kill.

Grant looked up in surprise as his leg gave out, causing him to fall face down. He then drug himself somewhat sideways into a half sitting position. He placed his hand into the injury, withdrawing his palm to examine the warm, dark blood in astonishment.

"You shot me," he said.

"Yes, and you won't die if you lie still and let me take care of it. Put the glass down."

He dropped the shard and sat open-palmed, expectant. I shooshed the glass away.

"Lie down."

He obeyed. I put my gun in the hand of my lame arm and patted him down with the good one, removing a small gun from under his pant leg. Obviously he hadn't had time to pull it when I barged in. I slid his gun out into the livingroom, well out of reach, and holstered mine. I grabbed some kitchen towels and pressured them into the injury.

"Hold those there."

Then I quickly tended to Cynthia, who was unconscious. Her cuts were not as deep or as severe as I had originally thought. I had been certain she would have bleed to death already, but now upon inspection I was more inclined to believe she would make it. On the one side and around the trachea the cut was superficial; it had sliced the skin and caused blood loss, but it wasn't going to be fatal. On the other side, the cut was much deeper but back farther, missing the main artery in the neck. The inconsistency in the edge and sharpness on the shard of glass Grant used had miraculously allowed her to escape without serious injury.

She hadn't lost enough blood to have caused her unconscious state. She was probably suffering from shock, most likely had convinced herself she was going to die and passed out. I shook her and called her name.

Rattling at the front door, and it swung open. A half dozen officers swarmed in using SWAT-type formation, preparing to sweep the room and put down any threats. I put my hands up, as far as the sling would allow, and indicated they could remove my weapon.

"I'm Paul Grey." I identified myself.

"We know who you are. You can put your hands down. Stand up and move away."

"It's about time you got here," I complained as I did as instructed.

"Did the best we could, sir. All the elevators were in use. We had to wait."

EMT's had been called and arrived to care for Cynthia and Grant. Watching as the men worked on stabilizing the wounds and listening to the men talk, it appeared both Cynthia and Grant would survive.

Jeffries arrived a few minutes later, sidling up to me. "Well, I know there's someone who'll be glad to hear this thing is over and will be happy to see you."

"Yes, where is Lindsey?"

"She's staying with Detective London Shope at her house in

Chamblee. I'll get someone to give you some directions, or, better yet, I'll have someone drive you."

"Great, when?"

"First tell me what's happened. Should we be arresting both of them?"

"Yes, both of them. Cynthia for the murder of Nikki Sills and Grant for the murder of Mark Sills, the attack on me at the park, and the attempted murder of Cynthia."

"Ah, give me a few minutes."

I nodded.

Jeffries wandered off to gather some more details and give a few orders, leaving me to ponder the case and to watch Cynthia and Grant being cared for.

"Two for the price of one," I commented as Jeffries returned.

"What?"

"Your arrests—two for one case. I was looking for one killer and found two. Now it all adds up. Cynthia was telling the truth, mostly."

"Think she'll still want to plea-bargain?"

"Do you think you'll have a strong case against her?"

Jeffries shrugged. "We have lots of circumstantial stuff. Maybe with the hypnosis and if we get a matching print from her to go with the glass we found in the apartment."

"It'll match. She's confessed. Check all her shoes in her apartment. I'll bet a pair will have tiny shards from the broken potted plant embedded in the soles. The plant broke in the struggle. Cynthia put the chair back upright before she left."

"That wasn't a smart move; it gave her away."

"No one said criminals had to be smart. I'm rather glad they do make mistakes. It makes it easier to catch them."

"True. What about Grant?"

"Any blood or hair from the park will match Grant's DNA. Prints on the knife will be his."

"Well, then, I think we'll have enough evidence to get them both."

"I'd ask about plea bargains then." I shrugged. "Heck ,Grant may know something. Between the two of them you might get a good case going. I wouldn't be too upset about that either."

"Still some unfinished business?"

"In a way." In the back of my mind I had been wondering about the more personal, final aspect of the case. The mob still needed to be dealt with. "If it's all right by you, I'll be going."

"I've got a car to drive you. You'll stop by for paperwork in the morning?" Jeffries asked.

"Will do."

The officer dropped me at Detective Shope's home. Although Detective Shope wasn't home, there was an officer on guard. Seeing my police escort and waving to my driver, he let me pass to the front door. I knocked. I heard rustling on the other side of the door as Lindsey checked the peephole then fumbling as she quickly unlatched it and swung it open. I stepped inside and pushed the door shut.

"Oh, God." She exhaled the words of relief. She hugged and held me so tightly it pained my arm, but I didn't care.

"The case is over," I explained.

"I gathered." Her reply muffled as she buried her face into my chest.

I stroked her hair and kissed her. She took my one hand in hers, then with her other hand stopped my caressing motion. She stepped back and looked me in the eyes.

"Things will change now, right?" she asked.

"Right. Absolutely." I shook my head in agreement, but still thinking about the mob.

She had a stern look on her face, the way my mother used to look when I'd been mischievous as a boy, like the time I put the cat in the hamper.

"I have to tell you something important. We need to talk," she said.

Oh, no. Had she changed her mind? Had she decided I wouldn't change or that I was a liar? Could she read the thoughts in my head?

"What is it? Is it bad?"

"No. I've tried to tell you, but couldn't, but it's wonderful."

"What?"

"I'm pregnant. We're having a baby."

"What?"

"Pregnant, we're having—"

"I know; I heard. I can't believe, I mean, when? How?"

"Well, *how* I think is obvious, don't you? I knew back when you first started this case. I tried to tell you."

"That day, the one when you said you had good news. We had lasagne."

"Yes."

"I knew you were acting weird. So how far along? I mean, why not tell me sooner?"

"About twelve weeks. I knew at nine weeks, almost ten weeks, but decided not to worry or stress you until this case was over. But now I want us to be clear on this—no more cases like this one."

"Yes, yes. Clear." I felt like a bobble-head doll. Words coming out, me agreeing, head up, down, up, down, but not connecting.

I couldn't believe it—Lindsey pregnant. Me—I was going to be a dad. Oh, God, a dad. Would I be a good parent? How would I know what to do?

"Are you O.K.?" Lindsey asked. "You look pale. Is it too much?"

"Yeah, not really sinking in."

"I think it has sunk in, judging by the worried look on your face."

I put my hand out to feel and rub her belly.

"You can't feel it or tell yet." She placed her hand over mine.

A flood of emotions—happy, surprise, euphoria, but also, as Lindsey had suspected, anxiety, fear, and worry—had all set in. I felt the warmth of her belly and her hand surrounding my hand. I knew how warm and cozy the baby inside must feel. I couldn't wait to tell people, yet at the same time a barrage of questions ran through my mind. Did we have enough money? Were we ready to be parents? Would it be safe to have a baby in our thirties?

"Are you healthy? I mean, with all this stress of me on the case, isn't stress bad for you?" I asked.

"I'm fine. A little stress and worry won't hurt. The baby's fine."

"What did the doctor say? How much do you know?"

"I've only been the one time, when I found out. At the time everything was fine. I go back in four days."

"Do you think everything is still fine? Do you know if it's a boy or a girl?"

She nodded and laughed. "It's too early to tell, honey. Do you care either way? I'm sure the baby's fine."

"Boy or girl, it doesn't matter. I'm just curious."

She smiled; her eyes shone. "Are you happy? I mean, it's good news to me. Is it for you, too?"

"Yes, of course. I'm surprised. After all this time, I didn't think it was going to happen."

Lindsey hugged me. I was afraid to hold her too tight; I didn't want to squeeze her.

"You can't hurt me, or the baby." She pulled me tighter.

My thoughts again came crashing in—how things would change

in our lives. My work would have to change for a baby. I couldn't be out all night on surveillance or running around with a gun. Maybe I would need to get rid of the gun? If I didn't do dangerous cases, I wouldn't need it. I wouldn't want to take on dangerous work. I wouldn't want to leave Lindsey a widow and a single mom and leave a kid without a dad. Right then and there in the foyer of the house, I swore things would have to change. Forget the mob. Forget it all. None of that mattered.

EPILOGUE

At the conclusion of the case, I was almost at the end of my two years with Morehouse Fidelity Insurance. State requirements mandated I have that much time working under a company investigation license before I could apply for and hold my own. When I told Glenn about the baby and my dilemma, he immediately agreed to switch job positions with me; he took my cases and I took his. This would reduce some of the risk. Mr. Moore had no objections, and for the rest of my term of work there he was supportive of almost anything and everything I suggested or needed. He'd gotten a nice pay raise and some kudos from the higher-ups since he'd turned over our "proposal." At the end of the two years, a few short months later, I said my good-byes to Morehouse, to Glenn and, to Shawn.

Within eight months my arm was feeling almost normal again. Therapy helped, but it never felt exactly like it used to. Sometimes it gave me a little twinge, a nice reminder of what I'd been through. All the more reason to begin my own business.

My own investigative company, the Paul Grey Detective Agency, was officially opened at Christmastime. What my company name lacked in creativity, it made up for in safety. Since I owned my own company, I could stick to only safe, non-violent cases. How much risk or trouble could there be in finding lost loves or biological parents of adopted kids? My work mainly focused on finding missing teens. Sometimes they didn't want to be found, but mostly it was safe, reliable work. And although I worked fewer cases, occasionally picking up work from overflow at other agencies, I actually made about as much as I had working for Morehouse.

In the meantime, Jeffries was busy developing a case against Vincent Artello of the Atlanta mob and others in Nevada. Cynthia and Grant both agreed to turn over evidence for shortened sentences, and between the two of them they were able to give plenty of information—names, crimes, connections, bank accounts. So in a round about way I got my revenge, too. I never had to take direct action against the mob for what part they had played in the case or what they had done to me. But indirectly, through the arrests of Cynthia and Grant and their willingness to bargain, some major mob leaders would be getting what they deserved.

Cynthia and Grant would both be given protective services. Their jail times and locations would not be given publicly; perhaps they even had their names changed before they went in. I figured Cynthia would get about eight years for her crime, then they'd put her in a small, dinky town in the middle of nowhere, someone keeping an eye on her. A small nowhere town would be exactly what Cynthia would want. She'd undergo another name change. Would they change her looks, too? Could I run into her again in the future and not even know it? Would I even recognize her? No doubt whatever town she ended up in, she'd open the pizza place she always wanted to own. For years afterward, when in a new town, I'd go in and try the local pizza eatery, thinking maybe, just maybe, I'd see her.

And while the mob case and the ensuing arrests made nightly news over the winter, Christmas was a special time preparing for our new baby. Lindsey was due in February. We'd decided not to find out the sex of the baby, to let him or her surprise us. We busily decorated, child-proofed, and planned. Things seemed to be running smoothly. The baby was born right on time—February 18th.

But then Stuart Newsome called. It was part of our deal, and I would have to do it. My precious baby was only three weeks old that first week in March when I packed to go to New Hampshire. I kissed Lindsey's cheeks, then the baby's tiny rosy cheeks, warm and bundled. Eyes opened lightly and gazed at me. Would I even be remembered if by some chance I didn't come back?

Then I headed out into the cold to catch a plane.

ACKNOWLEDGMENTS

Thanks to Leslie Santamaria, Ellen McRaney of McRaney Photography, Chuck McBrayer of Allen Investigative Services for his assistance with the legal issues of surveillance, Mary Chamier, Betty Lumpkin, Karen Nelson, Rebecca McRaney, and Diane Packard for being my test subjects and first line of defense against grammatical errors, and my husband for his input and technological help (I couldn't get anything done without him).

ABOUT THE AUTHOR

Cheryl Ritzel lives in Georgia where she spends time with her friends and family. She is the author of the Paul Grey series as well as several short stories and magazine articles which have appeared in Lifeloom, Mystery Scene Magazine, and The Forum. She's been a teacher of Social Studies and Creative Writing for over 14 years. Currently she is enrolled in a Private Investigator certificate course which she hopes will add realism to her mystery writing and eventually may lead to a career in investigative work.

Tolling Bell Books

5430 Jimmy Carter Blvd.
Suite 111
Norcross, GA 30093
Fax: 770-448-0130

ORDER FORM

TITLE	ISBN	PRICE	QTY
Beginner's Luck: A Paul Grey Murder Mystery	978-0-9740583-2-0	$12.00	
Runner's High: A Paul Grey Murder Mystery	978-0-9740583-6-8	$13.00	
Long Lost Teddy	978-0-9740583-3-7	$10.00	
Adventures of Huggaboo Bear	978-0-9740583-4-4	$10.00	
	SUBTOTAL		
	GA RESIDENTS ADD 7% TAX		
	SHIPPING ($1 per book)		
	TOTAL:		

Name: _____ Phone: _____
Street Address: _____
City: _____ State: _____ Zip: _____

Mail completed order form to the address above. Include a check or money order made out to Tolling Bell Books.

For information about our titles or forthcoming books visit our website.

www.tollingbellbooks.com